ELZA GATE

By

Danny Thomas

Koinonia Associates, LLC
Knoxville, Tennessee

ISBN 978-1-60658-028-8

Published by:
Koinonia Associates
7809 Timber Glow Trail
Knoxville, TN 37938

To learn how you can become a published author,
visit PublishwithKA.com
March 1, 2021

Introduction

Elza Gate is a work of fiction. All the incidents, dialogue, and characters---with the exception of some well-known historical figures---are products of the author's imagination and, thus, are not to be construed as real. Where real-life historical figures appear, the situations and details concerning those persons are fictional and are not intended to depict actual events or to change the fictional nature of the work. In all other respects, any resemblance to persons living or dead is entirely coincidental.

***

"From April 1, 1943 until March 19, 1949 Elza Gate was the primary entrance to the secret community of Oak Ridge, Tennessee, and, along with six other entry points, it was manned by armed guards. Elza Gate took its name from a local community that predated Oak Ridge." Tennessee Historical Commission

Elza Gate was where rural citizens of Anderson County first encountered military and elite scientific personnel assigned by the Army Corps of Engineers to undertake an unprecedented experiment---the development of the world's first nuclear weapon. Few, however, were familiar with the nature of the weapon at that time. Yet all were undoubtedly aware of drastic transformations surrounding them, challenging their customs and traditions, pulling them inexorably toward a formidable new existence.

Dedication

For my parents, Lou and Dan Thomas, the one
indomitable, the other a philosopher, who in early 1949
brought me across the Smokies from Durham, North
Carolina to Oak Ridge, Tennessee. Though I was just
three months old, I took root there.

Acknowledgments

I am grateful to Katherine Bartis, my editor, for her attention to detail, generous suggestions, continuous diplomacy, and impeccable good taste.

To Barbara Ferrell for being willing to receive a portion of the draft even though she was more than a little busy; and for being willing to put the book up for sale at her shop.

To Deb Kile Hotchkiss who knows Oak Ridge far better than I do; and because she's a phenomenal photographer willing to share exquisite, evocative images with me.

To Bonnie Albright Shoemaker who worked thirty years at Y-12, lives even yet in Dossett and has a full acquaintance with places like Marlow and Frost Bottom and the good souls who inhabit those rural communities.

To Ray Smith, the renown Oak Ridge historian, who shared resource materials with me and encouraged verisimilitude.

To Ed Southern, Director of the North Carolina Writers Network, for making time to consider fiction not his own.

To my daughter, Amanda Whalen, whose eye for image, color, and proportion shaped the photographic portions of this book.

To Mick Wiest, who providing advice and counsel about Oak Ridge history and provided valuable resource materials.

And, finally, to my wife, Cynthia, never reluctant to read another draft, never reluctant to add, "You need to fix a few things. I have a list for you." But then offering a kiss as consolation.

Table of Contents

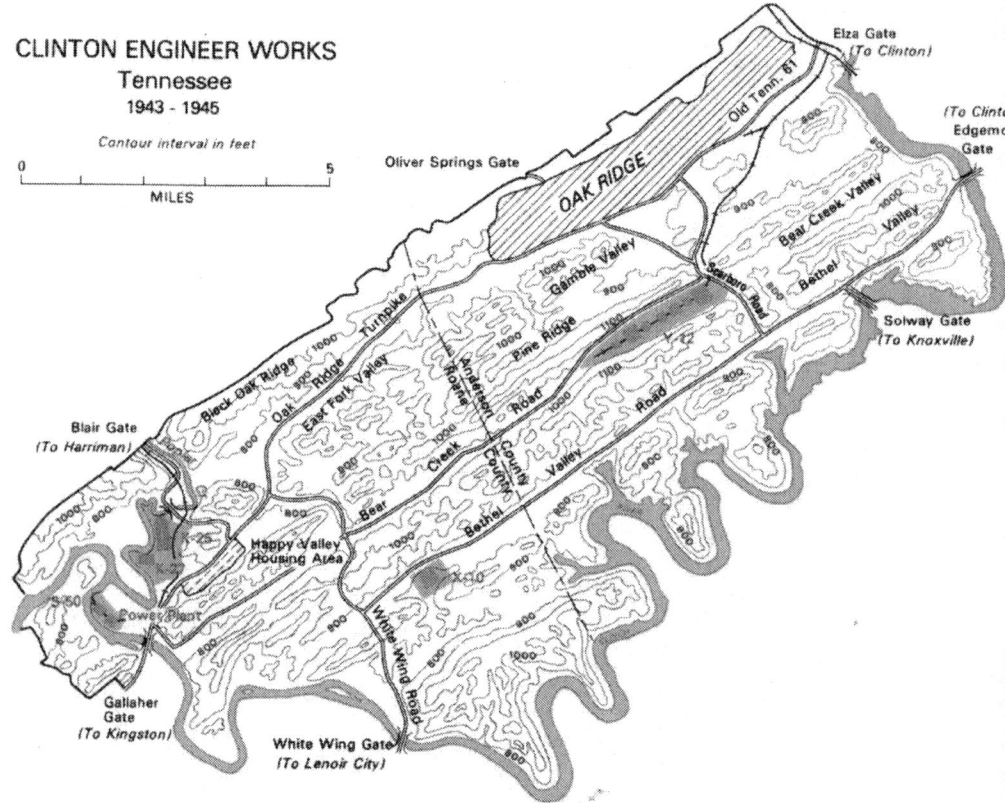

CLINTON ENGINEER WORKS
Tennessee
1943 - 1945

Contour interval in feet

0 — — — — — 5
MILES

Elza Gate
(To Clinton)

(To Clinton)
Edgemoor Gate

Oliver Springs Gate

OAK RIDGE

Old Tenn. 61

Bear Creek Valley

Bethel Valley

Gamble Valley

Scarboro Road

Solway Gate
(To Knoxville)

Pine Ridge

Black Oak Ridge

Oak Ridge

Anderson County

East Fort Valley

Turnpike

Bear Creek

Bethel Valley Road

County Road

Blair Gate
(To Harriman)

Happy Valley
Housing Area

Power Plant

White Wing Road

Gallaher
Gate
(To Kingston)

White Wing Gate
(To Lenoir City)

10

Foresight

On Thursday, the last time Kathleen saw the Sad Lady at the store, she looked tired, standing at the lettuce, fingering the green leaves without putting anything in her basket. Her face and hands were unusually pale, nearly white, and, she looked like she needed help. And, of course, Kathleen was the only one who could help her because nobody else even knew the Sad Lady was there. Kathleen could see things other people couldn't see. Sometimes that could get scary. The Sad Lady was a little like a ghost because while Kathleen was standing there, watching her, she simply disappeared. Kathleen quickly swept all that away, out of her head and went on with life.

Other than wondering about the Sad Lady, Rebecca Kathleen Woodson was feeling fine, like a princess. When someone called her Rebecca she was quick to say, "I want to be Kathleen!" So everyone called her what she wanted. Her older sister, Etta, should have been Kathleen's constant playmate, but Etta was always reading. So little brother Toby was the one she played with. He was a crybaby even when Kathleen let him be her prince. She liked telling him what to do all day. Toby was like their little black dog, Blossom, following her around, looking at shiny things, going after anything that might taste good. Blossom was an outside dog. Momma wouldn't allow her in the store or the house out back of the store.

Brother Ronnie always reminded Kathleen she was only five years old, and he was fourteen. But Ronnie was not the oldest. Hank was seventeen. Gary, ten, little brother Toby, three. That was all the boys. The girls were Etta, seven, and then

13

Kathleen. Momma always said, "That's the whole pack of Woodsons." And, of course, Daddy Earl and Momma Tilde.

Kathleen liked flowers, bushes, and weeds, but she liked red sumac leaves best. And she collected the smallest, greenest pine cones to keep on a shelf. Momma said, "Kathleen, your decorating touch is a gift magically bestowed on you somehow. Being as how we're at war with Germany and Japan, times are hard these days, so we need to make the most of everything God gives us. And that includes you." Momma gathered her up, hugging Kathleen to her front, the place called her bosom. Kathleen wondered if someday she'd have a bosom, too. She pretended she did with her doll, Suzy Polineau, who wore a blue and white dress and a permanently worried look. Kathleen carried her all around so that Suzy would feel loved. Suzy Polineau loved being held this way.

One time Kathleen forgot Suzy and left her in the Treasure Cave down by the river. She had forgotten about taking her down there because Toby had got muddy, and she washed him off so Momma wouldn't fuss. "Ewwww!" he said, making his unhappiest face. Kathleen jerked him straight like Momma did sometimes. "Stand still! We don't want you going back to the house so muddy." All this had combined to make her forget sweet Suzy, which in turn made Kathleen upset with Toby all over again. He stood still while she wiped off his arms and trousers. "There now," she said, like Momma. "You're clean, buddy."

Toby's eyes were handsome, especially when he was smiling. Blue eyes with a speck of brown in one. This was something she had not noticed before. Kathleen thought it was special to have two different colors in one eye, and she told him, "Momma needs to see your pretty eye. This one," she said poking him above the eyebrow such that he blinked and flinched.

14

Toby had found a little frog and didn't want to go to Momma, but Kathleen told him, "Come with me, Toby Woodson!" and he started crying because she said it so loud. She bent down, picked him up, and hauled him up to the store. He was littler than her, but heavy, too. When they got inside the store, she put Toby down, keeping a hand on his head.

Momma nodded, talking on the phone, "Yes...that's right...that's right. You only get as many shoes as the ration book allows." She wasn't even looking at Kathleen or Toby.

"Momma, Momma!" Kathleen said, holding Toby with one hand, grabbing Momma's skirt with the other. "Look at his eye. This one," poking her brother right above the eyebrow so he blinked again.

Toby screeched, "Eyaaah!" trying to get away, still holding onto the frog, which Kathleen saw was getting squeezed hard. She reached for the frog, but Toby squeezed it harder.

"Toby, stop!" she said. "You're killing your frog." She saw that it would be gone in a few minutes. A ghost frog. She knew about ghosts before others knew they were there. And that bothered her a little bit because she didn't know why she knew things ahead of time. One thing she did know: gone means dead. She told Toby, "Froggie's going fast, buddy."

He shook his head. "No, it won't."

"Yes, it is."

"No! No!"

He relaxed enough for her to snatch the frog and run into the grocery. She knew how to get into the pantry, closed the door, and put the frog on the cucumber shelf higher than Toby's head. Toby banged on the door, which she knew he couldn't open. She let him yell and hammer a while. Then she opened the door real quick, and he rushed in as she went past him back outside, closing the door on him. He couldn't get out now. Blossom stayed right outside the door, so Kathleen thought he was all right. Blossom saw things like Kathleen could. She was a good old dog, though she barked at the people and ducks in the fog down by the river.

"Your frog's on the high shelf, Toby. Feel around. You'll find it," she told him. "Play with him until Momma comes." She opened the door, saw him sitting on the floor with the frog in his hands, and he looked up.

"He's not wiggling."

"Let him sleep." But, of course, Froggie was like a ghost already.

She closed the door and went back to Momma, who wasn't on the phone now. "What is it, Kathleen?"

"Toby's got one eye that's brown and blue. Did you know that?"

Tilde Woodson smiled as she sat down in the rocking chair she used at the rear of Woodson's Grocery, beckoning her younger daughter to her lap. Once again she noted how different the girl was from her older sister, Etta, who clearly favored her father. Taller, with a longer face than this little cutie pie, Etta was serious and obedient. Kathleen favored Tilde with her straight auburn hair, her cupid's bow mouth, piercing blue eyes, and what some people would call high spirits, certainly not so obedient. The little girl had energy, an active imagination, and something else Tilde couldn't describe. She saw it, but couldn't identify it. Something special adorned her little girl.

"Now" she asked the child, "why couldn't you wait for me to get off the phone, young lady?"

Kathleen said, "Toby has a funny eye."

Tilde stroked the girl's hair as she spoke, a familiar,

16

calming maneuver that usually had the desired effect. "I know all about that, darling. I know everything there is to know about your little brother. And about you, too. I know about all my babies."

"I'm not a baby." She wanted to look at Momma's face, but Tilde held her close, so she waited to hear what Momma would say. Momma didn't know about the frog. She didn't know about the Treasure Cave, which Kathleen had discovered a month ago playing Hide and Seek. Kathleen was the best hider. Nobody else but Blossom and Toby knew about the Treasure Cave. And Toby didn't have the words to tell about it.

Kathleen felt the words that Momma would soon be speaking. When they were alone, just the two of them, sooner or later Tilde would ask, "Miss Kathleen, will you sing for me, please?"

Kathleen's heart would grow inside her chest as she sat up, escaping from the embrace, turning to face her mother, beginning to sing, "Hankie Doodle went to town, Riding on a pony."

Tilde laughed, "I do love to hear about old Hankie Doodle, Kathleen. Promise me you'll always sing about him for me." Kathleen would join in the laughter, too, knowing it was good for Momma to be happy. And that it wouldn't hurt Momma not to know everything Kathleen knew. Like how Toby had surely killed his frog. And Kathleen had taken pretty things to the Treasure Cave. And that Kathleen saw the Sad Lady at the Cave mostly, but sometimes in other places. Maybe Blossom saw her, too. Nobody else. People talked instead about the War, about the Bad Not-See's and Nips. The Sad Lady was a kind of Not-See, too. But a good one.

Nobody else could see the Sad Lady, which made Kathleen just the tiniest bit uncomfortable. The Sad Lady helped Kathleen with pretty flowers and weeds, and her name was

17

Bathsheba Kincaid, but she told Kathleen, "You can call me Bashie."

"Call me Kathleen."

"I love the name Kathleen."

"Me, too," she said, and that was when she decided to keep Miss Bashie all to herself, which seemed just fine with the Sad Lady. Kathleen noticed Miss Bashie never talked about the war, but maybe it was the war that made her so awfully sad.

Toby started making a big fuss in the pantry, which helped Kathleen remember how she'd left him, so she confessed to Momma, "I left Toby locked up."

Tilde took Kathleen's chin in her hand so she could see her face close up, and said, "Sometimes you're a little rough on your little brother. You need to be kind and gentle with him."

Wriggling out of Momma's grasp, Kathleen said, "I will. I'm going to turn him loose now, Momma," and she ran as Momma laughed some more.

The little frog was sure enough dead as a doornail. Momma shushed Toby, explaining, "We got plenty more frogs, buddy. You'll find yourself another before long." She wiped away his tears, kissing him on the forehead. He fussed a minute, but then got down. Blossom was right there with him, and, when he stopped to pet her, she licked at new tears rolling down his cheeks until he laughed.

The next day Kathleen visited the Treasure Cave down near the river in a hollow under a rock cliff where the sun couldn't find it, so it was always cool. She wanted to start a fire in the Treasure Cave to keep Suzy Polineau warm. Blossom, too. And she wanted to bring her jewelry to the Cave. The necklaces, the crowns, and her wand, which was broken. She had some matches, too, in a little box. Daddy fussed at the boys for taking his matches, and he looked straight at Kathleen when his face got red from fussing. But he never actually asked her about his matches, so she didn't have to confess she'd taken them. The Treasure Cave was just a little hollow place in the rocks, and she needed it to be a better place for the Sad Lady who was hugging herself as if she was cold all the time.

Miss Bashie had showed Kathleen how to wrap long pieces of Johnson grass around and around so they would fit on your head. If you stuck 'lellow' dandelions in the crown just right, you got a golden princess crown. "There you go," Miss Bashie said, placing the wreath on Kathleen's head, adjusting it so it was straight and proper. "Now you're beautiful."

"Am I?" Kathleen asked because Miss Bashie was herself beautiful. Her sun dress was white and 'lellow,' Kathleen's favorite color.

"Yes, you are," Miss Bashie said. "Your Momma would say so, too."

Kathleen walked a few steps to the other side of the Cave, acting like a princess would act. "I'm Princess Cinder Lella. That's my name. Cinder Lella. Do you have a glass slipper for me?"

The crown slipped a little bit, and they worked on it a while and talked about things a princess would do in her Treasure Cave. Now Kathleen had Miss Bashie, who would listen whenever Kathleen talked. She told Kathleen stories, too, and they had a fine tea party. Kathleen lifted one dainty finger while holding her imaginary teacup, and Miss Bashie chuckled, "Kathleen, do you know all your fingers? All their names?"

"Finger names?"

Miss Bashie said, "Here, I'll show you," and she raised one finger after another. "Here's Little Man. Ring Man. Long Man. Lick Pot, and Thumbo."

Kathleen grinned. "Let me do that." And she did like Miss Bashie showed her until the fourth finger. "Who's this?"

"Lick Pot," Miss Bashie said. "You know, licking something good out of the pot."

"Oh," Kathleen said. "Momma lets me get biscuit dough that way."

"When I cooked with my Momma, I liked that, too."

"Do you still do it?" Kathleen asked.

"Not any more."

Sadness started growing inside the Treasure Cave coming from Miss Bashie, sadness Kathleen didn't understand. "Why don't you cook with her any more?"

Right away Kathleen saw that what she'd asked was not good, but she didn't know how to undo it.

"Because she's long gone, that's why. I hold her memory in my heart, trying to find her again and again, but maybe it's not quite time yet. I know she's close, but I can't find her. When I cook, I remember Momma and how she always helped me if I came into the kitchen feeling bad."

"Like now?" Kathleen said.

"Why do you say that?"

"Because you're sad, and that makes me sad." Kathleen waited for Miss Bashie to talk next. But she was still quiet, so Kathleen picked up Suzy Polineau and nestled her baby in her arms hoping her new friend would explain when she was ready. Kathleen wanted to help Miss Bashie. She wanted to ask, "What's made you sad?"

Miss Bashie stood up and walked to the cave entrance, peering outside. "Do you know where there's a boat,

20

Kathleen?"

"Ma'am?"

Miss Bashie turned around. "I can't say why, but I have a feeling my Momma's on the other side of the river. I need to go over there myself."

"What?" Kathleen was confused. Something about the other side of the river felt scary. "I thought she was gone."

"Oh, she is," Miss Bashie said. "But I think if I was over there, I'd be closer to her." Her face was happy, but it didn't make sense.

Suzy Polineau was crying quietly. "Hush, now, Sweetness," Kathleen turned to her baby, patting her back. When Kathleen turned back around, Miss Bashie wasn't there. How did the Sad Lady get past her? She thought about telling Momma, but she was busy getting supper on the table. After supper it was Etta's turn to help wash dishes, and Kathleen didn't want her around when she talked to Momma. Then it was bath time. Finally, it was brush your teeth and bedtime, and that was when Kathleen said, "Momma, do you know your fingers?"

"Why do you ask?"

Kathleen held up a hand. "Look. Itty Bitty Man. Ring Man. Long Man. Thumbo. Lick the Pot."

Momma was scrunching up the pillow as she lay down. "That's good," she said. "Where'd you hear these names?"

"The Sad Lady told me," Kathleen replied. "I got em right, didn't I?"

"You did," Momma said, smiling. "A Sad Lady, you say?"

Kathleen cocked her head inquisitively. "When we were having tea this afternoon, she told me all the finger names."

"I see," Tilde said.

Momma always wanted to hear about what Kathleen had been up to all day long. Sometimes she'd say, "Dance, Kathleen, the way the princess dances at the palace ball." Kathleen could twirl and prance without any music at all, and Momma told her, "Your imagination's a blessing, darling."

In her bedroom Kathleen had already drawn a picture of Miss Bashie, but not just right. She was going to give it to Momma, but ripped the page out of the tablet, flustered so much she threw the pencil skittering across the floor. Momma got up to fetch it, trying to soothe her. "It's all right, darling. Your drawing's fine."

"But it isn't, Momma. I didn't do her eyes right. They weren't sad at all. The Sad Lady is really sad, and you can't tell that by looking at my picture, can you?"

Momma said, "Let's try again tomorrow night. Does that sound all right to you?" Kathleen knew Momma was trying to help, not unlike the way Kathleen was helping Miss Bashie. Kathleen lay back, but the pillow wasn't right. Momma said, "Sit up a second," and when Kathleen did that, Momma set the pillow just exactly right. She said, "Say your prayers for me," clapping her hands twice. "Hurry now. Chop, chop!"

So they did prayers, blessing all the boys, Etta, Suzy Polineau, Daddy, Momma, and finally Kathleen herself. Oh, yes, and Blossom, too. Momma kissed her on the forehead, turning off the light, leaving a crack in the door so the hall light shone across the floor for Etta when she came to bed later. Momma stood there in the narrow light, and Kathleen could feel the words coming.

"Kathleen, your imagination will be your blessing. But I also need you to tell the truth when I ask you a question. Understand?"

Kathleen said nothing, and Momma waited a little bit. "You understand?" she asked again. "You talk about this Sad Lady more than you talk about other make-believe friends. I want you to talk about all of them, not just the new one." She came back in the room over to the bed. "I need you to help more with Toby. Everybody will need to do more."

Kathleen said, "I understand." But she didn't, not really. How would she do it all the time? Things were getting heavier. More people would be like ghosts. It was happening too fast, which frightened her more than ever. The gone people were heavier every day, but there didn't seem to be a way to make anybody understand.

Momma backed into the hall as Kathleen suddenly felt really tired. But before she would let her eyes close she told herself she needed to ask Momma tomorrow about Rose Felt who would be going sometime soon. Before too long. Many people were going to cry when that happened. Too many to count.

She also remembered to bless the Sad Lady. And there were others who needed blessing. Miss Bashie's friends, the ones she had talked about, who had painted shining numbers on soldiers' watches so they could tell time at night. They licked the glowing brushes, and the glow went into their tummies. Soldiers in the war were fighting in darkness, and they needed glowing watches, but Miss Bashie's friends had the horrible glow eating their insides out. Miss Bashie couldn't see them, but Kathleen could. She didn't want to see them, but there they were.

Miss Bashie's friends, Polly Tadlock and Martha Jane Poteet, needed blessing. Kathleen had seen their ravaged faces, their terrible sore places. Miss Polly had an ugly torn place on the side of her face where her jaw should have been. Kathleen could see blood on her teeth and her damaged tongue. She made hurting faces every time she spoke. Miss Martha Jane's neck

23

was shrunken, bruised, and leaking blood down her front. The way they looked and suffered terrified Kathleen, and she wept when she saw them. They weren't gone yet, but they wanted to go soon. They didn't tell Kathleen they did, but they wanted to be gone. Kathleen didn't have to pretend they needed her. They were sadder than Miss Bashie. And even though Miss Bashie didn't know it herself, she was already nearly gone. Was she a ghost already? Kathleen could sweep that thought away if she tried real hard. She didn't know how she could feel everything that was coming at her, but feeling things, even the horrible things, was something she must do. Something she couldn't resist very long. She tried not to let the worst images take form in her head. That's how she withstood the horror of seeing things others couldn't see.

Tonight she was aware her heart was growing rapidly inside her chest again because of that man who was going to be a ghost next year, something which seemed to be approaching rapidly. Too fast for him. Too fast for Kathleen. Many people were going to cry about him being gone. He was important in the War. Important for the country. He was in newspapers. The family heard him on the radio.

"Frank Lindy Rose Felt," she murmured. "That's him."

And she did her best to sweep the thought of him away so she could sleep.

Photo courtesy of Deb Kile hotchkiss

Precious Cargo

Some folks are healed so they can get back to work. Some need to be talked through healing, and some need to be sung to. Some need loved ones holding their hands, and some need to be left alone in silence and darkness. I've been around all types, and I've learned ways to help the afflicted recover from whatever assails them. And, by God, you can count on me, Ida Rose Delap, the midwife. If I say I'm coming to help you, I'm coming, rain or shine, hail or Old Testament thunder.

Here's some things I know: natural remedies need to settle before they take. You got to abide patiently while waiting for a cure. And too much of anything can kill you. For instance, the pokeberry's something you need to take only as shoots, never its roots. The shoots can be boiled right soft and helpful, but the roots will light a coal inside you that won't go out. Pokeberry roots can kill you deader than four o'clock. But here and now, this evening I'm not messing with pokeberry. While it's cooling off I'll get started yanking Johnson grass and jimson weed out of my garden.

All this is on my mind as I walk out the front door, heading for the garden when I see him standing in the yard, hat in hand, waiting for me. "Hello there," I says. "What can I do for you?"

My visitor's a slender young fellow with problem skin, so I begin forming ideas about how to explain ways he can cure his acne, if that's what he's come for. His face is broke out and blemished. Taller than me, but not broad across the chest and shoulders, his dark hair's unruly, and he's got an anxious look. Not being one of those mind readers, I smile kindly as I can to

27

help him speak up.

"Hidy, ma'am," he says. "Am I speaking to Miz Ida Rose Delap?"

"You are," I say. "Who's asting?"

"I'm Gorry Jackson," he says. "I work over in the Clinton Engineer Works."

"Gorry, you say?"

"Like *sorry,* but with a G." He gives me a shy grin. "I'm the only Gorry I ever heard tell of." As he says this, he glances back over his shoulder at a red pickup truck parked a ways down the road, and I'm wondering why he didn't park closer.

I shake his hand. "What can I do for you, Gorry Jackson?"

"Can I show you?" he says, bending over so he's got both hands on his left pants leg, waiting for me to answer.

"Your foot?"

"My shin." Pulling up his pants leg, he reveals an ugly, weeping wound from ankle to knee. "I got burned last week," he says. "And a guy I used to work with, Ervin Davis, told me you fixed him up real good when he came to see you with his leg. He told me not to waste my time with the infirmary. Come see you instead."

"I remember him," I says. "Big hulk of a man. Maybe six foot four. He had that ulcer on his knee which had come to a boil, but never flinched when I lanced it."

"That's him," Gorry says, his face suddenly blushing red. "Mr. Davis says you're better than the doctors over at the Y-12 Infirmary. And you didn't cost him any time off neither. He couldn't afford to miss work. Neither can I. I need every dollar for---for---."

28

I wait for him to finish, but he never does, so I say, "Let me see that burn." I kneel down to study the wound where it's wept, crusted dry, and cracked open in a couple places. It appears he ain't touched it, just toughing it out, which is not the way to go. Painful and unsanitary. It's swollen with a pink tint just outside the crust, and, when I press around it gently, my finger leaves a shallow depression, paling until the fingerprint slowly disappears. All this as Gorry flinches just a bit, holding his breath while I poke him.

Standing up, I says, "You ain't put anything on it, have you?"

"I scrub it every morning with hand soap and again at night after work," he says. "It hurts when I do that, so I've been sort of gentle last two nights. Daytime I just power through, not thinking about it. Trying not to."

"You got a little infection showing," I says. "Let me scrub off the crust for you and use a poultice."

"Oh, would you?" he says, brightening up as if I'd just handed him twenty dollars. Once again he's looking back at his truck, nervous about it.

"Be happy to teach you to do it your own self."

"Oh," he says. "I don't think I could do it good as you."

"Let me work the way you need," I tell him. "Let me do what I do."

He's positively quivering, which ain't unusual with some of my patients, the youngest children or most delicate females. Not usually working men. Maybe he's hurt beyond what he's told me. My intuition tingles about this.

He says, "Not sure I can watch you. Is it all right if I turn away?"

29

"If you can make it to my house every other day," I say, "I'll clean it up and medicate you proper for a week or so. Maybe ten days."

"All right," he says, reaching for his wallet. "What do I owe?"

"I'll let you know next time you come. Set on that cinder block while I'm mixing up the ointment. Keep still while I'm working." He sets kind of fidgety and restless, so on a hunch I says, "What's Ervin up to these days?"

"I'm not sure," Gorry says, scratching his nose. "Pretty much the same old same old." He's wanting to look at his truck again, but he fights it off.

Back in the house I grab some primrose ointment in a jar, but I want to add a few fresh leaves, a little lard and salt. I boil water and pour the ointment in the pot, using a coarse sieve to thin out the mixture. It needs to cool considerably before he'll be able to stand getting it slathered on his wound. Out front I find him smoking a cigarette, his leg splayed straight out, pants rolled up to his knee. I put the pot down and go back in for soap and water. When I get back outside, I set down by him and ask, "How'd you get this burnt?"

"I'm a courier, delivering valuable items, packages and mail, all around the CEW, but every now and then they assign me to help the mechanics doing transmissions and mufflers, and one of them mufflers burnt the crap out of me last Friday."

"I'm going to wrap it up for you to keep your pants from sticking to the ointment. That ain't sanitary. I can show you how to wrap it."

He shakes his head. "I druther come back and let you wrap it, Miz Ida."

When the pot has cooled enough, I soap up the rag and tell

him, "Take it off slow or fast? It's going to hurt some whether it's took off long and slow or ripped off quick. Folks want to know how it's going to go with their pain instead of getting surprised."

He screws up his face, and whispers, "Get it over with."

Gorry's good when I scrub and scrape on his leg. He's looking the other way, taking deep breaths while I get that ugliness off his leg. Tenderly as I can, I ladle poultice on his wound and that's when I have myself a brainstorm. I run back in the kitchen, grab my honey jar, and come back to drip some slowly on the wound. Honey has its own enchantment. That's how I see it as I tear rags into strips, wrapping them around his leg.

When I'm done, I tap his shoulder, and he turns to look at me, his face having lost some color, but he seems all right. I ask, "I'd like to hear how Ervin's doing."

Gorry's face shows some tumult, shifting back and forth from obvious physical relief and gratitude that the hurt is over to some brand of regret. "I'm sorry, Miz Ida," he says, letting his breath ease out slow. His cheeks are blushing up again, "I ain't been truthful with you about Ervin and maybe waited too long to come see you."

"What is it?" I says. "Has something happened to him?"

"Naw, it ain't that," he says. "It ain't happened to him. Can I roll down my pants leg now?"

"Go ahead," I says. "But I'm getting the feeling something I did might have backfired on Ervin somehow."

He stands up and walks around in a tight little circle in my front yard. Finally, he says, "Come walk with me. I got somebody in my truck I want you to meet. That'll probably explain better."

31

I look at the truck, and I don't see anybody setting in it, but, as we get up closer, I can see there's somebody scrunched down in the passenger seat. She's a young redheaded teenager, pale faced, laying on her side, possibly napping. But when we get up to the window, I can see she's pregnant, belly big as a watermelon, her dress stretched tight across her front. She's a pretty girl with high cheekbones and freckles splashed across her face. She looks almost full term. I turn to Gorry to ask about her, but he beats me to it, saying, "Miz Ida, meet my wife, Judith. We're having us a baby any day now."

"I can see that," I says, reaching out to offer her my hand. "Hidy, Miz Jackson. Pleased to meet you."

She pushes herself up to a seated position and nods warily, shaking my hand. "Likewise, Miz Delap." Her eyes shift to Gorry. I get the feeling his introducing us wasn't expected.

I says to Gorry, "Is she what you haven't told about?"

"Well, yes and no," he says. "I should have come before now because of my leg. Should have spoke up before now about us having a baby because we want you to bring the child into this world." He checks with Judith before saying any more. There's something more important yet to be revealed. Gorry's absentmindedly scratching at his his burns so I grab his arm. "Stop that."

He says, "Judith is Ervin's daughter. We got a little ahead of ourselves with the baby coming, and that doesn't set well with him."

Judith says, "I never seen him so angry when we told him. He cussed a blue streak and said, 'I'm just glad your momma ain't alive to see this.' I thought he was going to bust a blood vessel in his brain. We been tippy toeing around him ever since."

I hold up my hand. I says, "Give me a minute to get all this

32

straight in my head." They look to one another, maybe grateful for my suggestion.

Judith gets out of the truck, and Gorry moves to take her hand as she takes short steps, like she's walking on egg shells. She goes around the truck to rest on the rear bumper. I note how slender she's built, wondering if her hips will be adequate for child birth. That could be a problem, but I hope not. She has just settled, resting against the bumper looking down the road when she says, "Oh, Lordy!" And I look to see what she's talking about. A vehicle's headed our way coming fast enough to raise a cloud of dust on the gravel road.

"That's him," Judith says. And the closer the truck comes, the better I can see it's Ervin's Ford. When he gets fairly close, he stops, and the dust billows past him toward us. He sets there in the front seat, and Gorry says, "You do the talking this time, Judith. He won't listen to me." She puts a hand on her belly like she's reaching for her child, squinting into the dust cloud.

"I'll talk to him," she says, "but be ready to go if he gets hard headed."

Ervin gets out of his truck, trudging our way, head down, studying the gravel under his feet. He's much more stout than his daughter, broad-shouldered and heavy in the chest, while she's a long, tall drink of water, slender and willowy. She must take after her momma. When he gets up close, his mouth is set hard, and I cringe because I'm better managing childbirthing than I am refereeing between hot heads.

"Judith," her father says a little louder than I'd wish. "I'm here to take you home unless you need to get to the Hospital." He glances at Gorry, then at me, but he's talking only to his daughter.

"Unless you're going to pay the doctor bills, Daddy," Judith says, "you don't have no say in this."

Ervin huffs his breath out, no actual words in reply. He puts his hands on his hips, glaring at everybody. "Judith Elizabeth Davis, you're not thinking straight. You never have."

"It's Judith Elizabeth Davis Jackson!" Gorry says, fierce as flint. "She's my wife. You don't get to decide about where our baby's born." His voice has got that shrill, hostile tone, and if them ain't fighting words, I don't know what is. Gorry's puffed up like a bantie rooster, but if things get physical it'll be no contest because Ervin's probably three hundred pounds to Gorry's half that. We're all four of us engaged in a staring contest. The only sound now is the chorus of cicadas singing in the trees all around us.

Suddenly, Judith lays both hands on her belly, and I recognize the gesture for what it surely must be. She wipes her hair out of her eyes, looking to Gorry, who had been looking at Ervin and missed what happened. I glance at Ervin, who did see it.

"I felt a jolt," she says, and now she's looking at me. "I think I wet my pants."

"Your water must have broke just now," I says. "Your time's coming quick."

Ervin and Gorry have forgotten their stand off, not knowing what to do. They've been struck dumb, so I jump into the situation as I typically do, asking Judith, "How old are you, darling?"

"Fifteen," she says.

"Too young to be having a baby," her father says, trying to explain, not angry, but more plaintive.

"It is truly a young age," I says, "but I expect you'll be strong, Judith, withstanding labor pains. And they'll be strong and fierce, believe me." I turn to the men. "I'm watching you two fools set against each other, arguing about someone you both love. Daughter to one, wife to the other. And then there's me right here with you, and I'm the one that knows what to do to get babies born. Gorry, you've brung a precious cargo to me, and that's well and good. But you two need to put your arguments aside and do what I tell you to do. Most likely, Judith and me will need help from the both of you. Like any child's birth, this is a serious situation we got here."

Ervin and Gorry have long faces, thinking about what I'm saying. I turn to Judith. "Come on into the house. We need to get you onto a bed." The men are staring at us, neither one budging an inch so I light a fire under them. "Don't just stand there, you two. Come in, come in."

I have them stay in the front room while I get Judith set up in my bedroom in the back. I fuss a bit at the men. "You two behave now. Don't start nothing in my house." I holler at them from the bedroom as Judith slides onto the bed here in the rear. "Take your shoes off," I says softly to Judith, and she does that with a curious look on her face, which makes me think she's got something to say about her father...or maybe her husband. Or maybe she wants to use my chamber pot. Not sure what she wants.

"You doing all right?" I ask, talking low so the men won't hear.

Now she's antsy, gesturing for me to come closer. I'm judging her condition as she drops her shoes by my bed, and I set myself on the edge of the bed so she can stretch her legs. If she's had her water broke, she'll be straining for quite a while. But it seems she must not be having contractions, at least, not rough ones. Sometimes this happens, so I'm ready to deal with a woman's anxiety and ignorance, what most first-time mothers go through. I know all the different ways delivery might test us.

But I'm not prepared for what happens next. She hops right

35

up from the bed, looking out the window, striding quickly around the bed so she's closer to the door than I am. She sidles up close to the wall, listening intently to the men in the front room. I hear the sound of their voices, but not the actual words. I watch her eavesdropping, and she seems satisfied with what they're saying. All I get is the basic notion that they're not angry with one another. They're not fussing.

She's examining my bedroom, all my nooks and crannies, my dresser and trinkets, coming back to the bed to set by me. She ain't in labor. I recognize that right away. She's in control. I can see that as she lays a hand on mine, asking, "How long can you spend with me?" No pretense she actually needs a midwife's help. She needs something else.

"I got some time this evening," I says. "But I need to be somewhere by noon tomorrow." I study her face a while before asking, "What do you need me for anyhow? Your water ain't broke, has it? What is it you're planning to do here?" I stare hard at her, but my questions don't faze her none. I don't think her water's actually broke yet.

"I'm trying to put out the fire between Daddy and Gorry while I've still got the strength to do it," she says. "I can't let the friction between them spark more than it already has. They could burn us all down to cinders. Including the baby. I need to fix things proper and do it right now, but I ain't one hundred percent sure how to go about it." She's still eye to eye with me, wavering a bit, slipping into uncertainty, but determined, too. I'm beginning to think more of her.

"I see your purpose now," I says. "And you're right to do it because giving birth don't always go according to Hoyle. It can lead you safely down one path and then backtrack the opposite way that's not so safe. You'll be worn down to a nub by labor pains because you can't tell how long that baby'll wait to get born. And fatigue makes cowards of us all."

36

I watch to see how she's reacting to what I'm saying. She's got her Daddy's mouth and chin, but pale blue eyes rather than his deep brown. And there's a quiet strength in her eyes. "I tell you what," I says. "You just follow my lead, and, if things go the way I want, they won't be no fire left to put out between those two."

The corners of her mouth start curling upward in a smile, but she keeps a straight face, and she says, "Thanks. I been all muddled up for a while, loving them both, not wanting to lose either one. They been talking mean to each other, and I'm afraid they're going to bust out fighting."

I think about that, stepping over to the window, looking out over my garden, considering exactly how to turn this from potential fracas to a proper welcome for a healthy newborn, but I'm curious about one particular thing. I turn to Judith, asking, "When did you get the idea that you should be the one to calm those two down? You got enough to do, getting ready for the baby."

"I first come on the idea when I heard them arguing about my name. And I figure the baby changes everything, I guess. That's when I understood what Gorry and my Daddy's got in common instead of just listening to them fuss about what they got against one another."

Just then she lurches, putting both hands on her middle. "There's another jolt," she says.

"Do you still feel it tightening in your middle?"

She colors in her cheeks. "Never thought about my middle the way I'm doing now," she says.

I pat her shoulder. "Let me check you. Lay back, and don't be shy. Maybe today your baby will come; maybe tomorrow. And that will mean we won't have to do no play-acting. This could be the real thing. Like I said before, just follow my lead

37

on this." She nods, laying herself back on my pillows, and I check her progress. She's pretty near starting, but not just yet.

I walk out to the front room and says to Ervin, "Go in there and get some of the cushions from the settee to prop up your daughter. Things are getting serious."

I tell Gorry, "Run yourself back home to get her some more clothes. Underwear, socks, any more gowns she might want, and her blanket."

"Her blanket?"

"It'll help her feel at home in bed, smelling her own bedclothes and such," I says. "Now don't argue with me. Get in there, give her a kiss, and then skedaddle back to your place to fetch what I said, and anything else you feel will comfort her." I turn to Ervin who's still standing there listening. "Let Gorry see her first. When he's gone, you get back in there to make her comfortable. Ask if she wants a back rub or if she wants anything rubbed. Feet, legs, shoulders, anything. Don't talk unless she asks a question. Be quiet as a mouse. This is about her and the baby, not you, not Gorry."

So I let the men go as directed. Gorry's quiet with Judith and out of the bedroom quicker than I'd have thought. Judith murmurs something to her father as he enters my bedroom, so quiet I can't make out her words. Her tone sounds right, so I busy myself in the kitchen, watering some of my little potted herbs, which have got too dry, thinking how to let this whole situation play out. Ervin's taking too long, so I waltz into the back room and shoo him out. "You've had enough time," I tell him. "Go out back of the house to my stacked firewood and bring me a dozen sticks of wood plus some kindling."

"What for?" he says, petulantly. "It's early August, woman. You don't need no heat in here."

"Ervin Davis," I says. "It ain't up to you to tell me what I

38

need. It's the stove I need because she may need some broth or soup. I may need boiling water for cleaning linens and towels. Don't be arguing against what I tell you." I take the broom and swat at his legs. "Git now! Do as I say."

Big as he is, he could withstand any battering I give him, but I'm more experienced when it comes to bringing babies into this world, so he's vacating the house, grumbling out the door.

It occurs to me that I ought to give Judith a tonic because this baby might decide to come when we least expect it. The first thing that comes to mind is Rosemary Tonic. It's rosemary, cloves, nutmeg, eggs, sugar, and a little scuppernong wine, and I keep some on my top shelf all the time. It prevents miscarriage, and, Lord God, that's exactly what we need here, a regular, normal childbirth. So I get that tonic ready, but I also prepare some Saffron Tea, which refreshes the spirits. It's good against fainting and palpitations of the heart. I measure out a quarter glass for Judith and full glasses for the men, recalling that too large a dose brings heaviness to your head and sleepiness. It won't hurt Judith to calm down a little, and it'll do a world of good for the men to settle down even more. A few minutes later I go in to check her, and I can see her face is flushed, and she's breathing quicker. "I think I'm wet now," she says. And she's telling the truth now.

I tell her, "We're cooking with gas now. Try to slow down your breathing. I'll be back with you soon." Her face is tight, her eyes squinting.

Ervin brings my firewood into my front room, and I lay a fire in the stove, telling him, "Here. Drink one of those full glasses I just poured."

He's still cranky. "Why? What is it?"

I turn to stare him down, not saying nothing, waiting him out.

"Ain't you going to tell me?"

I keep on staring, breathing deep and slow, and after a minute he picks up the glass and drains it. I knew he'd drink it because of all the sugar I put in it. When Gorry comes back, he takes the things he's got in a tow sack in to Judith, and I give him a few minutes to love on her a little bit, to find out how she's doing. Then I call to him, "Gorry, come here. I got some medicines for Judith and you."

He answers just like Ervin did, "Why? What is it?" and I reply the same as I done for Ervin. I hand him two glasses. "This is hers, and that one's yours."

After he delivers Judith hers, he lingers next to her bed. I give him a little while, but eventually I call him back out. "Come here, Gorry. I need to tell you and Ervin what's going to happen next. Come on now. I need to say something, and I ain't saying it but once."

Judith says, "Sugar, do as she says. I'm feeling all right just now, but she says it can get rough in a hurry, and I need to be ready when it does. I'm putting myself in her hands, and I want you to do that, too." It's quiet for a while there, but I look over to Ervin who's heard it just like I did. We can hear Judith's voice, but not her words. I strain to catch anything Gorry's saying, but hear nothing. I whisper to Ervin, "Can you hear anything from him?" He shakes his head.

After another minute Gorry comes out, sees Ervin, and sets down across from him in a wooden chair at the little table by the cupboard. He's still holding his glass of Saffron Tea. "Drink up," I tell him, and he does it without comment. I get a brainstorm about another medicine, so I tell the men, "There's one more drink we're all going to have, each one of us, me included."

That raises their eyebrows.

"But first, Ervin here's the plan for you: put your hands on her whenever you can. Rub her aches away. Let your hands talk to her. Let them tell her how you adore her, how you're already adoring her baby, boy or girl. Can you do that for her?"

He whispers something I can't make out, nods solemnly, then stares at his lap.

"Now you, Gorry," I says, "let Ervin use his hands to embrace his daughter. But you...I want you to sing to her."

"Me sing?"

"You can sing, can't you? Does she have a favorite song you know the words to?"

He looks up at the ceiling, and I can see the cogs working in his brain, and he's got one. "I know of one she likes very much, I think." He looks proud for remembering, and I watch the cogs turning again as he's remembering the words. His lips moving silently.

He tries not to smile, but can't help himself as he gets up and walks back there to her. Ervin says, "You got any more of this?" indicating his empty glass.

"Sure do," I says.

While Ervin sips from the glass I've handed to him, I mix up lemon zest, cinnamon, crushed dandelion leaves, a little shine I been keeping, plus some sugar syrup, stirring the whole mixture fast as I can so it froths a white, bubbling head to it. I pour two glasses full.

"One for you," I says, "and one for me."

Ervin hesitates. "What's this? More of the saffron?"

"No, sir. It's a cordial I ain't made in a long time, an herb liqueur called Perfect Love."

41

He sips it, nods, and says, "Good. It's what we need."

From the back room we hear, "I was dancing with my darlin', to the Tennessee Waltz, when an old friend I happened to see---."

Gazing over the rim of his glass, Ervin's face has gone soft and calm. He looks back at me, murmuring, "That was her momma's favorite, too."

The End

Sin

When Miz Lockwood dropped her keys into Buckley's open palm, he saw how he could steal from her. She hired him late that afternoon, saying, "I need you to drive my truck up to LaFollette to pick up a load of marble tiles."

And he thought he could hear his Momma saying, "You can't never tell when a break is going to come your way, so you always got to be ready." As of January, 1943, she was dead now these forty years, but he abided by her words. "Time works in an eternal circle instead of running straight out of the past." So he was careful to watch how things came back around again, if you knew what to watch for. This ran through his head as he planned to steal copper wire and welding tools from the cabin on the Lockwood property out in Dutch Valley.

When Miz Lockwood gave him the keys, she was staring at him and he thought, *Uh oh, she's picked up on something.* He returned her stare, taking in those intense brown eyes, her dark hair, the inquisitive expression on her face. She said, "You drive careful, you hear? They'll be waiting on you at Curt Alley's office. I've already paid for the tiles, so you won't have to fiddle with finances. Can you be back here by seven thirty? I need to feed supper to my crew before we unload."

Wanting to lower her expectations for how long he'd be gone, he said, "Might take longer than seven thirty." Driving away, he started calculating how to pull it off. He decided to head down Tennessee Highway 61 toward Clinton, but then would double back on Sulphur Springs Road. He had worked for Miz Lockwood three weeks earlier with Ed Powell. That's when he found copper wire stored in the ramshackle cabin over in Dutch Valley. He'd looked through the window of the lean-to shed where they kept the old tractor, and that's when he saw the copper and the welding equipment.

He would run get that wire and the welding gear, carry them to Spessard's store, where Dave Woods would keep it all quiet until they could sell it in Rockwood or Knoxville. Dave and him had done this kind of thing several times before, no problem there. Then he'd drive up to LaFollette and come back with her tiles. When she found out about the theft, he could lay the blame on the Gilliam boys out in Frost Bottom. Those Gilliams were all mischief and plunder.

Miz Lockwood was always tied up with her six kids, three teenage boys and two younger girls, then a boy just three years old. As he was working things out, he pulled the pint bottle of Old Crow out of his jacket and took a swig, letting that golden burn slide down. He turned onto the dirt road, which was slick from rain, laughing quietly about what her face would look like when she found out the wire and welding gear were missing. He'd give anything to be there when she saw it was gone.

When he got up to the cabin, he shut off the ignition and sat, listening to the engine as it cooled off, thinking it all through again. He might split a hundred dollars with Wood for the wire, maybe seventy for the welding equipment. A quarter of it would go to Woods, and the rest---well, that would buy a shitload of Old Crow. Which made him thirsty again, so he took out the bottle and drained her dry, tossing it empty into the woods.

He checked at the shed, and the gear was right there. First thing he did was grab about ten pounds of copper and put it in a burlap sack and stash it under his jacket behind the seat. He'd drop the copper off at Spessard's before he went back to Miz

Lockwood. Then he lifted the tarp away and pulled on the near handle of the welder to see how much it weighed. "God Amighty!" he said. "Heavy as lead pipe." He worked five minutes to heft it into the truck, and he liked to bust a gut doing it. He'd need to move it all without getting a hernia, so he quit. That's when he recollected the old tractor. He could let the tractor do the work.

The lean-to shed was laid out on a little slope, but the tractor was sitting nose out under the tin roof. The key was stowed away in the battery box, and he knew Miz Lockwood had her boys disconnect the battery every time they put the tractor to bed. That was a cinch to reconnect. He found the gas can, which, by the heft of it, was about a quarter full. He poured the gas into the tank, found the key, got up on the driver seat, and turned the key as he shifted into forward. Nothing happened. "Shit!" he muttered. "Need to connect that battery."

He shifted into reverse and got down and inched around back of the tractor to get at the battery, sliding behind one of the big tires, which stood nearly chest high, contorting himself to reach the cables. He got the negative pole connected and wasn't sure it was on right. The bourbon was giving him a woozie feeling. He hadn't eaten since…when? Yesterday?

From the rear of the tractor, he reached across the driver seat to the ignition. Something told him how he was stretched out wasn't right just about the same time he turned the key in the ignition. The engine caught right away, and the tractor lurched backward suddenly, slamming him hard into the post at the rear wall of the lean-to. The tractor was grinding away on him. When he had hopped down to check the battery he hadn't pushed it into neutral, and now, damn! His ribs hurt already, and he was having trouble getting a full breath. Then he slipped down a little, and the big rear wheel was turning directly against his hip and right leg. Grinding, grinding.

45

He took in as good a breath as he could manage and tried to heft himself back away from the big wheel, which was turning slowly, but steadily, as if the infernal thing had a mind to run him over. It might just pulverize him as he stood pushing against it with both hands.

No good. He felt something pop in his right shoulder, and he felt the beginning of a dull throbbing pain there. All the while, the big wheel was turning, turning, turning, and his belt was getting hung up a little on the tire treads, pulling his pants down a little bit on every rotation. He could see an angry red scrape on the pale skin of his hip, and that wasn't where it hurt the most. Down lower on his leg where the tire was grinding away hurt like the dickens. Not to mention something gone wrong in his back. Bleeding, he thought.

He gave a mighty push against the big wheel to no avail. His heart was beating rapidly, and he couldn't seem to get his breath. The smell of rotting leaves and loamy soil inside the shed blended together as he wriggled first this way, then that way, struggling to get out from under that big wheel. He yelled loud as he could, "Hey! Anybody! I need help!"

But nobody was around to hear, and the only sound was that damned old beat-up tractor's engine running like a top, chugging along like it was taking him to the county fair. But it was taking him someplace different, banging, bucking against him, whipsawing now and then like it wanted to get out from under the lean-to. He tried again and again to free himself, yelling until he was hoarse and out of breath, his head swimming. The pain in his hip, his whole midsection, and his right leg was spreading somehow. Not to mention his back, which was feeling worse. He didn't know how it could, but that old tractor was pushing him into blackness.

His sleep was fitful. When he woke for good, it was near dawn. The tractor was quiet and still. Must have run out of gas.

His head ached, and he was worried about his leg, which he could not move or even tell if it was there. His shoulder was some better, but he didn't test it. His pants and underwear were soaked through with blood, and his midsection was very cold and tender to the touch, especially on his ribs. It had started raining, and he could hear dripping all around. The pattering on the tin roof, syncopated and almost melodious. He was chilled to the bone, but knew he was lucky because there was no frost showing on the leaves and grass. Just the same, his teeth chattered noisily.

In the dappling sunlight coming through the branches a few little brown wrens flew down in front of the shed, foraging for seeds on the bare ground. He studied them, wishing with all his might that he could acquire wings.

There. What was that? He thought he heard a low rumbling. An engine somewhere. Coming closer. He didn't dare count on anything, but he held his breath as much as he could, and it sounded like an approaching automobile engine.

Minutes later the engine in the distance was perhaps only one hundred yards away, and he heard it idle while the driver got out to open the gate. The engine picked up for a few seconds as the car passed through the gate. Idle again while the driver closed the gate. Then it chugged closer, approaching the cabin. Easing up right in the clearing. Stopping where he couldn't see it, but could hear a car door slam shut.

Buckley hollered, "Hey! Anybody there? Hello, hello!"

Then the sound of footsteps approaching the lean-to. Ed Powell's face peered around the tractor at him. His dark hair showing under the bill of his baseball cap. His beard, a stubble. A perplexed look on his face.

"What happened?"

"Long story," Buckley said.

Coming closer, Ed said, "Where's it got you?"

"My right leg," Buckley said. "And here." He looked down to see a large bruise across his stomach, lavender and yellow around the edges, as if he had caught a cannon ball in the gut.

"How long you been like this?" Ed asked, raking leaves away from the big wheel.

"Since yesterday evening."

Ed raised his eyebrows and said, "Miz Lockwood's a few minutes behind me. She's been worried about you. She's got some of her kids with her."

Buckley licked his lips. He hadn't counted on her.

Ed said, "She wants to haul some firewood I've cut back to her house. Plus she's taking one of her girls to a birthday party. She ast me where you were. 'He didn't bring my truck back last night. Do you know where he went?' I said, I didn't."

Buckley heard the Lockwood station wagon come up as Ed walked away. Buckley heard him talking to Miz Lockwood. Ed's voice, quiet and polite while Miz Lockwood's was stronger, easier to make out. I druther she just speak with Ed, he thought, not wanting to be under her thumb again.

"All right," she said. "Mr. Powell, will you take Pete in your truck to start loading up firewood? Girls, you wait in the car. I need to go talk to Mr. Buckley. I want to see how things stand."

"Yes,m," Ed said.

"Pete, do what Mr. Powell says. Janie, Reba, we'll be going soon as I find out a few things." There was some short-lived whining from young female voices, but she handled it straight away. "The longer you fuss, the longer it'll take to get to Bonnie's party. Is that what you want?"

Miz Lockwood came up to the lean-to. "Hello, Mr. Buckley," she said, but she wasn't looking at him. She was peering at the tractor, walking around behind the shed, coming back in front so he could see her. Finally, she made eye contact, asking, "How're you doing? Are you hurt?"

"Not so much hurt as caught," he said, determined to conceal his suffering.

She said, "I'm sorry you got into trouble." But he didn't like the way she was studying him. She would have a bone to pick with him beyond this tractor business. Directly, she'd be asking why he was out on the Dutch Valley property. He hadn't worked out the best answer to that yet. For all he knew, she was reading his mind.

"Ed might have something back at his house that would work to pull the tractor out of the shed. He'll show me. But, if he doesn't have anything, then I'll get some help. Maybe drive over to Woodcutter's Crossing, see if the guys at the sawmill got anything that'll help."

He felt better hearing that, but on a different level he was wary. He saw how she was zeroed in on his eyes, timing out when to change topics and ask about the welding gear. "I also need to get Janie to a birthday party," she said. "Let me think a minute." She scratched her chin. "If Pete and the girls stay here, I can go for help. Ed can do for you while I'm gone." She went out of the shed and spoke to the girls a minute, but then came back, and he braced himself for her questions.

She called out to the children. "Reba, Janie, stay and help Mr. Powell when he gets through hauling firewood. Mind him, and stay out of trouble. I'll be back directly. You can also sit with Mr. Buckley here. We're going to get him loose pretty soon. In fact, Janie, bring those cookies over here. Mr. Buckley might want one." She turned and smiled kindly at him. "Bear with me, Buckley. We're going to get you out, come hell or

49

high water." Then she was gone. He was relieved she hadn't talked about the welding gear.

Buckley thought about Momma again, and he had mixed feelings remembering her. She could tell him how to get things without working for them, and then she could preach to him. She used to preach about sin, which will take you farther than you want to go. "Sin will keep you longer than you want to stay and cost you more than you want to pay." He had to admit that's how it looked right here. Momma had always surprised him when she talked about the Bible, about doing good deeds for the poor. The way it had always seemed to him, he was his own poor self, and he needed all the good deeds done for himself. At any rate he was damn glad she wasn't around to hear him take God's name in vain, especially if he did it in front of the children---and he was pretty sure he'd done that a few times. And she'd be terribly disappointed to see the mess he'd got into. Seemed like everything she'd always said applied to him, but not the way she intended. She wouldn't be proud of him for stealing from as good a woman as Miz Lockwood. He knew that, and it was the worst part of his predicament.

He drifted a while, thinking about Momma, wondering how he could please her if she was here. The next thing he knew Ed was back and had brought a cedar branch and was pushing it down under the tractor. Ed also brought a large, flat rock, pushing it under the main body of the tractor to use for leverage.

"I'm going to heave it," Ed said, "and when I do, slide thisaway fast as you can. I don't know how long I can hold it." The Lockwood boy, Pete, was standing there, too, watching, and he was good size and might be able to add muscle to pushing the tractor, if it came to that.

Buckley watched Ed jump on his end of the branch, exerting lifting pressure on the underbelly of the tractor, which groaned metallic, but didn't budge. Ed leapt again, and this time the branch creaked in protest, with the same result. That big wheel still had Buckley under tread as Ed fell off his end of the branch and said, "No good."

"No shit," Buckley said. His ribs were sore, and he felt like it was more ribs than before.

Ed was gathering himself for another try when they heard a rumble of thunder over the ridge.

"Move it down this way a smidgen," Buckley said, patting the loamy soil close to his leg. Then the trees swayed way over as a gust pushed through.

Suddenly, the leaves were spattered with large raindrops, and Pete hurried inside the shed. The branches and boughs were straining against the trunks. Leaves blew across the front of the lean-to. Then the rain came in sheets sideways through the trees, loud against the tin overhead, water runneling under the back of the shed. Abruptly, the tractor slid on the slick, uneven ground and lurched down across Buckley, mashing against him, squeezing tight.

Ed got up on his knees. "Tell me what to do. I'll do it."

"I don't know," Buckley wheezed.

Ed scrambled over close to him and reached under him, pulling on his trousers, which had the effect of mashing him in the opposite direction from which he'd been abused thus far. He felt Ed, grasping and straining to keep him up. Finally, Ed fell backwards, and Buckley saw the tractor slide back a bit, resting on his leg again, only lower, which he thought hardly possible. But he did know one thing for sure now: he couldn't exactly feel either one of his legs. He didn't think his legs were broken, but he was sure they weren't working right.

The rain let up some, yet still cascading through the leaves overhead when Ed scrambled around next to Buckley. "You want me to git you some kind of cushion?"

Pete spoke up. "I can get a couple pillows off one of the beds in the house. I know where Momma keeps the key to the front door."

Buckley just looked back at him for a moment. Then he shook his head, muttering, "Anything to eat?" His mouth felt awful. He wanted to taste something. Anything.

The younger Lockwood girl said, "You can have a sugar cookie." She wasn't much over four feet tall with short blonde hair and large, bright blue eyes. Buckley hadn't noticed her standing on the other side of the tractor. Then he saw the older girl a little behind her, taller, with dark hair, wearing glasses. In their matching green sweaters, white blouses, and denim trousers, both girls had anxious smiles as they crept forward to get out of the rain.

"Let me see what you got," Buckley said, and the younger girl stepped forward, holding out a plate of cookies. He took two, murmured, "Thank you kindly," and it was crisp and sweet, and he put it whole into his mouth. Hungrily, he did the second one the same way.

The girls were curious, but shy. At least, the older one was. The younger girl would look to her sister to see if it was all right to be talking with the injured man.

"Girls," Pete said. "Come on in closer. You're getting wet."

They did as told, and Buckley tried to act normal. He was going to power through his situation. He said, "How old are you, girls? What's your names?"

The older girl said, "I'm ten. My name's Reba. And this is my sister, Janie. She's five."

"I'll be six next month," Janie said. "I'm going to have a

big party, too."

Buckley was pleased to have something in his stomach, and they sat a while listening to the cold rain, which gradually stopped. Buckley closed his eyes and dropped his hand onto his leg, just about played out. Ed went back out, and Buckley listened to a car door slam. Then a minute later another car door slammed. Then Ed was back with a hopeful look on his face and a coil of rope in his hand. "They wadn't much but firewood in my truck," he said, "but I did have this rope behind the seat."

"It don't look substantial to me," Buckley said, but he figured it was something, so he said, "Can you rig it up to drag this goddam tractor off me?" He glanced at Pete and his sisters because of his blaspheming, but the young ones didn't react to it, except to glance at one another.

"I can try," Ed said. "Pete, if I need it, can you help me push?" Pete jumped up to be ready, and Ed set about backing the Lockwood truck to the front of the lean-to, up pretty close to the nose of the tractor. He looped the line around the tractor's front left wheel, cinching it down tight. Then he squatted down to sight how it might get attached to a fixed point.

"I'd druther it was more level. Pete, will you stand right there," Ed said, indicating close to Buckley's head. "And let me know when I get close?"

Ed went back out of sight. Then the truck started up, and it first eased back toward him. Then forward ever so slowly until the rope tensed straight. The engine growled as the truck tires started grabbing onto the rocks in the mud. Buckley felt something let go in his middle as the pressure released just a bit, but then he heard a sharp sound, and the tractor was still right where it was.

Ed shut down the engine and came back to squat by him.

"Rope broke," Pete said.

Janie went to pick up one end of the rope, and Reba said, "Janie, come back here!"

"It's all right," Ed said. "Just hand it here."

Janie was tickled to be involved. Reba grabbed her by the hand and pulled her close.

Buckley said, "Let me think on it a while. Then we'll try again."

"I don't see how---," Pete said.

Buckley raised his voice, "Just let me think!"

Ed walked away a while. When he came back, he squatted down by Buckley and said, "You'll figger something out. Or Miz Lockwood will."

Ed looked to Pete. Then to the little girls who had sat down on a log that ran along the shed wall. The girls whispered to themselves a few times. He'd caught a glimpse of Janie sneaking a cookie off the plate while Reba was retying one of her shoes. Janie wasn't through chewing when Reba looked up and said, "Momma told us to save these for Bonnie's party." The plate had only three cookies left. "Jane Margaret Lockwood, where'd all those cookies go?"

Janie said, "Momma said to give some to Mr. Buckley. He must have---he---."

"Oh, no, you don't," Reba scolded. "He had two. You must have eaten most of them yourself. Mr. Powell didn't have any. Pete and I didn't have any."

Janie clouded up right away, her face twisted into a guilty mask.

Reba put a hand on her sister's shoulder, her voice softer now. "It's all right, Janie. Momma would tell us, 'When you make a mistake, find some way to make up for it.' Remember?

She always says, 'Look for ways to get forgiveness.' And I believe you need some."

Relieved at her sister's attitude, Janie said, "Could we give the rest to Mr. Buckley?" She looked from face to face. "But maybe one to Mr. Powell, too?"

Reba looked to the men, and said, "Yes, that would be best, I think. In fact, I think it would be sinful not to."

Janie hopped up and took the plate to Ed, who waved a hand. "Mr. Buckley needs them more than me." Buckley took all three, but not wolfing them down like before, just nibbling. His chest was quivering, his hands trembling. When Janie sat back down Reba said to her, "We need to tell Momma what happened. Do you want to tell her, or let me do it?"

Janie said, "Let me tell it."

Silence fell over the shed, and Janie placed the empty cookie plate on the log next to her, but it slipped off. Reba said, "Just leave it."

Janie said, "How much longer til Momma gets back?"

"Shouldn't be much longer," Ed said.

"I'm sorry you're hurt, Mr. Buckley," Pete said. The boy seemed to have come to grips with things in general, more at ease now. Buckley could sense him warming to conversation. Pete spoke up again. "In Sunday School Miz Rosenbaum told us, 'We're punished by our sins, not for them.' And I...well, I'm trying to figure out...Mr. Buckley, are you being punished? Or is this just bad luck?"

Buckley twisted uncomfortably. "Sure feels like I'm being punished."

"What for?" Pete said.

Buckley didn't answer, but started wondering about that,

too.

They heard an auto coming back up the road, and the kids went to greet their mother. When Miz Lockwood got out, Pete started telling her what had been tried and failed. Janie confessed about the cookies, and Reba shared something Buckley couldn't hear. Miz Lockwood simply said, "I'll speak to him about it. Leave it to me."

Then she came over to the shed, making her way up close, smiling as if she had a funny story to tell. She laid a hand on Buckley's shoulder. "I brought back a gallon of gas. We'll just make sure the battery's still holding a charge and the tractor's shifted into forward...and, if it's in working order, we'll drive it back off you." Her smile widened. "What do you think about that?"

He nodded. "Damn good idea," he said. "We should have thought of that ourselves."

Ed stood there, shame-faced. "You're right. We should have."

Dropping her grin altogether, she said, "Then, Buckley, we'll take you to the hospital in Oak Ridge."

Ed filled the tractor's tank and, pretty as you please, drove the tractor out of the shed. Miz Lockwood and Pete helped Ed carry Buckley to the station wagon where the little girls awaited him. After the girls piled into the back-back, she told him to lie down in the middle seat. Pete joined Ed in the truck, and they headed out ahead of her.

As she drove toward town, the girls were reaching over the seat, touching Buckley now and then on his shoulder. When he glanced up at their faces, he could tell they just wanted to know if he was all right. If he needed anything. When they went into a curve and the car slid a little bit, they'd hold onto him so he wouldn't slide off the seat. He watched the back of Miz

Lockwood's head as she drove, knowing sooner or later she'd turn on him. She'd start grilling him about why he was in Dutch Valley instead of LaFollette.

Janie peeked over the seat at him, and he thought she sounded like his Momma when she said, "You shouldn't cuss God, Mr. Buckley. You'll get punished."

He thought about that eternal circle, but was too tired and hurting too much to do more than to mull over it briefly. All he could do was sniff back at her indignantly, muttering, "Where am I? Sunday School?"

"No," she said. "You're going to the doctor." He made a noise of utter disgust, but the little darling just patted his shoulder. "It's all right, Mr. Buckley. You can get forgiveness soon."

That started him quaking in his boots because, if he got forgiveness at all, it would come from her that was sitting in the driver's seat. Not a damn thing he could do to stop it.

Photo courtesy of Deb Kile Hotchkiss

Won't Last Long

In late August, 1943 I took the train from Trenton, New Jersey to Knoxville, Tennessee where I would be picked up and driven some twenty miles west to the Clinton Engineer Works. I was irritable and conflicted. On one hand, the Movietone News reel playing at the cinemas was announcing General George Patton had captured Palermo on the island of Sicily. Which was good. On the other hand, my fiancée, Gabrielle DuBonnet, had dumped me, and there I was, riding in a Pullman car, holding a grudge against a beautiful woman. Which was definitely not good. As the train rumbled southward, I knew damn well I was still crazy about her. Still worshipped her. She had exquisite, almost feline features, shoulder length auburn hair; exquisite cheek bones; alert, pale blue eyes. I thought she was prettier than Rita Hayworth, and I could have cheerfully spit in her eye.

Ten days earlier she'd giggled, "Yes, Bobby Blankenship, I'll marry you. Yes, yes!" She'd been so coy, such a coquette, teasing me with luscious, lingering kisses. As she pressed her hand to my chest, breathing into me, she literally held my heart in her hands.

But a few days earlier while I was still celebrating on cloud nine, she changed course completely and dropped me flat for a captain who'd just transferred in from Minnesota. He outranked me, that was all it was. Well, he was rich and good looking, too. I have to admit that. It didn't seem to bother Gabrielle one bit to let go of me so she could get a hold of him. So there I was, miserable and stupid and bitter about her and everything else in my life.

I enlisted ten days after Pearl Harbor and left home in Morehead City, North Carolina, bound for adventure and glory in the Army. Ft. Dix suited me pretty well due to my two years at William & Mary. On qualifying exams I outscored most of my competition vying for lieutenant. That made Mother and Dad proud as they could be, but I wanted to get into the War wherever they'd send me. Counterintelligence was my area, but after Gabrielle I didn't feel very intelligent. I wanted to get the hell out of Dix, if I could, and go someplace where I could do some good. It didn't have to be headline news. I didn't need a promotion or fame or any recognition of any sort. But what I did needed to make a difference. It had to be valuable to others. Which would make it valuable to me.

Word had got around about my desire to get away from Dix, so Colonel Cooper called me to his office. "I think I can help you, Bob. Some higher ups have been looking for someone to take on a very special duty. Basic Intel work," he said. "Just short term. Three weeks tops. I can expedite a temporary assignment, but I can also get somebody else if you don't want it. Do you want it or not?"

I asked for more information, and Cooper spent a few minutes laying it out for me. "It's all hush hush down there," he said. "Something called the Manhattan Project. They're looking for someone to help set up an Intelligence and Security Division, but the guy they want to run it can't get there until mid-September. So, if you take it, it won't last long."

I'd be in charge, and it would just be interim. I could do that. It would be a complete change of pace for me. I'd be working on something important a long way from New Jersey. A long way from Miss DuBonnet. I said yes.

I read through my orders about the Clinton Engineer Works

60

in Tennessee, and I got the distinct impression the CEW was a military mystery, something to do with developing new weaponry for the War. That was better than being miserable and stupid and bitter. In Knoxville I was collected by a lanky, baby-faced, redheaded soldier with a speech impediment. Just my luck! As he hefted my duffel into the trunk of a dark coupe, I said, "How'd you know me, soldier?"

He pulled a photo from his pocket, stammering, "I . . . I got your. . . your . . .."

"Picture?" I said, completing the thought. "Jesus H. Christ!" I muttered. I didn't relish talking with a dimwit. This interim assignment wasn't exactly getting off to a great start.

He nodded, handing over my photo. On the back I read, "Lt. Robert Blankenship." Somebody had already done some homework about me. He opened the rear door for me, but I pushed it closed. "I'm sitting up front with you, Private."

"Yes, sir," he said. He was a healthy, athletic fellow whose cheeks tended to color quickly. Not exactly A-1 in my book. Once we were on our way, I questioned him: "What's your name? How long have you been at the CEW?"

"Carl Yoakum, sir. Seven . . .months. Since the CEW construction started. They're...they're still building night and...and...."

"Day," I said. "Where you from?"

"Lynchburg, Virginia."

"You single?"

"Married," he said, warming to the topic. "My wife, her name's Dorothy. I call . . .call her Dollie. We're . . .we're having a . . .a . . .baby next month." He explained she worked as a typist for the CEW Office of Price Administration, or at least she would until the baby arrived. Her work station was in the Administration building, which the Army called the Castle.

I would have resented somebody treating me the way I was treating him, but he didn't seem offended. Finishing his sentences wasn't a habit easily broken because I always thought I knew what he wanted to say.

"Who else do you work with?"

"Captain Bentley checks . . .checks . . .checks on us once a week. He'll be in tomorrow around noon. And there's one more man . . .Corporal Cavanaugh . . .He answers . . .the . . .the . . . ."

"He answers the phone."

"Yes, sir."

I'd ridden twelve hours on the train, and twilight was coming on. Drowsiness descended on me as we rumbled out of Knoxville through the back country headed for God knows what.

The CEW was a military industrial complex like no other I'd ever seen. The place was still in the process of converting from wilderness and rural farmland into a bustling, new metropolis, born amid dust and smoke. Very little grass remaining. Precious few trees still standing. It had rained earlier so there was mud everywhere. In early twilight the sky showed a line of molten gold where the sun would set beyond the ridge.

Yoakum turned in his seat as we pulled up in front of a guard gate. "We got…we got…we got to check in here."

A large billboard announced

SOLWAY GATE

Military Area

Weapons-Ammunition-Explosives

Cameras-Field Glasses-Liquor

Telescopes-Radio Transmitters

Prohibited

All vehicles & passengers subject to search

The guard house had five men, two carrying carbines. One of them walked around the car, motioning Yoakum to pop the trunk. He was busy in back while another guard approached Yoakum. "Show me your badge, soldier." Yoakum turned in the seat to show the badge on his breast pocket. The man turned to me. "Now yours."

"Reporting for duty at the Y-12 plant," I said.

"You got authorization?"

I gave him my military pass. He scanned it, straightened up, and saluted. "Yes, sir. Thank you, sir."

We drove on, exiting the Turnpike, cresting a swale to encounter row upon row of one- and two-story buildings behind chain link fence topped with razor wire. Plus another guard gate. Despite the late hour, the Y-12 complex was a bee hive of activity. We repeated the pass-through exercise with another guard. It was after dark now, but with lights high on telephone poles all around it was as if we'd landed on the moon, deep shadows outside the circle of lights.

The Intel office was housed in a two-story building on the Y-12 complex. Yoakum parked the coupe, and we walked inside. He led the way to a door marked Intelligence Division, a windowless room equipped with desks, chairs, filing cabinets, and telephones. Spartan and neat, the place smelled of fresh paint.

Shorter than Yoakum, maybe a little older than Yoakum, but thicker across the neck and shoulders, Cavanaugh's black hair was a little too long, barely regulation. When he saw my rank, he looked mildly amused, saluted, and said, "Corporal

Donald Cavanaugh reporting."

"Nice to meet you, corporal," I said. "Fill me in. Bring me up to date."

He said, "We get daily reports from all departments. That's how we begin our day." He started summarizing a report, studying me more than informing me until I finally raised a hand. "Listen. Right now I'm nearly out of gas. I'll see you at seven thirty in the morning." Then to Yoakum, "Where are my quarters?"

"Cheyenne Hall," he said. "Not far from . . .from the Castle."

Cheyenne Hall was a two-story barracks, consisting of thirty rooms and two central bath rooms on each floor. Men only. My room was stuffy, but that didn't matter. I dropped the duffel and collapsed fully clothed onto the cot. Out like a light.

The next morning Yoakum and I arrived at the Intel office a few minutes after eight o'clock. Cavanaugh was the one who drove around the CEW collecting reports. Every morning he made six regular stops---the Hospital, the Castle, the Central Bus Terminal, Public Health, the Guest House---which was the only first class hotel in the CEW---and the Town Hall. Each report detailed episodes of interest, violence, vandalism, infractions of protocol. Anything that rocked the boat even the slightest. When Cavanaugh dropped his reports in the inbox, I picked them right up, trying to get a feel for what I'd got myself into. Each report included a list of persons who would be dismissed from the area, specifying any reason for exclusion: theft, fraud, manslaughter, sexual assault, desertion.

Yoakum wasn't much of a talker, but his typed reports were well written---succinct, nuanced, insightful. He was definitely much smarter than he sounded, better on paper than he was talking while Cavanaugh's oral communication was obviously better than Yoakum's, but he just didn't impress me. I was intrigued with Yoakum. Cavanaugh, not so much. But the paperwork Cavanaugh delivered was critical for the department. No arguing that.

We took a break at ten, and, while Yoakum went for coffee, I busied myself reading trivial, mundane stuff until I happened on Bentley's observations on espionage: "We're in a race to develop key weaponry which could win the War. This depends on keeping our work secret, whether those secrets be conceptual, technical, or procedural." When Yoakum returned, I waved what I was reading at him. "Bentley writes,---" I tapped the paper "---about CEW secrets. What kind of weapons are being developed here?"

"Don't . . .don't know," Yoakum said. "We deal with any problem that . . .that slows down our personnel. Recently, we . . .we . . .we've dealt with bad whiskey. Making people real bad sick."

He handed me what he'd typed: Cavanaugh's report on bootlegging, a list of taverns and nightspots where moonshine had been showing up, some of it toxic. Seventeen soldiers had been sickened by illegal liquor. Three had died in an alcohol explosion.

"An alcohol explosion?" I said.

"Explosion," Cavanaugh said. "Somebody lit a cigarette too close to the bottle. The stuff's volatile, that's for certain. But it might have been somebody testing the foreshot and got blown up that way."

"The foreshot?" I said. "I don't know what that is."

Cavanaugh's face shifted from polite and deferential to what I took for arrogant. He enjoyed explaining the word to me. "Foreshot is what the moonshiners call it when they pour off the first drippings out of the still. That's the poison that can blind

65

you. And, since hard liquor isn't allowed in the CEW, most folks do their celebrating with beer. But them that crave the hardstuff crave it any way they can get it."

Yoakum said, "It can bling you or . . .or . . .or kill you."

"Sounds like a dangerous game to be playing," I said.

Cavanaugh wasn't finished. "They can tell when the poison is gone, but that involves lighting a match under a metal spoon full of the stuff. It all looks clear. White, they call it. You light it, and if the flame is blue, it's safe. If it's yellow or red, it's got lead in it." He just stared back at me.

"And lead's bad?" I said.

"They say, 'Lead burns red and makes you dead.'"

Yoakum said, "Tennessee hill folks have always . . .they've always . . .cooked up white corn whisky. Some call it hooch. Some call it moonshine. But when those men died, I was at the hos...hos...hospital, and I heard the doctors talking about methanol. The lead. Some . . .some . . .somebody must have been careless. Cost those men their . . .their . . .their . . .."

"Their lives," I said.

"Yes, sir. A few of the others got big problems. Some still . . .still in the hospital."

"What kind of problems?"

"Headaches, joint pain," he said. "One's still unconscious."

"He was in the explosion?" I said.

"No, sir. He wasn't. They said he was just drinking, him . . .him . . .him and two buddies."

"Are they all right?"

"They're blind," he said. "The doctors don't know if it's per

66

. . .per . . .permanent "

"Okay," I said. "So those guys had probably done a lot of drinking then?"

"Not necessarily," Cavanaugh said. "Ten milliliters can do permanent damage to the optic nerve. Thirty milliliters can kill you. A shot glass holds forty milliliters."

I didn't know what to say about that. Cavanaugh left to go collect reports from another office downstairs, so I went back to what he'd already brought in, plowing through page after page. Yoakum was busy at the typewriter. Five minutes later I found a series of numbers I didn't understand. 95-365 . . .414 100 . . .2-4294 . . .7-2772.

"What's this?" I asked.

"Oh," he said. "These are . . .these are license plate numbers that . . .that I found to be coming through more . . .more frequently at White Wing Gate. More often than any traffic through the other six gates. Ten . . .Ten . . .Tennessee plates. Cavanaugh thinks . . .thinks it's not worth checking."

Cavanaugh outranked Yoakum, but he wasn't around just then. And I didn't like what I'd seen of Cavanaugh anyway.

On impulse, I said, "Take me to White Wing Gate."

"Now?" he said.

I stood up. "I want to see for myself. We can leave a note for Cavanaugh." I stood up. "Let's get going."

While Yoakum drove, I skimmed seventeen more pages of traffic information. There was a handwritten note that said, "Search better." Yoakum's handwriting.

When we arrived at White Wing we parked twenty yards from the gate. It was hot, and traffic was fairly heavy. We checked off all the targeted vehicles. 95-365 would be a 300-

gallon water truck. Two negro male passengers. Driver---
Pompey Ellis, 111 Athens Road (in the Happy Valley
neighborhood, CEW). I could see him as a bootlegger.

414 100 would be a brand spanking new white ambulance.
Two nurses and a female driver, whose name was Billie Etta
Horton. All white.

2-4294 would a dark blue Ford sedan. White male driver,
Rev. Paul Ashford. Baptist. I couldn't tell about him, one way
or the other, but I told Yoakum, "We'll treat the pastor like
anyone else."

7-2772 would a green Chevy pickup. Three females, two
little white girls and the driver, also white, an eighty-two-year
old grandmother, Isobel Disney. Address 976 Bush Road, in
Dutch Valley, outside Clinton. Unclear about the purpose of this
vehicle.

Faces were critical. I wanted to be close enough to see each
driver's face. We approached the guards, who initially weren't
very helpful, partly because I let Yoakum do the talking. Not
the best idea. When he had finished explaining what we were
about, the guy in charge wasn't having any of it. "You can't
hinder this operation. Go get approval from somebody higher
up. We're doing a job here."

It was 11:15 a.m. when we ran into this particular brick
wall, and I had a moment of indecision. Stay to argue or what?
I decided to confer with Bentley when he came to Intel, so we
drove back to Y-12 to get organized for his arrival.

Bentley came in ten minutes early, banging through the
office door like gangbusters. Small and dark like Cavanaugh,
maybe forty years old, he seemed concentrated, like a coiled
fist, quivering and ready to strike. I wanted to look like that:
decisive, confident, ready to act.

"I'm flying to New Mexico at 1400 hours.", he said, sitting

in the chair and propping his feet on the table. "So this needs to be quick." He was attentive as I laid out the idea about license plates. When I finished, Bentley sat looking us over. Which was good, I thought, but also a little uncomfortable. Bentley wanted to hear everything so he'd know what we were up against, so I gave him every last detail of our bootlegging theory.

Abruptly, he dropped his feet off the table with a loud thump. "Private, I need some writing paper." Yoakum scrambled as Bentley said, "General Groves expects this bootlegging activity, which constitutes a chronic security breach, to be eliminated as soon as possible."

Yoakum handed him paper and pen, which he used as he spoke. "Let me get it down on paper. Then we'll talk."

Bentley scribbled nearly half way down the page. Then he asked Yoakum, "Get your Division seal." Yoakum got an embosser stamp from a filing cabinet, and Bentley slid the document into it and pressed it tight a few seconds. Thus embossed, his scribbling had become an official document.

Clinton Engineer Works

Clinton, Tennessee

To all departments including Medical, Transportation, Food Service, Scientific, Waste Management, Military Police, and Housing: You will see that Bearer of this Notice is allowed safe passage with or without showing Identification. You will further see that Bearer is supplied with necessary items including work space and any supplies or materials which he may request to Expedite his purposes. Requests for reimbursement must be documented.

By Order of the Officer Commanding, Intelligence and Security Division

Captain Hershel T. Bentley

August 29, 1943

Yoakum whispered, "Man, oh . . .man!"

Bentley waved the paper at us. "If someone balks, tell them to call the Office of Price Administration office. Colonel Dean in Logistics will vouch for you. I'm going to bring him up to speed about you."

Then he stood and said. "Blankenship, you're in charge of Intel and Security for the next nineteen days."

I jumped in to ask, "Can you tell us a little more about the . . .?"

Bentley held up a hand. "All will be made clear in time." He gave a quick salute. "Good luck, Lieutenant. First thing you do--stop the bootlegging." He didn't stand on ceremony, banging out the office door with the same forceful manner he'd exhibited on entry.

"Lieutenant," Yoakum said, "this morning Dollie had con . . .con . . .contractions. She might go . . .she might go . . .."

"Might go into labor?"

"Right," he said. "I might have to . . .take . . .take her to the hospital. So Cavanaugh might be . . .be . . .be better now. Better than me."

"I'll think it over," I said. "We'll check on Dollie this afternoon. That's the best I can do."

"Thank you, sir. I don't mean to be . . .be . . .be causing trouble."

"It's not really a problem, Yoakum. I look forward to meeting your wife," I said. I was surprised I'd added that last part, but had to admit I was curious about who would marry Yoakum.

He cocked his head to one side, studying me. "Sir, are you . . .mar . . .mar . . .married?"

"No, I'm not. Got close once, but I struck out."

When we returned to White Wing, the sergeant couldn't argue against Bentley's letter. He didn't like us going around him like we were doing. I told him, "If one of our target vehicles shows up, direct it over by the fence." And that was that. We were cooking with gas.

Traffic was steady again. In a way the watching was tedious, but it was also somehow galvanizing as I played out in my mind how the conversation would go when we found someone smuggling illegal whisky. It was helpful to focus on doing the job instead of grieving over Gabrielle. I wanted to think about anything but her. Wanted my mind clear.

We got lucky a little after 4 p.m.. Tennessee license 2-4294. Driven by a small man with brown hair cut short, gray at the temples. He was wearing a white short sleeve dress shirt with a dark, thin tie. The Reverend Paul Ashford was composed and self-assured, even when he got pulled over by the fence. He had merry eyes. Bright, expectant eyes.

I told him, "Please step out of the car, and tell us where you're going. How long will you be on Army property?"

I had a feeling he'd been expecting us, so I was on edge. He handed me his keys. "I expect you'll want to open the trunk." I tossed the keys to Yoakum who took the trunk while I slid into the driver's seat, feeling under the seat, coming up empty. Then the glove compartment. Same result.

"I'm going to the hospital," Ashford said. "I'll be visiting several patients there. One, an appendectomy. Another, a broken hip. I should be headed home before supper."

I pulled the hood release, got out, and opened the hood to

look through the engine compartment.

"My goodness!" the reverend said. "What is it you're looking for?"

"Just looking in general," I said. We came up empty, and Yoakum handed his keys back to him. He shrugged and got back into the car.

"I hope you find what you're looking for," he said. Now he seemed as innocent as the driven snow.

After he drove through the gate Yoakum said, "I'm sort of glad it wasn't...wasn't him bringing it in. A preacher...I mean, that's not...that's not...."

"Not right," I said. We resumed our places as it began drizzling. Yoakum produced oil skin caps and slickers to keep us dry, and it wasn't ten minutes later that the ambulance arrived. The driver, Miss Horton, was an attractive blonde. Stunning actually, like Gabrielle. A real head-turner. The nurses were not so pretty as the driver, but all three of them seemed amused as we did our sweep. The guards were not unhappy that Yoakum had the women stand under the overhang by the guard house. The nurses were giggling and flirting, but Horton got much more attention. We were through pretty quickly, and they were on their way. Without meaning to, I compared them to Gabrielle, and it wasn't even close. I was a fool to even think of her. Yoakum and I weren't making much progress.

An hour and a half later the rain had let up, and there came the green Chevrolet pickup, driven by an old woman with two little girls on the seat next to her. The guards had to stand in front of her truck and force her over to the fence. I came to her window and explained our process, but she scowled at me. "What kind of search you talking about, buddy?" she said, exhaling cigarette smoke right in my face. Then she turned to the girls. "Set still, like I told you to." A big-boned woman, her

72

gray hair tight in a bun, she wore a dark brown shift and men's work boots, spectacles pushed down her nose so she peered over them. The little girls' garments were loose, far too large, draped across the bench seat. The girls were two little lumps, most likely wearing hand-me-downs they hadn't grown into yet.

"Ma'am," I said. "May I ask your name?"

"Miz Isobel Disney," she muttered. "What business is it of yours?" She blew smoke at me again.

"It's the Army's business," I told her, adding a little flint to my voice. "Where is it you're headed?"

"I'm taking these girls to see their momma when she gets off work," she said, glowering at me. "She stays down at East Fork Valley in one a them hutments with two other women. They all of em work at one of the plants. You don't need to ask what work she does. I ain't got no idea."

"How long will you be on the Area?" I said.

"Til tomorrow morning around six or six thirty. I keep my daughter's girls during the work days." She turned back around quickly and said, "Luellen, what are you doing? I told you all to set still, didn't I?"

The bigger girl, perhaps five or six, had sandy blonde hair, short as if bowl cut, and anxious brown eyes. Her little partner, maybe three years old, resembled her around the mouth, but she had darker hair and those same brown eyes. Luellen said, "Sorry, Mamaw. Jackie couldn't help it" indicating the smaller girl who began sniveling, her face flushed, tears trickling down both cheeks.

We didn't need to watch more of this. "You all can go stand over by the guardhouse to sort things out," I said.

Mrs. Disney said, "We won't do no such thing." Her voice, louder than it needed to be, not trying to gloss over anything.

73

She said, "Jackie, the little un's had a accident, so you're just going to have to work around us. That's all they is to it. I ain't going to be a party to embarrassing a little lady." She snuffed out her smoke, let it drop between my feet.

Both girls stared abjectly at their laps. This probably wasn't the first such accident they'd had. I didn't want to give in completely, but we didn't have time for this kind of thing either. I said, "Pop the hood for me, Mrs. Disney. I'll look at your engine and glove compartment. Then you can go."

Yoakum and I did our search. Nothing out of the ordinary under the hood. I shrugged as we let it back down and latched it. I went around, reaching through the passenger window to search the glove compartment. Jackie and Luellen flinched when I withdrew my hand. Not sure why removing my hand bothered them. But there was nothing to see there. I looked to Yoakum, who nodded back at me. I said, "Thank you, ma'am," and she turned away, just like that, and they were gone.

We settled back into our routine, which added to my anticipation about the water truck we hadn't yet seen. I wanted to believe Pompey Ellis was our bootlegger. Either that or we needed to go back to the drawing board. For some reason I thought back about that captain from Minnesota, wondering if Miss DuBonnet was slow dancing with him, breathing in his ear, nibbling on his neck. I dwelt on that too long.

At 5:20 p.m. Pompey Ellis showed up in the tank truck with another negro in the passenger seat. We went into our routine, and I didn't waste time chit-chatting with the big man. Ellis was probably six foot four, balding, square-jawed, his muscular arms swollen against his shirt sleeves. He could have been forty years old, give or take, and his partner, a scrawny, darker fellow with moustache and chin whiskers, looked scruffy. In my book Ellis didn't fit with his partner. Maybe it was his buddy who was bringing in the moonshine.

74

"Where you headed?" I asked. "How long will you be on the area?"

The big man was nervous. "Going to the Central Bus Terminal topping off radiators. Then up to Happy Valley, picking up septic from out houses. Probably on the area til dark."

"You do all that in this vehicle?" I said.

"Uh, No, sir. We leave this truck at Central Terminal. They give us another kind of truck for toilet work. We unload the . . .the . . .."

"Sewage," I said.

"Yes, sir. We dump all that behind Grove Center. They's a spot back there for it."

Yoakum brought a broom from the guard house and climbed onto the tank while I got Pompey and his buddy out of the truck. "Stand next to the fence, boys," I said. "I'm going to check inside the cab." Pompey grabbed his partner's arm, tugging him to the fence. The little man looked like he was about to bolt, which gave me the feeling we might be onto something. These two might be our bootleggers. Yoakum had seen it, too, and he hesitated climbing onto the tank.

"Go ahead, Private," I said. "Everything's under control." I checked inside the cab, finding nothing, listening to hollow reverberations resounding from the broomstick Yoakum was banging around inside the tank.

After a moment he climbed back down. "I . . .I . . .I didn't find anything."

"Well, shoot!" I said. We needed to regroup, so we let Pompey Ellis and friend go. Then notified the White Wing Gate guys we were pulling out. The sergeant smirked. "Come see us any time." I didn't rise to his bait.

75

Half a mile down the road Yoakum pulled over onto the shoulder. "Sir, I recommend we . . .we come back again tomorrow. Do . . .do . . .do it all over again. Better than today."

"What was wrong with how we did it?"

"I don't . . .don't know. We just need to do it better," he said.

I was dejected at striking out. Part of me wanted to find some other strategy right away. Go hard with a new plan. We'd already had what I'd thought was a good plan, but we somehow missed the mark. So maybe he was right. Yoakum's expression didn't alter one iota, and the longer I stared at him, the more I felt he probably was right. It wasn't exactly something he did; it was something inside me, easing onto his way of thinking.

I said, "All right, Yoakum. We come back tomorrow."

He grinned and said, "I was hoping you'd say that. Now can . . .can I ask a favor?"

"Sure."

"We're going to go…go right by the Castle. Is it all right if we stop to see Dollie? I'm ank . . .ank . . .anxious about her."

I clapped him on the shoulder. "Sure. Drive on."

Ten minutes later we pulled up in front of the Administration Building. The man at the desk greeted Yoakum, "Carl, how you doing?"

"Fi . . .fi . . .fine, Barry, fine," Yoakum said. "Going to visit . . .with . . .with Dollie, all right?"

"Sure," the man said, but then he looked at me. "This officer with you?"

"I'm Lt. Robert Blankenship," I said.

Barry stiffened. "Anyone unaffiliated with personnel here

is prohibited from entry unless properly authorized."

Yoakum said, "How about this? Can you phone Dollie? Tell her . . .tell her to come up front?"

"Can do," Barry said, picking up his phone.

Minutes later an attractive woman came down the long hall, obviously pregnant and heavy-laden; her gait more waddle than stride. Wearing flat heeled shoes and a flower print skirt and maternity blouse, she was striking, especially her face and hair. It struck me she might have been Gabrielle's sister. The resemblance was easy to see. Dollie's hair was a little different shade, but it had that same shimmer. And the shape of her mouth, the look in her eyes---they were Gabrielle all over. I tried not to stare.

Yoakum gave her a quick embrace, then pulled back to look at her. "Are . . .are . . .are you feeling all right?"

"Hush, Carl," she said. "I'm all right. No contractions since breakfast. I'm fine." She looked back at me. "Introduce me to your lieutenant." I was struck with how warm and self-assured she was. So genuine and open, unlike Gabrielle who always held you off, always tested you. It was always a teasing, flirtatious game with Gabrielle. Talking with Dollie was a profound relief. Neither husband nor wife was aware of my agitation. How could they be? I couldn't believe it myself.

"Hello, Lt. Blankenship," she said, extending her hand.

"Nice to meet you, Mrs. Yoakum."

"Call me Dollie." Her smile was friendly and intimate. Gabrielle had always smiled for bystanders to admire her. Standing there in the hall, I realized I was infatuated with Dollie Yoakum.

Yoakum asked, "You tired, Honey?"

77

Dollie said, "Sure am." She looked at me, adding, "My boss, Mr. Koontz, told me this morning he doesn't think I'll be working more than about another week or so." She didn't dwell on that. It didn't seem to faze her. She asked, "Are you married, Lieutenant? Do you have children?"

"I'm not married," I said. "Not even in a relationship just now."

"Well," she glanced at Yoakum. "Why don't you join us tonight at Grove Center? We're going to the bowling alley and then the Waffle Shop. We can show you around. Introduce you to some people."

Yoakum's face turned scarlet. "Is it all right, Lieutenant? They haven't put in an Officer's Club here."

I didn't know how it would feel going out with Gabrielle's double. I couldn't see myself sipping a beer if Dollie and Yoakum got up to dance, and I was left sitting at the table. So I said, "Is it possible you could find me a date?"

"Oh, sure," she said. "I've got girlfriends I can call." She looked to her husband. "Maybe Lorna? Or Allison?"

Yoakum nodded. "You know bet . . .bet . . .better than I do."

"Leave it to me," she said. When she turned her smile on me, it felt awfully good. She was open and sincere, trying to please me. At least, that's how I saw it. I was intrigued by the prospect of the evening. I'd be in the company of someone like Gabrielle, but better than Gabrielle. I didn't take time to figure it out. I just let the feeling flow through me.

Dollie had to get back to work, so Yoakum and I went on to Y-12 and sorted through paper. "Let's go at each vehicle in a different way," I said. "You talk to the driver and do the interior. I'll look at the trunk and check under the hood."

78

He looked surprised. "You want . . .want . . .want me to do the talking?"

I said, "You've got good ideas. Sometimes you have trouble getting them out in the open, that's all. Keep everything short and to the point. You can do this." I patted him on the shoulder. He looked sheepish.

"Let's...let's have them empty their pockets," he said. "Or any bags they might have."

"See?" I said. "Short and to the point, that's the way to go. And emptying pockets and bags, that's good," I said. And it was. I was at loose ends about the bootlegging thing, but I was feeling better about Yoakum.

I said, "How about dropping me off at Cheyenne so I can freshen up? I need to change clothes before Grove Center."

"Yes, sir. Thank you, sir. About . . .about . . .about how to talk with people." He was studying my face. "Short and sweet."

"That's right. All business."

I showered, shaved, and changed clothes and went back down to the lobby to wait, settling into a chair, collecting my thoughts about bootleg whisky. I couldn't concentrate very long. I kept drifting back to Gabrielle and her captain. I didn't know what I wanted from her. I didn't know anything about the captain. I was at a loss about them. *So why am I still thinking about her?*

Yoakum and Dollie came to collect me, and we drove to the Grove Center bowling alley where we'd connect with my date. She turned out to be a tall, heavy blonde with a round face and a peaches-and-cream complexion. I guessed---twenty-one or twenty-two. From the looks of her, she was happy to see me, bypassing a hand shake for an enthusiastic embrace, as if we'd known each other quite a while. I took this as a good sign.

"Lieutenant," Dollie said, "this is my friend, Allison Sheridan. She works at Y-12, so you might run into her in the hall sometime."

Allison said, "Lt. Blankenship, I'm glad to meet you." She glanced at Dollie. Assessments were being made by both females, which they seemed to communicate without words. I'd run into this little routine of charades with Gabrielle and her girlfriends in New Jersey, and I never did understand their parlance either. I was going to give Allison a chance. But maybe that was what she and Dollie were communicating to each other: give this guy a chance.

Allison was one of those people who likes to stand close when talking to you, invading your space. I didn't think anything about it when she and Dollie hugged and whispered to one another. But when Allison clung to Yoakum, whispering in his ear, she didn't step back, and a twinge of discomfort washed over him like a wave rushing to shore. I don't think it was what she said, but how she said it. When she stepped up close to me, I didn't mind sharing my space with her. She was taller than Gabrielle, bigger-boned, and obviously athletic, as if she was a centerfielder with a good glove and a strong arm. I doubted Gabrielle could even find center field.

One thing I knew for sure, and it surprised me how good it felt when Allison came close. I wanted to get to know her better, even if it was just for one night. I wouldn't have minded that at all. I was a starving man just walking into a banquet.

As close to full term as she was, Dollie looked uncomfortable bending at the waist when she was bowling. Allison saw that and said, "Carl, Dollie's having trouble. Let's just go get something to drink, maybe something to eat." Again, it wasn't something I'd ever run across with Gabrielle who only thought about herself. Or what you could do for her, not the other way around.

80

The bowling alley had beer, but Yoakum thought we'd be better off at the Waffle Shop. I'd missed supper by going back to my dormitory, so I was famished. The four of us walked down the next block to the Waffle Shop which was doing a big business. They had a juke box cranked up loud, too, so the waitresses had to maneuver between tables and jitterbugs. Yoakum located a table, and we ordered beer. There was an awkward moment as we sorted out who would sit where. As she sat down Allison's thigh brushed mine. She smelled faintly of gardenias, and there was a small blush area on her neck that I wanted to touch. I resisted that, but stared at her too long, and Dollie saw me doing it. Maybe that was sending a message too early in the evening because almost right away Dollie and Allison went to the ladies room, leaving Yoakum and me working silently on our beers, watching couples on the tiny dance floor the Waffle Shop had created. Couples holding onto each other, slow dancing, just shuffling their feet, embracing each other to the music.

"I appreciate Dollie finding Allison," I told him.

Yoakum said, "She had a guy she . . .she . . .she was crazy about. A corporal. David Thornton. He got killed a couple months ago over in Africa. This is the . . .the . . .the first time I've seen her since then."

"She was pretty serious about him?"

"Dollie says she was in . . .in . . .in love with him. Wanted to get married. Have a family. But…but…but they held off on that. She didn't want a war baby."

Allison Sheridan was deeper than I'd first thought. I wondered what Dollie had told her about me. Wondered how she saw me.

The girls returned, and I asked Dollie how she was feeling now. Absentmindedly touching her middle, Dollie talked about her morning contractions. "Six or seven pretty strong ones. But nothing this afternoon. It happens like that most days recently. I'm not ready yet, but I better be ready soon."

"You'll be ready," Allison said. "I don't know anybody more careful than Dollie. She's going to be fine. You hear me, Carl? Dollie's going to be just fine, and you'll be fine, too, so long as you do everything she says. Pamper her every which way. Take the best possible care of her."

Allison seemed like a true friend to the Yoakums, but mostly a kindred spirit to Dollie. Which puzzled me and intrigued me at the same time. Yoakum and I mostly listened and sipped our beer, letting the womenfolk take the lead. The juke box played song after song, the music loud enough now so you had to shout across the table to be heard. Bing Crosby singing *Oh, What a Beautiful Mornin*. Eventually, I stopped even trying to contribute to the conversation, shouting over Bing, and I sat watching the girls talking. Dollie seemed pleased with how the four of us were getting along, and I was impressed with how comfortable everything was. No keep-away games going on. We weren't beautiful or handsome. We were just ordinary folks. I realized I wasn't concerned much about how nice Allison was. In fact, I was hoping that in another way she wasn't that nice. More beer would help that kind of thinking. I should have had some supper a couple hours ago, but now I was enjoying the beer. The place got suddenly quiet as Vera Lynn sang "We'll meet again, Don't know where, Don't know when, But I know we'll meet again some sunny day." It slowed everybody down all through the song. But when it was over, it got loud again.

Twice Allison's hand landed next to mine, just barely touching. I wasn't unhappy she'd done it. She looked at me, inhaling deeply the last time she did it. That was all. No frown, no grin. Just stared at me. I wondered about her guy who'd got himself killed. David Something. Had she been saving herself

82

for him? Or did they do anything? Then it hit me that maybe I'd saved myself for Gabrielle. It didn't sound right to think I was holding back somehow, but the more I thought about that, the more it seemed likely, and I didn't want that. I wanted just to go with the flow, and I was hoping Allison would feel the same.

It was after eleven when we left the Waffle Shop, and Yoakum drove us to the Central Bus Terminal where Allison got out of the car, so I did, too. She said, "Thank you, Carl." Then she explained to me, "He knows I want a candy bar. They've got them at the concession stand, which is open all night." She reached for my hand and said, "Won't you come with me?"

"Sure." There was no way I'd let her go by herself.

When we started walking, she held my hand and said, "My dormitory's not far. We can walk."

"Mine's close, too," I said.

She stopped us and said, "Wait here for me. I need to tell Dollie something. Be right back."

The night air was just cooling down, which was very welcome. I'd had four beers without the benefit of anything to eat. I should have eaten something. Not a good practice to get buzzed on a first date. I was disappointed with myself until I realized I hadn't thought about Gabrielle in hours. I was distracted by Mrs. Yoakum and Miss Sheridan who didn't play keep-away games. So there was that. Not disappointing at all. And it wasn't like I was in the middle of something that would last forever. I was assigned here three weeks, tops. So carpe diem, right?

When Allison came back, she almost glowed, looking pretty good in a way I was appreciating more and more. She'd be a real handful if we got friendly, and while I was contemplating that, she caught me studying her.

"What?" she said.

"Nothing really," I said. "Just that I've had a good time tonight. That's all."

"Me, too," she said, taking my hand again. We got her the Tootsie Roll, but she didn't unwrap it. "I'm saving this," she said. "I need to cut back on sweets, but I just can't. I treat myself like this a couple times a week." She shrugged, smiling at me. "Tonight seems like a special treat. Very special."

I didn't know how to take that.

As if she was reading my mind, she nodded slowly. "I told Dollie and Carl you'd walk me home."

"Are they still waiting for us?" I said, craning my neck to look for Yoakum.

"I told them to go on. Dollie's really tired."

Cheyenne Hall was on the way to her dorm, so we stopped by there. I had a brainstorm about getting some private time with Allison, but the desk clerk said, "No females in the rooms." I thought I'd reason with him, but I was more tired than I thought, my tongue thicker than it should have been, and I stammered a bit just getting started. Rather like Yoakum. And that gave the guy opportunity to stand his ground. "No exceptions."

"Let's go outside a minute," I said, tugging Allison out the door. I didn't know what else to do. If I was seeing things right, she was a little wobbly, too. I put my arm around her shoulders to steady her. Which she appreciated because she lingered against me. I was enjoying how she lingered as we walked to a bench out in front of the dorm. Then she turned abruptly, took my face in her hands, and planted a long, open-mouthed kiss on me that got my attention. Holding hands, we circled back to Cheyenne Hall and sat on the bench outside the entrance. I put my arm around her, and she leaned into me, yawning.

"I was hoping I could show you my quarters," I said.

She nodded, but said, "I don't think I could stay very long and then be able to make it to my own dorm." She raised up to look at my face. "So I need to beg off tonight." She kissed my cheek. "Can I get a rain check, Lt. Blankenship?" Then she yawned again.

I wished she hadn't said the part about a rain check, and I wished she hadn't called me Lt. Blankenship. I thought about talking her into just going to my room for a little while. That's all it would take, but that last yawn of hers was infectious. I fought to repress my own. I even resorted to pinching myself to try to wake up and get something special started. Pinched hell out of my arm just behind the elbow. But after I let go of myself, the pain subsided, and I knew it was no go. Both of us were goners.

"Come on," I said. "I promised to walk you home."

It was getting a little cooler, fireflies abundant and active. We didn't talk as we were walking, which let me do some thinking. If we'd got to Cheyenne an hour earlier...if I'd had something to eat...if I'd limited myself to only two beers or even just one...it could have been a night to remember.

But none of that happened, and nothing else did either, except I walked Allison about 400 yards to Arapahoe Hall where we had to pound on the door a while to get somebody to open up. Allison almost missed my mouth altogether when we kissed goodnight. She glanced off my jaw, then said, "Thank you, Davey...I mean Bobby. I had a good, good time with you." She was sleepy.

I walked rapidly back to Cheyenne, wide awake and energized by the time I got there. All wired up, ready to go, but nobody to go with. I lasted for about ten minutes. That was all

I had in me.

At breakfast I was famished. I kept thinking Allison Sheridan was a veritable tonic for me. But I had to admit I'd missed an excellent opportunity with her. I wasn't sure there would be more chances like that. I felt really good and close to her, but how long would this feeling last?

The next five days were feast or famine with her. I worked long hours getting better informed about the CEW. I toured Y-12, which was huge. I visited the site of K-25, which was still under construction. I even visited another site where they'd just broken ground, a place that would be called X-10. While I was concentrating, trying to take it all in, Yoakum was invaluable, explaining the geography and some of the differences between the various plants. He didn't know much, but what he told me stretched my understanding. Helped me get a better picture of the Clinton Engineer Works and its military potential.

When I was off duty I saw Allison four of those five nights, twice with the Yoakums when we got something to eat. They wanted me to sample the best restaurants, and the four of us got to know each other better. Allison and I went out on our own twice. At Grove Center we caught Gary Cooper in *For Whom the Bell Tolls*. A really good war movie that had plenty of romance. Ingrid Bergman, who played the Spanish girl, Maria, had very short hair, but even so I thought she looked like Allison. Natural, wholesome, and, I hoped, passionate. Two nights later at the Center Theater down the street from Jackson Square we saw *A Guy Named Joe*. I liked Spencer Tracy in every movie he ever did.

I was getting more and more comfortable with Allison. After Spencer Tracy we got some beer and just talked a while at T and C Café on Jackson Square. Then, as we were walking arm in arm back to Arapahoe, one thing led to another, and she squeezed my arm, whispering "Can I redeem that rain check

86

tonight?"

"You most certainly can," I said, trying not to sound too ecstatic. She kissed me again while my hands did some wandering along her waist and hip. I was taken by the way her lips lingered on mine as she breathed into me. The way she gazed at me told me she was going to keep some kind of a promise she'd made to herself, not just to me. I let myself get a little more aggressive, both of my hands on her hips, sliding behind her until she caught her breath and shook her head.

"Not here, mister," she said, stopping my hands.

No guessing game. No keep away.

We walked up to Cheyenne Hall, and I was doing my best to work up a plan on how to get by the receptionist, but when we got to the desk, he wasn't there. What the hell?

We slipped on down the hall to my room where I was able to surprise Allison a little bit. Myself even more. Naked in bed, we rushed through everything without speaking, except for little cries from her throat---without saying what we wanted. Gradually, we warmed up pretty well and melted together. Twice. I craved the taste of her, and when I was spent, it was like falling off a cliff into oblivion. It might have been a dream, but she found her voice before I did. "Oh, my sweet Davey," she murmured. "Stay with me." Not sure I'd heard her right, but I would definitely be staying.

But in the morning it was Allison who was gone, and I was disappointed. I didn't know what I expected. Just that she would be there. I tried to go back to everything that happened, but it was s ort of fuzzy. Allison had been insistent and more than willing. She had wanted the same thing I'd wanted. When you think like someone again and again, you just click with them. You know you're going to agree about things. I was sure of her that way, and that had helped me sleep like an innocent babe.

There was a note on my dresser. "Call me at 2482 after 6:30 p.m---AS." I didn't want to hurt anybody's feelings, but I wasn't ready to call her. Her leaving me asleep had stumped me. I wasn't planning anything at all except to find out who was bringing bad whiskey into the CEW. That was my job. After that, maybe I'd be able to call.

When I got to the office I was self-conscious, struggling to pay attention to our investigations, but simultaneously enthralled with Allison. I was content at work. I was content when I was with Allison, but the transitions from one to the other were tough. I could handle the one or the other, but could I handle both? This part of the CEW, these people I was working and socializing with, they were different from those I'd known at Ft. Dix where everything depended on rank and appearance. I had a split-second flash of Gabrielle's face frowning at me, but I repressed it. Yoakum and Dollie had done what they could to take care of me, and I was grateful. Maybe things with Allison had gone further than they'd expected. Further than she'd expected. Than I'd expected. All of us were a little further along than expected. Other than Cavanaugh, I was with people who actually cared for me.

But when Cavanaugh arrived at the office that morning, dropping reports in the inbox, he looked different. Not so breezy and casual. He looked almost grim. "The Hospital reports five alcohol deaths over the past seventy-two hours," he said. "More bad whisky down by Grove Center. Some at the Townsite, too. Two gunshot wounds, not life threatening, but we're dealing with guns now, Lieutenant."

I asked Yoakum, "What are the chances our targets had anything to do with this? What do you think?"

He pondered my questions. "We've got a good plan," he said, and I noted not only what he said, but how he'd said it. Just stating the obvious. Short and sweet. What we'd started, we needed to finish.

Whoever was bringing in the bad whisky was killing people, and it wasn't slowing down. It was picking up. It was mean business. The CEW prohibited hard liquor, allowing sale of beer only. Not even allowing wine. But illegal moonshine, white corn whiskey, was too tempting for many of the civilian workers and soldiers at work on Y-12 and the other plants being constructed. The hooch or moonshine, whatever it was called, it was irresistible. Some of it was potent and provided the desired effect much quicker than beer. It was powerful stuff, but some of it was plain old murder.

We had a theory about how it might be coming in, even if the notion was only slightly more than nothing. Focusing on White Wing Gate was worth trying. Yoakum and I were feeling copacetic with our plan. And now I even felt better about Cavanaugh.

Yoakum and I went back to White Wing to start over, getting there just in time to see Ashford. Ellis came through ten minutes later. Yoakum did all right doing the talking, keeping his comments short. His stammer not so pronounced. The nurses came through after noon, and the guards got in the way again. I had to growl at them so we could do a more thorough search. "Back off until we're done," I told them. The sergeant grumbled, and I thought he might give us real trouble. I sure as hell didn't want to bring the MP's in, but he finally left us alone. There wasn't anything in the ambulance, not that we could tell.

We realized Isobel Disney would have brought her granddaughters through before 7:00 a.m. so we'd missed them going out, but I thought we'd catch them coming back in around 6:00 p.m..

At 1:15 I told Yoakum, "Let's get something to eat and talk things over. We've got to have a backup plan if Mrs. Disney isn't hauling it. Otherwise, we're hunting needle in a haystack. There's just too many cars and trucks to account for."

"You don't...don't...don't think she's bringing it in with her little girls in the truck, do you?"

"No, I don't," I said. "Maybe we missed something on the water truck when we let Pompey Ellis go. We should check him again, but let's search Mrs. Disney good and proper when she comes back through. Finish what we started. In the meantime, let's figure out something else."

"Do you want guns?" Yoakum asked. "I don't, but I thought you might."

I thought about that. "No, we'll let the gate personnel be our muscle. Use their carbines if they need to."

We got something to eat at the Central Bus Terminal and then swung by Y-12. When we walked in the door, Cavanaugh piped right up. "Lieutenant, it would save time if you use the phone at White Wing. Instead of driving back and forth to see what's come in while you're out of the office. I can give you an update whenever you call."

I asked Yoakum, "Did you know they've got phones at White Wing?"

He shook his head. "No, sir."

Cavanaugh grinned like a Cheshire cat. "They just got phones at White Wing a half hour ago. All the gates are getting phones. I heard about it at Public Health. There's no phones in trailers or hutments, but they're starting to put phones in the flattop houses and the dorms. The whole CEW is getting downright civilized. We can stay in touch with each other. You know, speed things up." He was proud as a peacock. "So there's that," he said, studying my face.

I was about to tell him "Good work," but just then the door

opened, and Allison stood there, her smile cordial, almost formal, as if she hadn't been introduced to me. I didn't know what to say.

"I'm delivering your ID badge," she said. "You'll need to wear it all the time." After she said her piece, she ignored me, greeting the others. "Hi, Carl," she said. "Hi, Donald."

I attached the badge, thanking her, and there was another awkward moment of silence until Yoakum said, "Dollie says hi, too."

Turning to him, Allison asked, "How's she feeling this morning?"

"Fine," he said. "No contractions. She'll be all right."

"From your mouth to God's ear," Allison said, glancing at me as if something else was going to happen. Was it my turn to speak? I couldn't think, my head, still throbbing. Allison looked fresh as a daisy. I was anything but. There she was, waiting on me. Cavanaugh and Yoakum were waiting, too, but they stepped away, Cavanaugh retreating to his desk in the far corner, Yoakum to his typewriter, which he loaded with paper and got busy. Allison, still awaiting some signal from me. The moment dragged on. Finally, she took a step forward and under her breath said, "You're a fool." Nobody heard it but me.

"That's okay," I said, caught off guard, not knowing why she said it. "I've been a fool before." Trying to make light of things.

That did it for Allison. She left without closing the door, marching down the hall. Cavanaugh was shuffling papers, seemingly unaware of her exit, but Yoakum was watching. He shook his head and said, "She's mad. She'll...she'll beat you til your name is Jesus."

"Huh?"

"Don't overthink things."

I skipped a beat, thinking about not thinking, which didn't make sense. But I trusted Yoakum. He wasn't trying to finesse anything. He was giving advice.

"I'll be right back," I said. I hurried down the hall and, at first, couldn't locate her in the coming and going. Striding rapidly, I made my way past the few people in the hall and around a corner, and there she was, unaware I was trailing her. I flashed on something: Gabrielle would have played this as a prima donna, traipsing down the hall at a speed designed to let me catch up with her in a dramatic confrontation. But Allison was trucking it down the hall. I called out, "Allison, wait for me. Wait!"

She turned, huffy and impatient, not inclined to wait. I felt her heat right away, but I didn't want things to keep going like they were. Allison was so distinctive, so unique, so very different from what I was used to I wasn't sure I knew what she wanted. She hadn't given me a chance to telephone her after work. She'd come early to the office. That was good, but I wasn't ready. Didn't know what she wanted. Shoot! I didn't even know what I wanted.

"Well?" she said, plainly irritated with me.

I said, "What did I do? Why are you angry?"

She stared back at me, breathing through her nose, huffing audibly. Cogs were turning in her head as she deliberated about how to answer such stupid questions. I thought she would blast me, but she resigned herself to something else. She just glared at me. "Well, if you don't know," she said, "I'm certainly not going to tell you."

She let that sink in, then turned on her heel, and marched away. I was absolutely flummoxed as I walked back to the office. She was a complete puzzle. If I didn't understand why she was put out with me, and if I asked her to explain things to me, and if she outright refused to explain anything at all---well, how do you deal with that? Who thinks that way? She'd left me without a single clue.

We had already proven we could make sparks fly, and those sparks were, in my opinion, spectacular, bright, and golden, but I didn't really know Allison Sheridan. Didn't know what her job was, where she was from, her family, her background. Didn't know diddly about her, except what she enjoyed in private. I needed time to work things out in my head, and it wasn't like I didn't have anything else to occupy me. I was torn up trying to fit Allison into my life. Or me into hers. I didn't have time for a capricious female just then. I'd be okay seeing her again, if she'd let me. And I'd like to be with her in the dark again, but I wasn't sure all that was still possible. I didn't know how to calculate which way to go, what to do, but it felt right somehow to hold onto her, if I could. She could be real, real quick like Gabrielle. Or she could be forever.

When I got back to the office, Cavanaugh was gone again. Yoakum said, "Cavanaugh's done some work on...on...on the other six gates' reports. He's found that Mrs. Disney's been leaving sometimes through Elza Gate. Highway 61."

"Highway 61 goes where?" I said.

"To Oliver Springs, a small town north of us. Clinton, the county seat, is east of us if you use Elza Gate," he said. "Eight miles away. It's . . .it's . . .bigger than Oliver Springs."

"Bootlegging territory?"

"Oh, yes." He handed me a sheet of paper. "Here's a list of Mrs. Disney's exits over the past ten days. From White Wing and...and...and from Elza."

"No other gate? Not at Gallaher?"

93

He shook his head. "No other gate."

I looked at her times, coming and going, trying to see a pattern. Her entrances were sort of scattered, but all occurred in the evenings---5:15, 5:45, 6:10, 6:55, 6:22, 5:31. Her morning exits were more consistent---6:14, 6:11, 6:23, 6:11, 6:17. She was using both gates, alternating back and forth for a while until the last three trips, all of which were through Elza.

"Yoakum," I said, "can you tell what I'm thinking?"

He grinned. "We're going to Elza Gate?"

"You got it."

It wasn't far. When we got out of the car, I went to the sergeant in charge and told him who we were looking for. I was ready to flash Bentley's letter, but the guy said, "Yeah, I know who you're talking about. Old lady and two little girls. Comes through regular as clockwork. Never says much though. She's got this take-charge attitude."

"Did she leave here this morning?"

"Yes, sir," he said. "A little after six o'clock. What you want her for?"

"We want to search her vehicle for bootleg whisky."

He laughed out loud. "That old witch? I wouldn't put it past her." Then his grin slipped a little. "She wouldn't bring in hooch with little girls in the truck, would she?"

"You never know," I said.

We waited and waited, but never saw Isobel Disney. I called Cavanaugh at the office, but he never answered. "Probably gone home," Yoakum said. "We've missed her…and…and him, too."

"All right," I said. "Let's go see if Cavanaugh left us anything on his desk and then call it a day. We'll try Disney again tomorrow."

Cavanaugh hadn't left anything important, so Yoakum drove me to Cheyenne. I laid down in my room a few minutes before walking over to the Terminal for a burger and fries. I didn't have anywhere to go or anybody to go with. I went back to my room.

Lying on my cot, I started thinking about Dollie, wondering how she was coming along, but pretty quickly I ended up wondering some about Gabrielle. There was clear juxtaposition between the two of them. One petite, glamorous, capricious. The other, sincere, honest, and straightforward. Gabrielle was such a knockout, such a prize, that I had let myself be led around like a prize bull, happy just to be close to her. Happy she'd lay hands on me now and then. Ours had been a relationship built on appearances and physical sensation. Like any guy, I wanted somebody nice looking, somebody attractive, and there were plenty of those around. Allison was one of those although her demeanor was nothing like Gabrielle's, who seemed always to be one or two steps ahead of you, and if you disappointed her, she just ignored you. Forgot you. She didn't really care about your feelings. It was always about her.

But Allison showed how she felt right away, and didn't mind making it real clear to you. She had a hair trigger. And she was more than a handful. She didn't have to tip toe to look me straight in the eye. I thought for a while about how healthy she was, dwelling on every single detail about her, everything about her I'd already discovered. I went back through our first episode a couple of times, lingering on how it had felt to be with her. I shivered uncontrollably at the memory of one especially delectable kiss, unable to stop myself from smiling at the thought. I was pretty mellow considering what we'd done, but it was probably going to fade. If I was going to have some, I needed to taste it soon. Savor it. All this until I fell asleep.

Yoakum and I spent the next two days trying to locate Isobel Disney, but it seemed whenever we zigged, she zagged. I had a few thoughts about giving up on her to start on some other theory, but I was stubborn. Once I started a job, I had to finish it. I only had a few days left in the CEW. If I was going to nab this bootlegger and do something worth a tinker's dam before the next officer arrived, I needed to get on the stick. I was running out of time.

We tried Elza first, then White Wing, but no Isobel. We checked the gate tallies and found several times she'd come through minutes before. She wasn't exactly consistent any more, and it seemed she was aware of being hunted somehow, figuring out where we'd be before we figured it out ourselves.

One of Cavanaugh's reports told us there were four more guys in the hospital due to bad whisky, and we went to talk with them, but we got nothing. "Shoot, man," one said, a short, stocky blond fellow with gauze over both eyes. "I was three sheets to the wind when somebody gave me a glass of hooch. Rum and coke, I thought, but it didn't taste like rum, and it sure as hell had a kick to it. Lord, God, I got the worst damn headache I ever had in my life. And now I can't see shit! I'm still hurting, man, and I'm in the dark forever! Can we quit talking? Please, can we just stop?"

Back at Y-12 we checked in with Cavanaugh, who said, "Why don't you wait somewhere halfway between White Wing and Elza, maybe at the Terminal, and have the guards call you when Disney shows up? They got phones at the Terminal."

"So they just hold her until we get there?" I said.

"Why not?" Cavanaugh said. "Surely, they can hold onto an old woman for you."

Yoakum said, "Let's contact all…all…all the gates. Get her held until we can get to wherever she's tried to come through."

96

We tried to set that up, but not all the phones were connected. It would take another day or two to get a phone installed at every gate. The CEW was growing fast, but not everything was coming in on schedule. So we drove around to the ones that didn't have phone hook-up yet, and I had to show the Bentley letter at each gate, which smoothed the way for us, and we began the waiting all over again. It was after one thirty when we returned from the Oliver Springs Gate. I didn't really think Mrs. Disney was our smuggler, but we needed to check her off the list. Then maybe we'd need to go another way. My tenure at Intel wouldn't last much longer. I'd been counting down the days until the new man would arrive, and all this would be over for me.

But I was wrong about that. Cavanaugh brought me a telegram from New Mexico. This is how Bentley put it: "Replacement delayed in San Diego hospital. Continue in position until notified of reassignment. Do some good."

I folded the telegram and put it in my pocket, thinking about those last three words. Yoakum said, "Good news?"

"You could say that," I said.

We got lunch at the Waffle Shop, which looked different somehow in the daylight. Allison's face flashed by me, and I regretted not doing better by her. I would have liked to start over with her.

Yoakum asked to use the phone behind the counter to call Dollie. There was only one phone at her office, and it was busy. When he got back to the table, he looked anxious. I asked him, "How'd she do last night?"

He nodded. "Had pretty strong contractions. But…but…but nothing this morning." He was calm on the outside. I wondered if he was on the inside, too. I liked him. Liked her, too, but didn't know them well. Had to admit that. Good people, I thought, but who knows how they'll end up? Sometimes the feelings of somebody you care about can rub off on you. Can change you. I wished I could see me the way they saw me.

"I think Dollie's going to be fine," I said. "I think you two are going to be lucky in the important things. Like having babies."

"Thanks," he said, sipping from his iced tea. "Let me tell you about my Daddy. He worked on…on…on the railroad more than forty years. He always told us kids…he said, 'Look on the bright side.' Us Yoakums, we…we've always been lucky. Whole family's been lucky."

"That's good," I said. "A good way to be."

"Yes, sir." He blinked and sipped again. "But…but…but Daddy told us, 'You'll lose it if you brag about it.' So I don't even bring it up most of the time."

"Then why tell me?"

"You're…you're different. Dollie likes you. We both do. I want to serve. I'm willing to sacrifice. For Dollie. For our baby. For you. For America. I might not…not…not be saying it right, but all this is inside me. Does this make sense?"

"I understand," I said. But I wasn't sure I did. I heard his words, but didn't share the feeling. I didn't have somebody like Dollie. Didn't have anything to brag about. I felt empty.

The waitress brought our sandwiches, and we got busy eating, but I was struck by what Yoakum's daddy had said. The part about not bragging. My mind was unsettled about things: Isobel Disney, Allison Sheridan, bad whisky, White Wing Gate, and Elza. I'd need some time to get a handle on things. I could do investigating. I could romance Allison; one or the other. But how do you do both?

Yoakum sat pushing his food around on the plate with his

98

fork, not eating much, so I said, "Go call her again. You'll feel better."

"Yes, sir."

He hurried to the phone, but got back quicker than he should have. "Still busy," he said. "I dialed three times."

"Eat up," I said. "We'll try again at White Wing."

He heard me, but he didn't eat much. Five minutes later we were in the car. At White Wing we parked by the fence and went to check in at the guard house.

"Lieutenant," the sergeant said, "your driver just got a call. Name's Yoakum, right? His wife's gone to the hospital. Baby's coming."

Yoakum went pale. I told him, "Go on to the hospital. I'll get a ride later." I was happy for him. Right away he was moving light on his feet, but stopped suddenly right in his tracks, staring at something.

"What?" I said. "What is it?" I turned to look. The green Chevrolet truck with Isobel Disney at the wheel was just pulling into the gate. Without a word, Yoakum and I walked briskly toward the truck where a soldier was approaching Mrs. Disney. The sergeant in charge was there, too.

"Sergeant, Sergeant," I said, raising my voice. "Hold up there." I headed for the driver side window, pointing Yoakum to the passenger side. Mrs. Disney wasn't happy to see us, and she turned away to say something I couldn't hear. She was speaking to the girls beside her. I was almost up to her door, when the truck lurched forward a foot or two, then stopped again. Two armed guards stood in front of the truck. She wasn't going anywhere.

"Mrs. Disney," I said. "Shut off your engine. Step out of the truck. The girls, too."

Yoakum was at the passenger side window, peering across at me. "Go ahead, private," I said. "Help the girls out of the vehicle."

From that point on, everything happened in a kind of slow motion. Mrs. Disney brought out a large, antique pistol, swinging it around to bear on me. I yelled, "Gun! Gun!"

She pulled the trigger as I was twisting away, clenching my eyes closed. When it came, the shot was like thunder. My head slammed back as I fell flat on my back, stunned like I'd been hit with a sledgehammer. The guards were shouting, "Drop the gun! Drop the gun!"

The older girl shrieked, "Mamaw! Mamaw!"

I was flat on my back, breathless, my face numb. So dizzy I didn't know which way was up. I touched my cheek gingerly, holding my fingers up to see if I was bleeding. My entire hand was bloody. My teeth ached. I tasted blood in my mouth. Wet. Salty. I spit trying to sit up, but was restrained by someone. The truck engine revved up harsh and shrill as if grinding against the gears, and I heard Yoakum. "Shut it down!" He was in front of the truck, coming around to the driver side, holding the smaller girl, blanched and stoic in his arms.

The truck lurched forward again, the fender ramming into him, knocking both him and the girl to the ground. She landed on top of him as his head rebounded off one of the stanchions at the guard house. The guard at the driver's window used his carbine to smash Mrs. Disney in the face. She collapsed across the seat, the truck engine slowing and coughing, eventually going silent. Stopped cold.

They let me sit up. I felt blood slipping down my neck, and I swallowed so much I coughed, spewing some on my shoes. My cheek felt like it was sinking into my face. A guard called out, "Roy, get the medical kit. And bring something to wipe up

100

the blood."

Then to me, he said, "You don't want to lie back down?"

"I think I'm good." I was aware of Mrs. Disney still lying across the seat. Not moving.

The guard spoke to his buddy, "Check around the other side of the truck. Find that other girl."

Yoakum sat up, still holding onto the smaller girl, who seemed none the worse for wear. Yoakum struggled regaining his feet holding onto her. He brought her over to me and set her down. He told her, "Let's see about your granny."

"Mamaw," she murmured.

"See about Mamaw," he said. As he leaned into the cab, he put a hand on the seat, and the upholstery must have shifted slightly because he jerked and stiffened to keep his balance. I heard an unexpected sound. A clink. He studied something, then stood back up, turning to look at me. He looked tired.

"What?" I said. "What did you see?"

He blinked and shook his head, but said nothing. He paused as if he heard a distant call.

Two more guards came up to the truck. One said, "Let me check on the woman." Yoakum backed away. The smaller girl reached out to hold onto his leg, hugging him, trying to keep him from going anywhere.

Someone brought me a hand towel and said, "Let's see what's going on with your face."

He was maybe forty, forty-five. Brush mustache. Sandy hair. He wiped my chin and neck, then dabbed tentatively above my wound. "I'm going to wipe careful as I can where you got hurt. Just take a quick look."

He put two fingers behind the towel, gently touching my cheek, proceeding in a circle around the wound. While he was so engaged, my teeth throbbed, and I got slightly dizzy. Still not actually in pain, but maybe in shock. Maybe some vertigo. When he finished, the towel was heavy with blood. "The bullet didn't go through your cheek. That old pistol misfired. It wasn't fully charged. You're a lucky son of a bitch." He took a few steps around me, bent down, and picked something out of the gravel. "Here it is," he said. "Looks like a lopsided minie ball."

He dropped it into my palm, a bloody, misshapen lump. Then he said, "I'm going to check on everybody else. Do you want to come inside and sit in a chair? We'll take you to the hospital to get a doctor to say grace over you. Same for the old lady. And your driver, too."

"Yoakum?"

"Is that his name? Yeah, he hit the ground pretty hard. Seems okay now, I guess." He shrugged. "We need the docs to look at him. Better safe than sorry."

I saw the wisdom in that. The guard handed me a new towel. "Your wound's seeping blood." Somebody was at the driver door, tending to Mrs. Disney, so I went around to the passenger side. I pushed at the seat, and a squared-off section slid onto the floorboard. Where the section had been was a crate with a dozen mason jars filled with a clear liquid. We had probably found our whiskey. We'd need to get it tested to make sure it was what we thought it was.

I made my way inside the guard house and found a chair, but I only sat a minute before I got up to look for Yoakum. He was around the corner of the guard house, sitting on the ground with both girls, backs against the wall, legs splayed out in front of them. One girl to his left, one to his right. None of them said anything. It was like they'd just sat down there after a long walk. A brief, peaceful moment. Yoakum's right ear looked odd. His hair looked scruffy, like he'd slept on it wrong.

"You all right?" I said.

He nodded, but he didn't elaborate, which made me uneasy. I moved a little to the left so I could see his ear better. Was that blood? I stepped closer, and it certainly looked like blood. Just a trickle.

"Yoakum," I said. "Do you know me?"

He smiled faintly and nodded.

"Okay," I said. "We need some help here."

I directed the sergeant to seize the illegal whisky and keep it under lock and key. "But give me one jar," I said. "I'll send for the rest later." The guards brought up two jeeps, and they loaded Mrs. Disney into the first one, along with two men to ride with her. She was unconscious. The rest of us got into the next jeep. I rode shotgun, pressing the towel to my face, wincing at every jolt or pothole, feeling the impacts in my sinus. Yoakum and the girls rode in the back.

At the hospital I lost track of Mrs. Disney. Two nurses escorted me into a small examination room and had me lie down. There was a little kerfuffle around Yoakum because the girls wanted to go with him into a room adjacent to mine. That's how it worked at the start, but after a few minutes Yoakum was laid out on an examination table, and the nurses wanted to move the girls to another room. That didn't go over well. The younger girl, Jackie, started screaming, scrambling past the nurses to latch onto Yoakum's legs. He raised his head to see what was going on, but made no move to deprive her, so the older girl, Luellen, did likewise. They were caterwauling and screaming, and the noise hurt my face. I had raised up too quickly on one elbow to watch. The nurses asked me how I'd been hurt, and I told them, "The old lady shot me. She's the one that came in with us. Do you have any idea how she's doing?"

"Not yet," the brunette nurse said. "We'll let you know when we find out anything. You want me to take that?" indicating the jar of hooch cradled in my arms.

"Well, yes," I said. "Can you keep it safe for me? It's evidence."

"Evidence of what?" the white-haired nurse said.

"Smuggling," I said. "Bootlegging."

"That's not really a crime, is it?" she said. "Not here in East Tennessee."

Her partner said, "It's a way of life in these parts. That's what I've always heard, but we'll hang onto it for you."

They were busy moving me around on the table, placing pillows under my shoulders to keep my head elevated, removing my bandage, looking me over. They took my pulse and stuck a thermometer in my mouth for a while.

"It's illegal to sell toxic liquors," I told them. "This stuff can blind you if it doesn't kill you."

After they used some soap and water to wash away the blood that had dried on my face, the white-haired nurse said, "Yeah, I took care of three guys who'd had bad whisky. Two of them are blind. The other one's dead." She spoke to her partner. "Bad moonshine."

Both nurses told me to lie still. "The doctor will come see you soon. Are you hurting? We can give you something for pain."

"It's not too bad," I said. "I've felt worse."

They left me, but the white-haired nurse named Murtaugh came back with a glass of water and two white pills. "Here. Drink these down. You don't need to be a hero."

The doctor hurried in, a short, bespectacled fellow in a white coat. "I'm Dr. Burgess," he said. "What do we have here?"

"Gunshot wound," I said. "Not serious, but...but...."

"But needs tending," he said, turning my face into the light. "Keep still," he said. "I need to see which muscles are affected. How deep the wound is. So far, it doesn't look too bad." He moved my chin left and right, then asked a nurse, "Can I have a probe?"

He wiped my face carefully. I was still bleeding, but not so much as before. He probed lightly the circumference of the wound, finally announcing, "I'm going to wash out the wound. You got some black grit in there. You'll need about ten stitches, I think." Fifteen minutes later, he was through with me. The man had a delicate touch.

"Murtaugh," he said to the white-haired nurse, "bring a mirror so the lieutenant can see what he looks like. Then bandage him up good and proper."

She handed me a small mirror, and I thought I looked like I'd lost a knife fight. But it felt all right. A little tight at the cheek. I tried to keep a straight face.

I asked her, "Do you know how Yoakum's doing? He's my driver."

"I need you to sit for ten or fifteen minutes. If you're feeling okay after that, you can see him. Dr. Burgess has already seen him."

She led me to a corner of the waiting room where she pulled a curtain to keep me out of harm's way. Where I was out of sight. She hadn't made eye contact with me when she said her last few words, and I didn't care for that. "I'd feel better if you'd tell that last part one more time," I said, and she finally

105

looked at me. "I'm concerned about Yoakum. I'd appreciate it if you could tell me about his condition."

"We're not supposed to do that," she said. "You're not family. I can only tell family and staff about his condition. You're neither. But let me do some checking," she said, leaving me behind the curtain. I tested my bandage a few times, but the bulk of it prevented much sensation except for how tight my cheek was. I was grateful the Novocain was still working, but it made my head feel huge.

After a while I heard footsteps, then I heard Murtaugh talking with the younger nurse, "Jenny, did you hear anything about the driver? How's he doing?"

"Dr. B believes he's had a concussion plus a small brain bleed. Which has stopped. Burgess checked everything, his vision, hearing, sensation, reflexes. He reacts to being pinched, and his reflexes seem fine, but his eyes are fixed and dilated. He'll answer you most of the time. Not all the time. It's like he's got a short circuit."

Murtaugh came over to check on me, pulling back the curtain, placing her fingers on my forehead to check for a temperature, smiling briefly. Very businesslike.

"Thanks," I said.

"For what?"

"I think you know."

She smiled again and said, "No fever that I can tell. Dr. B says you can see your driver now. But don't get him stirred up. He needs x-rays, and he might be spending the night here." She lost the smile. "That's all I can tell you. Shouldn't have told you as much as I have."

I got up, and she pointed, "Last room on the left."

Yoakum lay on his back, staring at the ceiling without acknowledging me. "Hey, buddy," I said, laying a hand on his shoulder. He looked at me, but his eyes were glazed over. I didn't think he knew who I was.

"Yoakum, do you know me?"

He gave no indication he did. He seemed to be resting for a while, perhaps gathering words for a reply.

"Short and sweet, partner," I told him. "Come on now. Tell me something."

I watched him a while, as he stared at the ceiling. I was worried about him, but there wasn't a damn thing I could do. It was up to doctors and nurses.

What was up to me was getting the moonshine tested, and I remembered I'd left the jar with Murtaugh, who was nowhere to be found. I did find Jenny. She rummaged around in a cabinet and then handed me the jar. She was busy, I could tell, but before I left she said, "Have you seen Mrs. Yoakum?"

"Mrs. Yoakum?"

"One of our orderlies told me a Mrs. Yoakum has had a baby, and she was worried her husband wouldn't know she was here. I put two and two together. I mean, Yoakum's not a common name. She's up on the second floor with her brand-new baby girl. I don't think she knows he's been injured."

I went upstairs and asked for Dollie. The nurse at the maternity desk said, "Mrs. Yoakum's in room 223. Are you a relative of hers?"

"Yes," I lied. When I got there, Dollie had just finished nursing the child. When she saw me, she said, "Lieutenant, come in, come in. Come meet Emily Gail." She was happy as a lark, but, when she saw my bandaged face, she had questions.

107

"What happened?" She skipped a beat before she said, "Where's Carl? Where's my husband?"

"He's downstairs. He fell and hit his head. He was all right for a while, then sort of slowed down. Maybe a concussion? They're not sure."

She took a deep breath, and I saw how she was struggling to compose herself. She offered a brief, fragile smile. "What happened to you?"

I explained, but was talking too fast, saying too much without thinking it through. I was trying to reassure her, but from the way she was looking at me. I wasn't doing it. Not at all. I fully expected her to melt into a puddle, but she didn't. "When the baby goes back to the nursery," she said, "I need to see my husband."

"I'll get a nurse."

"That would be good."

She was all business, no artifice whatsoever. Determined. Beautiful. My heart went out to her.

I went back to the maternity desk and explained that, "Mrs. Yoakum's husband is downstairs. He's injured. They don't know how bad. She wants to see him."

The nurse said, "Let me get somebody."

I told Dollie, "They're coming." I wanted to tell her how I'd seen him, but I was afraid she'd ask what I thought about his injury, and I didn't want to tell her about that. I wanted to help her. To talk about the baby. To wave a magic wand and have Yoakum up and about, smiling, holding the child in his arms, looking back at her beaming face. He wouldn't have to say much. Wouldn't have to say anything at all.

Finally, a nurse came in, gathered up Emily Gail, who had

thick dark hair and looked sunburned red. They took her to the nursery. Dollie got out of bed gingerly, and I found a wheelchair in the hall and we used it to get her from her room to the stairs. She crept down the stairs behind me as I rolled the wheelchair step by step down to the first floor. I wheeled her down the hall until we ran into Jenny, who said, "He's down in room four."

Murtaugh had just come out of Yoakum's room, and I said, "This is Yoakum's wife." Murtaugh took her in like she was Dollie's sister, gently, full of sympathy and understanding. "We took x-rays," she said softly, but with a tenderness I thought was just right. "We're worried that he had a brain bleed, but the pictures show that's not the problem. He's got a slight skull fracture. Which is something we watch very carefully."

Dollie's face lost color. When she saw that, Murtaugh touched her arm. "Do you want to take a minute before we go in?" she said. "Before we see him?"

Dollie took another breath, but said, "I'm ready now."

I followed to the threshold, watching as Dollie sat on the side of the bed, her hand on Yoakum's chest, speaking quietly to him. "I'm here, Carl. Right here with you."

Murtaugh stood close by for a moment before retreating out the door. As she went by me, she gave a nod, indicating I should follow. When we got to the nurse's desk, we stopped, and I spoke to the nurse, "Let me ask you something. Is it common for someone to hit his head and there's no trouble right away? Then later problems show up? Is that normal?"

"Sometimes it happens that way," she said. "Each case is different. Depends on the person. How strong he is. How healthy. Lots of things. Sometimes it comes on like this, and then it goes away. It's not always permanent. But it's always a horrible waiting game to play." She sighed. "And you don't get better with practice."

Dollie stayed with Yoakum for nearly half an hour before they came to get her. She needed to nurse the baby. I walked back with her, but didn't stay. "I've got to check on some things," I told her. "I'll be back. I'm sorry, Dollie. I feel like I'm responsible for…it happened pretty fast. I don't know."

She reached for my hand. "Did he get hurt before or after you were shot?"

"After."

She touched my shoulder. "That's what I thought. You wouldn't have let anything bad happen to my Carl, if you could help it. But you couldn't help it. So it's okay. My Carl's always been lucky."

The nurse brought in Emily Gail who was fussy. I wanted to say something, but I didn't know what it might be. I went downstairs to the emergency desk to find out about Mrs. Disney. The nurse said, "Are you family?"

"I'm the one she shot," I said, which caught her off guard. "More importantly, I'm in charge of the Intelligence Division here, and I need to question Mrs. Disney. We're arresting her on charges of attempted murder. Now where is she?" I said the last part a little stronger than I intended, and it had the opposite effect. The nurse got her back up and said, "You'll need to talk with Dr. Cadwallader."

She directed me to Cadwallader's office. He had a slight build and was neat as a pin, but reluctant to do as I asked until I showed him Bentley's letter. That did the trick. He asked if there was anything he could do personally, and I said, "Lead me to Isobel Disney."

"You won't get much out of her," he said. "She has a broken jaw, and we've sedated her heavily."

"Why the sedation?"

"She was unruly. We had to get her calmed down. With her jaw wired shut we couldn't understand what she was telling us." He grinned. "We were pretty sure she was cursing every one of us, slapping and kicking to beat the band."

"I'd like to see her anyway," I said. "Even if it's just to take a look."

I didn't really have bad feelings about her. I was impressed with her devious audacity, bringing in illegal whisky accompanied by her grandchildren. I didn't like her using little girls as part of a smuggling enterprise, but she had pulled it off, hadn't she?

Our work wasn't finished. Where'd she get the whisky? Who was she delivering to? What did they do with it? How could we trace them? Put them out of business? We had plenty of work left to do. Miles and miles of it.

This was in my mind as Cadwallader and I went to Disney's room. He was right; she wasn't helpful. She was sound asleep, and they even had a restraint attached to one of her ankles anchoring her to the bed. I took a look at her jaw, which was swollen and misshapen, and I couldn't help touching my own bandage. The Novocain was wearing off. The whole side of my face felt too tight now.

Cavanaugh came walking in, proud as punch. "Lieutenant, I've got a jeep outside whenever you want to leave."

"How'd you know to come here?" I said.

"White Wing called the office and made a report. I thought you might need some help. I asked at the desk, and here I am." Then he stared at my bandaged face. "You all right, sir?"

"I am," I said. "Yoakum's not."

"Huh?"

"Let's see Yoakum before we go. I just want to check on him one more time."

Jenny didn't make eye contact as we passed her in the hall. Inside Yoakum's room Cavanaugh stepped over to the bed and said, "Yoakum, hey, buddy. It's me, Cavanaugh. How you doing?" He grinned at me, then at Yoakum, but when nothing happened, his grin gradually disappeared. Cavanaugh was trying to help, but didn't know how. Watching his frustration, I could relate to him a little better.

We went by White Wing to check with the sergeant. The Disney truck had been moved up next to the fence, and the keys were still in it. I talked with the sergeant, with the other guards, and finally with Cavanaugh about how to get the crate of whisky tested. We had a choice---to deliver it to the MP's or find a lab at Y-12 that could analyze it. I had them send it to the MP's.

The rest of the day was a comic opera. I developed a dull headache, which might have been due to the Novocain. I called the hospital to find out what had happened to the little girls. Cadwallader said, "I'll have to check on that for you." Mrs. Disney's condition was the same, as was Yoakum's. We needed to investigate where the whisky connections were. Cavanaugh helped me start listing steps to take, but I had trouble concentrating, making mistakes just writing things down. My own personal motor was sputtering and stalling out. Finally, I said, "Cavanaugh, take me to Cheyenne Hall. We can pick back up on this in the morning."

"Sure thing," he said. "I'll drive you. No problem." He was delighted to be taking care of me.

I picked up a clipboard, thinking I might make a better list at the dorm, and we were just starting down the hall when I saw

Allison approaching. She didn't notice us until the last second. She halted abruptly, her brow wrinkling as she recognized me. When she saw it was Cavanaugh with me, she said, "Where's Carl?"

Cavanaugh didn't help when he said, "I'll bring the jeep to the front door." The way he said it and hurried out made Allison anxious.

I said, "Carl's at the hospital. So's Dollie."

Allison's face brightened. "So the baby's come?"

I smiled. "Emily Gail Yoakum's doing fine. So's her mother."

"Oh, my goodness!" she said, touching my arm. "A little girl."

She gazed at me in the same way I'd been gazing at her, and finally she pulled me close again. "Hold me," she said. "I need you to hold me."

I was pretty good at that. She molded herself into me, which told me more than words could ever tell, and that made a big difference. She pulled away. "It's only twenty-five minutes until I get off. Will you take me to the hospital when I get off?"

"Of course."

"And do you love me?"

"Yes," I lied, thinking she was a little crazy. But maybe she was right. Or maybe I was the crazy one. Whatever it was, things seemed right this way. I didn't really care what she said, only that she was there.

She went back to work, returning ten minutes later. "They said I could go early," she said, and we headed for the jeep. When we got to Dollie's room both women wept while Dollie tried to explain about Carl. There'd been no change since I'd

113

seen him. Then a nurse brought the baby, and the tone shifted from alarm to joy.

Emily Gail's ruddy face contorted from grimace to grin. Her eyes opened wide.

"Dollie, she's perfect!" Allison said. "Just look at her. She's got your mouth. So sweet, so pretty." There were tears again, but they were more hopeful.

I left to see about Yoakum. I found Jenny first. "Can you give me an update on Yoakum?"

Jenny wiped a stray lock of hair behind an ear. She looked tired, but she drew herself up, smoothing her skirt and blouse. "He's hanging in there," she said. "He seems a little quicker when you walk in on him, quicker to focus on you. Still not talking, but he seems more aware of his situation. That could be good…if he keeps it up."

"Can I see him?"

"We're bringing his wife down in 45 minutes. It would be best if you saw him same time she does."

"Dollie's got a friend visiting with her right now," I said. "And she'll want to see him, too. Is that all right? The three of us?"

Her brow wrinkled. "We try to keep visitors down to one or two." She looked as if she might cave in if I pushed her, but I didn't do it. "Best hold it to just two people with him for now."

"I understand."

Dollie needed Allison more than she needed me. I touched the bandage on my cheek, more sensitive than I'd been earlier. My headache was worse. I checked with Cadwallader about the little girls, and he told me he'd found an off-duty nurse to take them until they could contact their mother. Mrs. Disney was still

114

under sedation, sort of a twilight sleep. "Much easier to treat her that way," he said. "She'll probably be ready to leave the hospital in a couple of days. Maybe three more days. Remember, she's in her eighties."

"Thank you, doctor," I said. "You've got a lot going on here. I appreciate what you're doing."

"You look like you're about to say, 'but,'" he said. "What's still bothering you?"

"I'm just trying to make sure that the women are okay with Yoakum's situation. They ought to be thinking about the baby, but now they've got to worry about the husband."

"And how do you know him?"

"We work together," I said. "He's my driver. And he's one of the good ones, you know what I mean? He's solid. I rely on him." I shrugged. "Don't want to lose him."

Cadwallader nodded, and I got the impression he was waiting for me to tell him more. It was as if he knew something I didn't. I had an inkling of something unresolved, something I'd overlooked somehow.

I went back to Dollie's room, and both women looked at me quickly when I came in, and then looked away. I thought they'd been talking about me. Allison's face was getting red, but she came right over to me. "Can we see Carl now?" she said. She was up close to me, and I wanted to put an arm around her shoulders and hold her for a while.

I explained that two people could visit him in about 45 minutes. "And that's when the two of you need to be with him. I'll see him again later." I started making a list of everything he and I'd need to do to find out who Mrs. Disney was taking the bad whisky to. Did she know it was deadly stuff? I hoped to God she didn't.

We talked a few more minutes about the incident at White Wing Gate, and they took close looks at my face bandage. Allison raised a hand to my cheek. "I won't get close to the wound or anything. I just need to see how you are," she said. Her palm, warm and soft on my cheek. She kept it on me, the first message I'd had no trouble understanding. I was keen on her, heedful of everything about her.

I went out into the hall so the women could praise every inch of Emily Gail to their heart's content, and I considered where we had come. The day had dragged on and on, and it would continue relentlessly, blending work with longing. I considered how Allison had reacted to news of Emily Gail, news of Yoakum, news of my injury---all of it. I'd treated her unfairly, imposed on her, but when she'd held my face in her hand, everything turned over inside me. She was still a mystery, but she was nearby, and of her own accord. Allison and I didn't have to pretend something. We just needed to experience what we had to the fullest as long as it lasted. To endure and savor it. This whole notion, this fateful realization came like a bolt out of the blue, leaving me shaken and bewildered, but strangely hopeful.

Hackworth House

General Leslie Groves was distracted. His driver, Sergeant Marcus Brummett, didn't know whether to open the car door or not. Marcus stood a moment with his hand on the door handle, staring at the big man in the back seat. The sedan itself was unmarked and unremarkable. That is, there was no lettering on the side of the vehicle designating it as a Clinton Engineer Works administrator's mode of transportation.

Poised where he was, Marcus could see his own face in the side mirror, tie slightly askew. Ever so slowly, he reached to adjust it, trying not to attract the General's attention. Marcus was lucky to have visited the barber at the Townsite just yesterday. This fellow, Groves, the man he secretly referred to as High Pockets because he wore his belt so high he looked like a spud stuffed into trousers, was a stickler for maintaining proper military appearance. Marcus's dark brown hair was not exactly military cut, but it was neat and trim so he breathed a little easier.

Marcus had been driving the highest ranking officer in the area around the CEW for eight months now in the unmarked car not because of any humility Groves might possess---which Marcus thought was scant---no, the General traveled around the Area without fanfare because it was more efficient. He could get wherever he wanted without anything slowing him down, and that's the way the General liked to operate. He didn't want people at the three plants, Y-12, K-25, or X-10, to know he was coming. He liked to surprise people. Catch them off guard. Of course, Groves would never admit as much. He always said, "I just want to see how you're coming along without wasting time sprucing up the place for the brass, without preparing for inspection. We shall succeed by doing what we need to do exactly right as quickly as it can be done." General Groves always finished up such conversations by asking, "Do you understand me, sir? Surely, you can see how it's got to be if we're going to win this war."

The inevitable reply was, "Yes, sir."

Groves was a big man physically, weighing over 220 pounds. He had a barrel chest, steel gray eyes, and a short gray mustache. He was a confident man who didn't mince words, never cursing or even raising his voice, though he was often sarcastic and demeaning to those who had displeased him. Marcus had never witnessed the man losing his composure. Groves knew what he wanted about 95 percent of the time, and the other 5 percent he had a knack for figuring out what fit the situation best, moving rapidly toward that end. By 1943 Groves' twenty-four years of experience with the Army Corps of Engineers had enabled him to be very near the top of that part of the Army. Before he'd come to East Tennessee, Groves had been stationed in Washington, D.C. where he had supervised the construction of the Main Headquarters of the Department of Defense, which some called the Pentagon. The amazing five-sided, three-story building covered about ten acres of land enclosing millions of square feet of military office space. It was a gargantuan construction project which he had personally overseen. He had already succeeded on a huge military project, and Marcus was swept along on the man's momentum every time they went anywhere in the hubbub that was the CEW.

Throughout this southwest corner of Anderson County, Tennessee, only about twenty-five miles from the Knoxville city limits, thousands of civilian workers were busy obliterating hundreds of acres of forest land all through the valley to make way for various warehouses, plants, roads, houses, trailer parks, and the necessary shops needed to support the sudden influx of civilian personnel. This was where Groves was going to build something as big or bigger than the Pentagon. Three industrial complexes under construction out of sight of the houses and stores along the Turnpike were hidden from one another because of the natural ridges comprising the foothills of the Appalachian Mountains referred to locally as the Great Smokies. These ridges divided one valley into several parallel valleys, but unless you were on official business with a high priority like Groves enjoyed, you were clueless about the work going on across the next ridge. The planned X-10 site would be separate from another designated Y-12, and Y-12 wasn't proximate to the planned K-25 site and not far from the S-50 site. Neither were the respective sites laid out alike. One was a long oval-shaped structure. Another was three or four stories high, yet without such an expansive footprint. Groves had set about keeping each of these three facilities oblivious of one another. Questions were discouraged. Secrecy was paramount. The War Effort required it.

Y-12 ran twenty-four hours a day with at least three separate shifts of men and women employed. Hiring for K-25 was on-going now, and interviews for X-10 and S-50 jobs would start soon. Thousands of civilians had found jobs in the CEW, doing every conceivable task to construct and operate these plants. Whether a plant was still under construction or fully operational, activity on site was continuous. Buses ran to each site, dropping off and picking up the hordes of workers. It was never still. Never idle. The Clinton Engineer Works was like a living thing, a monstrous military organism. You heard its rumbling heartbeat day and night, and the beast was growing constantly throughout the valleys, surging up onto the ridges.

Groves was in charge of this beast, and he was an ambitious taskmaster. All business all the time. Brash, assertive, pompous now and then, impatient, shrewd, and a little hard to take once in a while. He had a swaggering ego and certain idiosyncrasies that let everybody know that, when he was ready to go, he was going to go, even if you hadn't had all your say. The white-coated, scientific types got irritated when he cut them off before they could completely make their factual case. Lieutenants, captains, colonels, and even lesser generals gave High Pockets the evil eye after he dismissed them and was walking back to the car. But, as dictatorial and decisive as he was with everyone else, Groves had never really given Marcus a hard time, and Marcus was a mere sergeant. High Pockets was actually a pretty nice boss, a good passenger. Marcus's future depended on keeping the General happy, on time, and where he wanted to be every day all day long. That is, when High Pockets was in town.

Groves traveled often, apparently all over the country. Sometimes out west. Maybe somewhere in New Mexico. Or maybe Washington state. Maybe both. And he was in Chicago now and then. Also in New York City, and, of course, Washington, D.C. Marcus would get a phone call at the Guest House where he lived and served as a glorified taxi driver when Groves wasn't in town. Groves' assistant in D.C., a Mrs. O'Leary, would call and say, "He's coming in from Chicago. Pick him up at the Knoxville train station tomorrow at 9 A.M. He'll need your services for the next six days."

Sometimes it would be just two days. Sometimes ten days. And other times Groves would be set for the six days or whatever time period it was, and then change his mind. That would be another phone call any time of the day or night to or from the front desk at the Guest House, a new guest accommodation not yet completed, situated on one of the ridges that provided a nice view of the Townsite and the Turnpike that ran through the middle of the burgeoning community which was growing every single moment.

120

The girls at the front desk would either phone Marcus's room, or, if he wasn't in the room, they'd go hunt him down in the dining hall or outside on the patio. Marcus wasn't allowed to stray from the Guest House when Groves was in town. If he was delivering a passenger somewhere else on the Reservation, he checked in with the Front Desk to give his reason for departure along with an estimate of how long he'd be absent. Upon his return, he was required to let them know he was back. It was a peculiar way to live, but Marcus rather enjoyed it. He was a VIP in the CEW.

Groves did not use the Guest House himself, and that, too, was peculiar. Before the Castle had been readied for visiting dignitaries, Groves was put up for the night at a little stone house near Elza Gate which had been owned by the Hackworth family. The place had been acquired by the War Department as had nearly a thousand other properties in this part of the county. Most of the existing structures inside the CEW had been demolished after the farmers and other residents had been relocated elsewhere, but somebody---maybe Groves himself--- had decided to use Hackworth House, a charming little stone cottage, nothing very special, probably only about a thousand square feet all total. Two bedrooms, a living room, a dining room, and a nice kitchen with ample pantry space. In the beginning Groves would spend his CEW nights either in the maternity ward at the hospital or at Hackworth House. Marcus really wanted to know how that maternity ward arrangement worked out. It was pure Groves to get his rest someplace where you'd never look for him.

The Hackworth caretaker, Theophilus Kincaid, took good care of the General. He cooked and served his meals, kept the place in good order inside and out. Marcus often saw Theo mowing the lawn, watering the flowers, attending to all the outdoor chores. Kincaid and his wife had originally sought a quiet life completely removed from the War Effort, but, of course, that was no longer feasible. While Mrs. Kincaid was a shy one, Theo was a congenial, fair-haired fellow, not quite six feet tall, trim like an athlete, light on his feet. Marcus considered him a little different, distant now and then and somewhat distracted, but with his wife's help Theo took very good care of their Very Important Person, General Groves. Mrs. Kincaid's given name was Bathsheba, although her husband called her Bashie. Marcus often stopped by the photographs displayed on a shelf in the living room to gaze at what were obviously Kincaid wedding photos. He considered Bashie a beauty, that's for sure. The couple were nearly ideal caretakers of Hackworth House.

But now, quite abruptly, the General looked up at Marcus, as if just realizing the car had come to a halt in front of Hackworth House. "Oh," he said. "I was thinking about something else." He thrust papers into his briefcase, latched it, and got out. Marcus had once made the mistake of trying to handle a particular suitcase, but Groves corrected him sharply. "This one I'll always carry myself. Be mindful of that, Sergeant." High Pockets kept it with him in the back seat along with an overstuffed leather briefcase. Secret material, to be sure.

Theo stood at the front door, which was how he usually greeted them. He seemed to be watching for them whenever they were headed his way. "Welcome, General," he said, smiling warmly. "Sgt. Brummett, how are you?"

"We're hungry," Groves said. "What have you and Mrs. Kincaid planned for supper tonight?"

"Fried chicken, General."

"And...?"

"Mashed potatoes, green beans, biscuits with gravy."

"And for dessert?"

122

"Pecan pie," Theo answered. "Just as you requested last month."

"Ah, Sgt. Brummett," the General said, "we have hit the jackpot."

"Yes, sir, I expect we have."

Theo took a suitcase from Marcus, leading him to the General's room, a modest, neatly appointed bedroom, lit by windows facing north and west, a sturdy spool bed accompanied by a walnut dresser and matching nightstand with telephone. There was an oak rolltop desk on the opposite wall with a Tiffany lamp illuminating the room.

Marcus began placing the General's clothing in drawers as Theo hurried back out to tend their guest. Groves told Theo, "Let me have a glass of tea, please. I have some reading to do before supper. Then a phone call to make. I'll be ready in about twenty minutes."

"Yes, sir."

Theo delivered the tea and walked back into the kitchen to find Bashie seated at the counter, her head in her hands.

"Are you all right, darling?" he asked her, making sure not to let the others overhear.

She sat up and took a deep breath, nodding, "A little tired, is all. Is the General ready to eat?"

"He said twenty minutes."

"We can wait a bit more," she said, turning to face him. He saw she was not feeling well. Either that or thinking again about the baby.

"Try to stay busy," he said. "Think of other things."

She looked up at his face. "Not so easy as you might think,"

123

she said. "This sickness, this affliction I got, it ain't what I ever wanted for our family. You know that."

He poured two glasses of tea. "I know. I know."

"I still get the weak trembles," she whispered, and she saw him flinch. "Oh, not now, Theo. Not now. Earlier. Before you walked in. I'm feeling a little bit better. I am. You worry too much. You know that, don't you?"

They stood in silence a while until he said, "Let me go check on things. Back in a minute." He held her gaze an extra beat before taking the tea to the table.

As she listened another wave of exhaustion washed right through her, and she felt light-headed such that she grabbed hold of the counter with both hands. She took two quick breaths, and the dizziness lessened. After the spell passed, she did as Theo had suggested, thinking of other things.

She focused on their most recent outing. It had been Theo's idea nearly two months previous on her first day back from the hospital. He hadn't told her what he was going to do, abruptly turning north on Florida Avenue, which had just been graveled. Compared to other roads through the Townsite which had been graveled weeks earlier, Florida Avenue seemed like part of a grand boulevard extending up the slope of Black Oak Ridge. It was wider than most other streets in the CEW, and the scent of fresh-laid gravel seemed to make it a smoother ride, so much so that Bashie had been thrilled to realize that the sounds emitted from her throat were laughter instead of mourning for a stillborn child. The bumps and ruts on the road were gone. Now it was a smooth ride.

Theo had been so delighted with her sudden expression of joy that he took them all the way to Outer Drive, found a circle which turned them around, and then brought them back down Florida again, smiling when she exclaimed, "Oh, Theo, do it again. Can we, please? Again! Again!" There was little traffic on Florida Avenue, but each driver they encountered seemed as enthralled as they were with the new gravel macadam. And it was on the way back up to Outer Drive the second time that she glanced over at him, wanting to know if he was as happy as she was, that she saw him wiping his eyes. She was astounded because he was always cheering her up, urging her to find ways to cope. He was the constant optimist. Usually. Not now.

"Stop the car, Theo!" she said. "Stop! What's wrong? Why are you...what's wrong?" He found another turn-off, a little cul de sac called Fulton Lane, which sloped downhill to a turnaround, where he stopped the dark blue Studebaker. A bulldozer had been busy here, making a clearing for a new building, but there were a few trees left.

Bashie slid over closer to him as he was smiling back at her, a thin, quiet smile that was all too brief.

She said, "I've never seen you like this."

He shook his head.

"You want to wait a few minutes?" she asked.

He nodded, then opened his door and walked over to a willow tree running his hands down among the long slender low-hanging curtains of willow branches. She saw him take a deep breath and nod his head a couple of times before turning back to the car. Back inside with her, he said, "It's been so long since I'd heard you laugh."

"What?" She couldn't believe her ears.

"I was afraid you'd never laugh again. Never smile for me again. I wasn't ready when you did. Sorry."

"Oh, Theo," she said.

She wanted to hug him tight as she could for as long as she

125

could, but she knew he wouldn't let her, given her condition. Instead, she put both hands on his closest hand, which seemed to warm him considerably. She could see him absorb her emotion. As he breathed, he got better right before her eyes, and she was relieved when he said, "Let's do another outing like this next week."

"An outing?"

"Sure," he said. "Another drive like this. We ought to try to find something positive every day. You know, to think about something else. Something happy."

She nodded. "You're right. It's a wonderful idea."

So they started taking drives, their outings, one afternoon each week. But later they decided once a week was silly, not nearly often enough, and they started taking an outing every time they went out for any reason. They usually made it all the way to the end of Outer Drive to stop and look west at the Cumberlands until sunset. On the third such excursion they went to the Clinch River where they watched ducks feeding in the grass on a sandbar until Bashie discovered two male kingfishers feuding over a female perched in a nearby stand of sumac.

On the fourth outing they went to The Music Box, the record store at the Townsite where they entered the private booth and listened to Al Dexter and His Troopers playing *Pistol Packin Mama*. Then Theo asked the clerk to play Judy Garland singing *Zing Went the Strings of My Heart* which was something Bashie wanted to hear five times in a row. Then there was Bing Crosby's *Oh, What a Beautiful Morning* and finally Tommy Dorsey's band playing *Boogie Woogie*, which inspired Theo to dance around inside the little soundproofed room. Bashie laughed so long she wept tears of joy all over again. This she was recalling and savoring while Theo was tending to the General and the sergeant.

126

Voices in the other room ceased, and Theo came back to her, saying, "They're ready." He hesitated. "You okay?"

"Fine now," she said. "It was like the owls had caught me for a while, but I'm back."

Theo took the platter of chicken in, and she made sure the mashed potatoes were ready. Then she went in, and General Groves said, "Mrs. Kincaid, I do declare you are a bona fide national treasure. I hope you will forgive me for keeping you top secret." His laughter was loud and hearty, "I just wish I were here more often. Truly, this is my second home."

Someday Soon

"Come on, Blossom. Come on, girl!"

Kathleen waited for the old dog to come out of the Cave. Blossom's long black hair made her look longer than she was tall, and you could tell when she was happy because her wagging tail would say she was. And she was happy most of the time, but not as fast as she used to be. She limped now. One of her back legs was the limping leg so Kathleen didn't go fast with her. She liked to have her hand on Blossom's back as they walked.

Momma saw them coming from the river, and when they got close, she said, "Kathleen, make sure Blossom stays outside. We're going to be shelling beans, and I don't want her in the strings and such."

So they washed the beans first. Then took a lap full each of beans to pull strings off. Then snap them into two littler pieces or maybe three. Then dump snapped beans into the pot on the floor between them.

"Momma," Kathleen said, "have you had hickory cakes?"

Tilde Woodson said, "Hmmm. I think so. Long time ago when I was little."

"Can we do some?"

"Well, I suppose so. It would take some doing. We'd need to gather hickory nuts, of course. And then I'd need to find the recipe because I don't recall anything about how to do hickory cakes."

"I think I know some of it," Kathleen said. "And I will be glad to get hickory nuts. I can get Toby to help. Maybe Etta, too. Is that all right, Momma?"

Tilde nodded, glancing at her daughter. "Sure, it's all right. But it might take some work to do everything. Are you sure you can do it?"

"I'm pretty sure. It'll be easier if I can get some help. Do hickory cakes taste good?"

"Well, yes. Not like chocolate cake though. Not sweet dessert. They're sort of nutty, and you put butter on them. They're good. You'll see when we're done. Things like hickory nuts are like all the wild greens out in the fields. They grow where God plants them." She held out her hand. "Give me the beans, will you? And you scoot out of here now. I got more to do. But I thank you for helping shell."

Blossom was ready right outside the screen door, and she followed Kathleen back through the field winding around through the jimson weed and briers to the Treasure Cave where the Sad Lady waited for them. "Hi there, Blossom. Hi, Kathleen."

They went over to the old log where Miss Bashie sat, her arms crossed, looking cold like always. She looked different somehow, and Kathleen thought maybe she was tired. "Hi, Miss Bashie. Are you tired? You look tired."

"I am," she said. "Feel like I'm wearing out like a cake of soap. And my hands are so cold they feel like they're crying. Even though I'm a native of right here," she added, "but I swan I can't seem to warm these hands. Ever since..." She halted mid-sentence.

Kathleen jumped up. "Let me build us a fire. That'll warm us both up. My hands probably aren't so cold as yours, but I got matches and kindling."

Kathleen would glance now and then at Miss Bashie while gathering the little sticks and dry leaves. Kathleen knew how to pile up kindling with dry leaves, and she tore the driest leaves into little pieces so they'd catch fire easy. She went to the rock shelf where she'd left the matchbox and knelt by the fireplace and struck three matches in a row before a leaf flared and then sputtered out. And that's the way it went for all the matches. Just brief flames out too quick.

"Durn it!" she muttered.

"I thank you for trying," Miss Bashie said. "I'm not sure it would have helped much. My circulation isn't what it used to be. I'm chilled almost permanent. Especially since I...lost something precious to me."

Kathleen said, "Was it somebody precious?"

Miss Bashie gave her a look. "How'd you know that?"

Kathleen tried to go another way. She said, "Listen. I talked with Momma about hickory cakes, and she said fine. So will you tell me again how to cook em? What do I do?"

"I tell you what," the Sad Lady said, sounding better. "You tell me where you found the fiddleheads, and I'll tell you step-by-step how to cook hickory cakes. Can you remember everything?"

"Oh, yes. I got a good remembery." Kathleen twirled around real quick and asked, "What's fiddleheads?"

Miss Bashie chuckled. "A fiddlehead is the tip end of a certain type of fern. The coiled tip end. Twisted around in a tight circle. If you break it off a few inches from the end, it will look like a fiddle. If you collect fiddleheads, the coiled tips, and wash them in cold water, you can cook them in butter. I salt them, too. They're good. But they're not easy to find. Where have you seen them? Down here by the river?"

"No, ma'am. I've seen them on that little rise in the patch of woods by Preston's pasture. Past where the stink weed grows and the cow path gets muddy. I can show you."

"Maybe later. You brought me some wild lettuce, too. Where'd you find that?"

Kathleen leaned against the big log. "That was over near the railroad bridge. On that little hill. Why do you want to know about that stuff?"

The Sad Lady sighed. "I'm hoping it will ease my headaches. If you use it to make a kind of tea, it gives relief from all sorts of pains. I could use some relief. And wild lettuce is supposed to help a body sleep."

Kathleen pulled her hair behind one ear. "What about that little white flower I brought you? What do you call it?"

"Little mouse-ear," Miss Bashie said. "It's just a favorite of mine that spreads like chickweed. I'm not certain it cures anything. I just like the way it sleeps at night."

"Huh?"

She smiled again. "It goes to sleep when the sun goes down, its leaves curling up, and its blossoms do, too. They open back up when the sun comes up in the morning."

"That's nice," Kathleen said. "I like talking with you about flowers. Can we do it some more? I mean, another day?"

"Sure, we can, Kathleen. I'd like that. I enjoy seeing you. Being with you and Blossom. She's a sweet dog."

"Maybe we could give her some of that special tea. The wild lettuce tea. Her leg's been hurting her for a long time now. I don't want her to hurt so much. I don't want anyone to hurt. And something makes me think she won't hurt much longer. She'll be gone."

Miss Bashie froze when she heard that. "How do you know that?" Her face was afraid.

Kathleen looked down at her feet, then back up again, pulling hair behind her other ear. "Sometimes I can see what's coming. And other times I can see someone a long way away. I can't tell exactly when something will happen. Just that it will. And sometimes when I see the person who's not here, I can see what's happening to them. And maybe hear their name. I don't know why I see them. It makes me sad because I don't know what to do about all this."

"I'm sorry," Miss Bashie said. "Sorry you see things like that."

They sat quietly a while, and Blossom lay between them, muttering in her sleep.

"Let me tell you about baking hickory cakes," Miss Bashie said. And she went on to describe how you save the nut kernels in water a day or so. Mash them up into paste. Add cornmeal, flour, and a little salt. Mix in two eggs along with some bacon drippings. Stir it up good, frying it in grease to make little pattie cakes. "Can you remember all that?"

"Let me tell it back to you." And so she did, forgetting only one thing.

"Add a pinch of salt," Miss Bashie said.

"A pinch?"

"That means just a little bit. Maybe a quarter spoonful."

"I can do that." Kathleen nodded a few times, fixing things in her head. "It won't hurt Blossom if I give her some, will it?"

"No," Miss Bashie said. "But it won't make an old dog young again. You know that."

"I know."

"So why do you want to give her hickory cake?"

"Let's just let her get a happy taste of it before she goes. She'll be gone from us pretty soon. I want to remember her as happy as possible. Blossom's my true friend."

"Kathleen," Miss Bashie said. "That's a sweet notion."

"A what?"

"A notion is something you believe. It's the way you see things. What makes sense to you."

Kathleen nodded, thinking, *I got plenty of notions nobody else can have. Just me.*

On the walk back to the house Kathleen walked as slowly as she could with her hand on Blossom all the way. For a while she thought the dog had lost her limp, but when they got to the back door it was back again. Blossom stood panting, her weight mostly on just three legs. Kathleen went straight in to Momma asking about lettuce tea, and Momma stopped mashing potatoes to ask, "Where in the world do you get these ideas, Kathleen?"

"I'm not always sure, Momma. I got this one from the Sad Lady. She's like a queen, Momma. A fine lady."

Tilde shook her head as she returned to the potatoes. "My goodness gracious sakes, child. You are an amazement to me." She dropped a piece of potato skin on the floor and said, "Oops. Will you pick that up for me, darling? Just toss it in the garbage."

Kathleen picked it up, asking, "Can I feed it to Blossom?"

"She won't take it. Dogs don't usually go for vegetables." She glanced at her daughter. "But you can try. If she refuses, toss it in the garbage."

"Good." She took the scrap outside to Blossom and knelt to offer it to her. Blossom licked at it and took it in her mouth, but let it drop a moment later. Kathleen patted her on the head as she went to the garbage can.

Back in the kitchen she asked, "Momma, if I bring you wild lettuce, can we make some lettuce tea?"

"Wild lettuce? Goodness, Kathleen. Did you hear about that from Etta? She's reading *Peter Rabbit* these days. Is that where you heard it?"

"No, Momma. The Sad Lady's the one who told me. It's supposed to ease pain."

As she continued with the potatoes, Tilde looked over her shoulder at Kathleen. "This is one of those times when I need to hear the truth, Kathleen. Are you sure the Sad Lady told you about this healing tea? It wasn't something you heard elsewhere? You didn't make this up, did you?"

"No, ma'am. She told it to me. And she told me about fiddleheads and little mouse's ears, too. But the lettuce tea is what Blossom needs to get rid of her limp." She was going to talk more about what the Sad Lady had told her, but Momma had stopped doing potatoes, and she was looking at Kathleen's face, studying her such that the girl thought better of it. *Maybe Momma doesn't need to know everything just yet. I'll tell her, but maybe some other day. Someday soon.*

She went out the back door and sat by Blossom who licked her hand, and she pulled some cockleburs off the dog's ears. Toby came and sat down close to Blossom's tail, holding something in his hands. He said nothing because he had the hiccups, and when he looked up, he was grinning. She was going to ask what was he holding onto when he said, "Worms." He held one out to the dog, but Blossom wasn't interested in worms either.

"Hey, Toby," she said. "Want to go help me find wild lettuce for Blossom?"

135

"Uh huh."

The children headed into tall grass, and the dog limped after them as they wandered past the crabapple trees into the sumac.

Photo courtesy of Deb Kile Hotchkiss

Tainted Seed

We had our boy Bill in 1923, five years after losing our first three children to the Spanish Flu. After Glen, Teresa, and Jimmy died, I lost something inside me. I told my husband Phillip I didn't want any more children because I was scared of losing them, but Phillip begged and begged me. He swore he'd help take care of any child we had, and I knew he'd be sweet to any new baby just like he was to the others. So eventually I gave in, and that's how we got Bill.

But Bill never was any good even when he was little bitty. When I nursed him, he seemed to bite me more than any of the others did, staring up at me, calm and content every time I yelped. As a toddler he fought me when I put him down to nap, striking me in the face with his fists, screaming and crying while he did it. When he was older, he never did as told unless you were right there, making him do right. I don't have any idea what Phillip and I did wrong with him. As a teenager he cussed and defied us both, and he broke my heart a thousand times with meanness. Some way somehow we messed him up, treating him like a little king. That's what we did, but he still hated his Ma and Pa, and he was always mean as a snake.

He joined the Army right after Pearl Harbor, but eight weeks later he got stabbed in a alley behind a bar at Fort Benning. They said he bled out right there in the gravel and weeds. I mourned him, but I never thought that boy loved us or respected what we did for him. That made it easier to keep on keeping on without him, but I still have a tender spot right in the

137

middle of my heart that craves a child or grandchild, especially since Phillip died in a car wreck a month after we lost Bill. That was nearly a year ago, and ever since, I been feeling old and lonesome on my own. Without my man, without my boy.

But here's the thing: I'm still right here. My salvation's been that work is a good thing to live for. If you don't work to earn something, you never really appreciate the true worth of it. That's the way I see it, and it's the way I live. Nowadays my work is partly in the garden and partly with people. I tell them, "Yes, I'm Ida Rose Delap, the midwife," but I do more than bring babies into this world. I treat the injured as well as the sick. Them that need healing of any sort come to me, and I do best I can for each and every one of them. I've learnt to pace myself because Nature works in her own time. You don't want to ignore signs that something's different inside you. Foolish not to pay attention to your body.

This evening it's cooled off some, though still awful muggy, worse than it ought to be during July in East Tennessee. On top of that, I might need to do some self-doctoring. Could be I've picked up some kind of asthma or hay fever maybe, but I don't know. It's late in the year for hay fever, and I ain't been asthmatic in all my sixty-seven years. Maybe I've just reached the age such that it's all catching up with me. I'm not so quick to bounce back from illness as I once was, and my neck's a little tender to the touch, so I'm going to see about that soon.

Now as the gloaming shadows deepen, I'm heading outdoors, and I glance at the hall mirror, staring at a stranger in the glass. An elderly female creature wearing dungarees under a worn, brown apron. My face is craggy and wrinkled, especially along the wattles at my neck, and I can see deep crows feet around my eyes where the skin is dark and pouched.

I feel sorry for myself sometimes because, if you knew what I've lived through, you could see it plain as day on my face.

I've come undone a few times, forgetting important things. It shakes me up a little to know that's happening over and over, more often than before. I wonder how much more it will happen. And will I realize it when it does?

A couple days ago I had to take care of a little girl over in Oliver Springs. Sweet little thing just four years old. Sharon Freels was her name. Had the impetigo, and I had to teach Mrs. Freels how to treat the sores and blisters. How to wash the little darling with her own soap, her own washcloth, dry her with her own towels. Not to let anyone else play with her nor use her soap neither. Keep her separate from the rest of the family, and wash good and proper every day. Anyway, I got into that in a big way, feeling true affection for that young un. Sometimes I was a thousand miles away in my head, dreaming how it would be if she lived with me.

There are times when my brain gets addled somehow. Sometimes I can misremember the simplest things. I'll see something in my mind's eye, but can't always keep the details straight over time. I can't seem to remember so good. Not all the time. But some things can come back to me. I recall six weeks ago when that fellow had come to the door. He was young and slender, taller than me by maybe six or seven inches. His Adam's apple stuck out on his neck, and his voice broke a couple times while he was visiting with me.

He said, "Hidy, ma'am. My name's Walter Lancaster, and I'm testing a new fertilizer for some folks the other side of Oliver Springs. You know the Stooksbury farm?" he asked. "They hired me to spread new fertilizer for them, and I did it one, two, three, just like that...or thought I did. But as I was making my way back to town, a bottle of the stuff rolled out from under my seat. And, well, I don't want to turn around and go back to Stooksbury. And I wasn't going to throw it away." His face turned red, and he gave me a shy grin. "I need to tell you. I got myself a date tonight, and I'm running a little late."

"So, what do you want from me, Mr. Lancaster?"

"Please call me Walter."

"Well, call me Ida Rose then. I'm Ida Rose Delap."

He blinked. "Would it be all right if I spread this last bottle on your garden? I see you got a few rows out back. I got more than enough fertilizer. They say it's going to be real, real good. Fantastic, they claim." He blinked and took a deep breath. "I'll check back with you in a month or so. But I wouldn't tell anybody else about it, if I was you." He offered another gentle smile.

When he said that last part, I saw how much he resembled my own Bill. He was about Bill's same age before Benning, only a few years out of school. I was looking him over, noticing things about him and couldn't help but see he had ants in his pants, wanting to see his girl.

"What time do you pick her up?" I asked.

"We're to meet outside the bowling alley at 6:15," he said. I thought he was holding his breath as he waited on my answer, which touched my sympathy and tickled me, too. I was craving to help him any way I could. "All right, Walter. If you'll answer my questions about this stuff so I can get some idea of what in tarnation it is, I'll let you do it."

He picked up the bottle and turned it around a few times so we could see it clearly. What I noticed was something like coarse, black sand, greasy and shiny, with streaks of other colors layered inside the bottle. Brownish black mostly, but some gray, and even a smidgen of olive green. It was like nothing I'd ever seen.

"It's tailings from a mine in Africa," he said.

"What's tailings?"

140

"It's better known in mining as overburden."

"Well, what in tarnation is overburden?" I say. "You got more explaining to do." I was beginning to think I'd turn him down.

"Overburden is waste rock dug out of a mine without being processed. It's right next to whatever it is you're mining. It ain't usually worth anything, but normally miners dig it up, too, because you might be able to filter it and find a little extra gold or whatever it is."

"Why're you offering it up as fertilizer? That don't make sense, son." I surprised myself calling him son. I felt tremors of sentiment deep down inside me.

"The miners who dug this up weren't looking for gold. This stuff's called pitchblende."

"So what's it good for?"

He shrugged. "That's what we're trying to find out. They grind it up and add water to make a dark slurry and do different things with it. The Army does. Their scientists do. They're hot after it." Then he leaned in confidential and said, "The big bosses are having us be extra careful with it. I don't see the need for it, but they got us wearing special gloves when we handle it, special protective gear. Weighing what we start with, then what we get after we're done."

I studied on that a while. "So how'd you get these bottles full of it if they make you account for every little bit of it?"

"We substituted coal dust and gravel, and just in time, too. Later that very same day, they brought in inspectors to watch us every single minute. Me and my buddies were just plain lucky to connect with Stooksbury, who's like us, trying to find some way to make some money out of all this new Army business. We ain't real happy with the price freezes and the rations and all

141

the new rules that's coming down on us. We're determined to make a buck our own way, not the Army's way. And we've used this pitchblende stuff, this new fertilizer, and it works fantastic. We got it all figured out, but figure we need to try it out a few more times to make double sure. It's a new day, Ida Rose."

I saw his grit and cleverness as he was telling me this, and I had to agree the new Office of Price Administration rules were a lot of trouble for farmers and laborers, even for me although I don't live on the Army base. I asked a few more questions, but didn't learn much. So finally, Walter said, "Do we have a deal, Miz Ida? Can I spread some around here and come back and see how it's all going for you? Is that all right?"

I said it was, "But how about giving the corn a extry dose? You can dust everything I got, but hit the corn a little heavier, would you?"

"Yes, ma'am!" he said, turning back to his truck. "You're a life saver!"

I watched him spread the black slurry over every row I had. It looked like a fairy had sprinkled night dust on the leaves and vines in every row. At least, that's how I remember it now. I probably would have thought more about it, but I got busy with babies and a spate of flu, sore throats, and all manner of aches and pains in a ninety-two-year-old lady that lives over in Dutch Valley.

Then I delivered triplets for the Rabbs, which was a long labor, tough on the mother. Marjorie was one of those plump, healthy girls that didn't look like she'd be able to work through the worst that comes. But she surprised me, coming through just fine, and I told her I'd stay with them a week or ten days to make sure everybody was still good after all. Her husband, Douglas, kissed me three times, once for each boy and again for the little girl. I stayed with them over in Dossett longer than they really needed help. Some of it was for my own sake. While I was staying there I felt something like heartburn for a minute or two. That puzzled me because I've never had digestion problems. It was a burning sensation for just a short spell. Then it was gone. I wondered if it was me loving those triplets too hard.

But finally, I went back home. I was conflicted about leaving, but realized they weren't my children, and I was sure I'd be finding others in need pretty soon. When I got up to my front door, there was a note pinned to it. Since my reading's none too dependable, I slipped it into my bosom, thinking I'd get somebody to read it later.

That's when Ronnie Woodson came by to fetch me because his brother, little three-year-old Toby, was in awful pain. His folks, Tilde and Earl, run Woodson's grocery just outside Elza Gate. They'd already took him to the Oak Ridge Hospital, where the doctors said he had Rheumatic Fever. They said he was getting gradually better, but his legs from ankle to knee were awful tender such that he couldn't stand you to touch him there. Couldn't stand the weight of the sheets on his lower legs, crying and pleading for momma to take the hurt away. "Momma, help me. It hurts and hurts! Please, Momma!" And Tilde was just beside herself, unable to bring him onto her lap to comfort him. Earl had driven them home from the hospital and pulled the boy's bed out onto the covered porch and tenderly laid him down. They took turns setting with him, day and night. They got six children, four boys and two girls. Toby's their baby so everybody got involved, which warmed my heart clear through.

I told Tilde to bathe his legs with sweet marjoram, but he just squalled loud and pitiful. Finally, we ladled mustard on his knees, letting it slide down his shins, and he didn't protest that. I wasn't sure this was doing much to ease his pain, but his eyes looked better. His breathing improved. His oldest brother,

143

Ronnie, said, "I think he's doing better, Miz Ida." And my heart was tender again when I thought about these boys, the littlest one as well as the biggest. I cherished them right then and there. Remembering my last boy, Bill, the absence of hate was enough for me.

And I started feeling tuckered out. Tilde asked if I needed anything, and I recalled that paper I'd put next to my heart. I handed it to her, and she read it out loud. "Mrs. Delap, I need to talk to you. Please call me at 1371. It's important. Walter"

"Who's Walter?" Tilde said. And for a minute I couldn't place him. Then I saw his face in my mind's eye. And at the same time I thought about what he'd like to eat, hoe cakes or maybe some biscuits. I'd use bacon grease, Martha White flour, and my cornmeal harvested from the stalks where he sprinkled that black fairy dust. Walter might like to butter them still warm from the skillet and drink some sweet tea or maybe some buttermilk, whatever he wants. That would be what I'm hoping for. To have man or boy looking forward to my cooking. I know how good my biscuits are because I been eating them ever since he first visited me.

"He's a feller that was helping me with my garden," I said. "Can you call him up for me?"

"Certainly," she said, and quick as a wink, I was speaking to him on their phone.

"There's a problem with that stuff I put on your corn," he said. "I need to come see you. There's some other people that'll come with me." He didn't sound happy to be telling me this.

"Walter, what is it?' I said. "Are you in trouble?"

I heard him let out his breath. "Not any more," he said. I wished I could see his face when he said it, and for a tiny minute I was asking myself, *What if Walter's done something wrong not knowing when he did it that it was wrong? And the*

144

authorities has caught him, and he's trying to make things right? Could that old boy ask me anything, and I'd do it, no questions asked?

Yes!

So Walter told me he was going to meet me at Woodson's Grocery, and he'd be bringing some of the big bosses with him. Half an hour later a car load of men wearing white dress shirts and dark ties shows up plus one fellow in a long white coat. They call me over to where they're sitting. They use this contraption they call a Geiger counter, running it very deliberately down my left arm to my hand. The dang thing lights up and waves its hour hand all over the place, and I wonder if that's bad.

The man in charge is a young fellow, maybe thirty-five years old, who sounds like some kind of Yankee. Slender, with dark, slicked back hair, and big ears, he's calm and fairly solemn controlling the whole thing. Everybody looks to him before they speak. He's taking in everything, nodding and taking his time deciding what he wants.

"Mrs. Delap, I want to thank you for waiting on us," he says. "My name is Jeffrey Stauffenberg, and we're not going to keep you long. We're here about the black slurry Mr. Lancaster shared with you. Actually, it's waste material he and his friends pilfered from a secure site they shouldn't have been able to get into. He understands why he shouldn't have taken it, and he's helping us get it back, if we can. The Geiger reading we got on you was much higher than it should be. Something you've been doing or someplace you've been could be very dangerous to you and to others."

I realize I ain't said anything yet to Stauffenberg, who's a nice young man, so I say, "I'm just a old woman, nearly sixty-eight years old. Give me a minute to get my thoughts straightened out." And that's when it occurs to me how I ought

145

to explain things. Stauffenberg's just doing his job. He makes me feel important, which is a proud feeling, but also frightening. I'm not sure if I'm in trouble like Walter. Might be. I can't tell.

So I smile at Stauffenberg, and the words just flow like a waterfall out of my mouth. "All right, young man. Let me say first of all that I myself rely on natural remedies. I don't know what's going on all around us here on the Army property. You scientific types know much more than I do, that's for sure." I'm studying his face hard as I can to see how that's going down, and I study the others' faces, too. They seem interested in everything I got to say, so I plow ahead with what I know best. "Let me tell you what I use the most: cayenne."

"I beg your pardon?" Stauffenberg says.

"It's a kind of pepper. I got teas and herbs of all sorts," I tell him. "And I know exactly how to make a healing butter from caraway, ginger, and salt. You grind em up together and work it and work it and work it. It's good for what ails you. And, if you ain't ailing, this'll keep you from even starting to feel bad."

But wouldn't you know it? That's when my throat is tickled just a tiny bit, and I cough a while. I try to stop coughing, but my little fit lasts longer than I want it to, and I feel like there's a sharp scrape down my throat somewhere that hurts like too much pepper on your tongue. That's a new worry, but now's not the time for it. When I'm through choking, Stauffenberg has seen it for what it is and asks, "When's the last time you went to the doctor?"

"Haven't been in a long time."

"More than a year?"

"Oh, sure, yeah. I'm fairly hardy myself. And I'm a midwife my own self. Bet you didn't know that."

146

"Yes, I was told that," he says. "You've been bringing babies into the world for quite some time now. Am I correct?"

"I done more than just welcome young uns to the earth. I treat the sick and injured, too, whenever they come see me." And I tell him about Sharon Freels, Marjorie Rabb and her triplets, and Toby Woodson.

Stauffenberg nods slowly, studying me a while. I don't know what he wants to do nor what he's able to do to me. I druther he be a little stern with me instead of so sympathetic. I druther argue with him than deal with his respectful difference of opinion. The corners of his mouth soften into a smile, and he says, "We're going to take you to some of our doctors at Y-12," he says. "To make sure you're all right."

Well, that wasn't what I was hoping, but I need to show how I can cooperate and not make waves, so I tell him, "I got no problem with that, but your Army doctors and me don't exactly see eye-to-eye. Like I said, I use herbs to keep well. Grow most of them my own self. I generally stick to the old ways, and I work hard at it every day."

I've probably said too much. Talked too fast. I focus my attention on these young faces around me, young modern fellows who seem to be deciding something about me without speaking aloud to one another. I end up staring back at Stauffenberg, thinking I ought to add one more thing.

"I'm a firm believer of the tried-and-true. The old ways. They brung us through tough times in the past, and they'll see us through challenges still coming at us. The old ways will surely save us. They have so far."

Stauffenberg smiles ruefully. "Wouldn't it be nice to think that could always be true?"

I smile right back at him, determined to answer all his questions while keeping quiet about where I buried the last of my seed corn in an enchanted, secret place on the far side of Walden Ridge far from the Federal Reservation. After Walter had sprinkled that black dust on it I took a handful of kernels and laid it under a blanket of cushion moss at a tall black oak tree, a very distinctive tree with black, gnarly bark I know I can find again. I guarantee I can find it. Deep in the woods where other oaks, hickories, dogwoods, and redbuds have been woven into a quilted canopy over that section of Frost Bottom. So far from the Army it might as well be buried on the far side of the moon.

I just need to be patient and count my blessings. Have faith in God Almighty. Breathe deep and slow so long as I can. I know the true worth to let Nature have her way. And, if it can heal them that seek a midwife, it can heal the midwife herself.

But now there's something new I must get a better understanding of. There's that black fairy dust from Africa. I'm pondering these things, and without any warning, my tender heart begins to shrivel, and a fierce coughing fit comes on me with a vengeance. A searing pain is suddenly scalding through my throat and chest as if I'd swallowed barbed wire, and Stauffenberg has started pulling it out of me. When I take my hand down from my mouth, there's blood dripping from my palm onto my shoes.

Silver-Tongued Devil

Outside the Administration Building, there was a handwritten sign reading "Wipe your feet." Rain had been so continuous that mud surrounded the Castle's front steps, making it impossible to mount the steps without bringing red clay mud. It was a soupy mud. There was also the spoiled and sour smell of something organic down in that mess.

Gazing down the slope from the Castle Buckley saw several bulldozers mudbound and quiet for the time being. They'd been busy until the rains shut them down because there were large muddy mounds scattered about, as if some giant's child had been playing in the muck. There was red mud all around. The dozers had pushed down all the undergrowth, the sumac, briers and honeysuckle, and all the mature hardwoods, black oaks, red oaks, hickories, maples. Pines and cedars, too. Everything green---grass, weeds, shrubs, saplings---all of it had been ripped up and pushed into mounds of branches and limbs to be burned instead of hauled away. Some of it was still smoldering even though the rain had been fairly recent. Some still waiting for government arsonists. Nearly all the grass and wild flowers and weeds had been scourged from the valley. There was more brown and red showing than green. The dozers had also dug out roads which would be graveled soon, but remained mud now. Yet high up the ridge, the woodlands continued untouched, wild and natural, stretching all the way to higher, distant ridges and finally to the Cumberland Plateau.

This building, this modern Castle, a long two-story wooden

structure, was the largest building in sight, brand new, yet lacking basic amenities. Most of the buildings on the Federal Reservation were accessed by boardwalks instead of paved sidewalks like those in the nearby county seat, Clinton. None of the roads within the confines of the CEW except for the main road, the Turnpike, was paved.

Jeter Buckley wore a slouch hat pulled low. He was a short, slender man in his early 60's, wiry and ropey, tanned such that he was sometimes mistaken as Arab or Greek. His cleft chin and slicked back hair revealed years of wear and tear. His nicotine-stained fingers perpetually holding a cigarette, he had a skeptical look to him. He thought *You got to be impressed with all this industry, all the activity going on around here.* He had noted something about this strange new world coming to life in southern Anderson County. The birds were gone. There were no birds visible, no birdsongs, no avian flitting and chittering in the branches and grasses. But now and then he heard a mysterious rumbling originating in the distance somewhere in the next valley.

What the hell's going on over there? he wondered.

Opening the front door he found two uniformed guards right there in the hall.

One said, "State your business."

"Looking for a job," Buckley said.

"Go upstairs. Take the first door on the right. That's Personnel."

"Beg pardon?"

"That's where they do the hiring."

Buckley said, "Thanks, fellas," starting up the stairs.

"You better wipe your shoes," the other guard said. "Make

a better impression that way."

Buckley looked around, uncertain how to clean up.

"Bathroom down this hall on the left. You can freshen up in there."

"Thanks," Buckley said.

In the bathroom he took a few minutes wiping his shoes off with toilet paper. Also to eliminate some dried mud on his pants leg. He took a look in the mirror, thinking, *Probably should have shaved this morning. But no use crying about it now.* He ran a hand through his hair, smoothing gray strands among the darker ones before wiping Brylcreem residue on his trousers.

Upstairs a woman sat behind a big desk. When she looked up at him, she handed him a clipboard. "Fill out this information. Have a seat with the others. Wait there til your number's called." She tapped the clipboard where the number 47 was scribbled in the top left corner. Buckley found men seated on wooden chairs on both sides of the hall. He estimated maybe 60 males staring at each other, mostly young fellows. Some wearing Sunday go-to-meeting clothes. Some in overalls or jeans and work shirts. Down at the far end were three sad looking Negroes, staring at their feet. No one was talking. He figured he was the oldest guy in the hall.

"Damn!" he muttered, walking past the men toward empty chairs down at the far end. There was a large round clock on the wall that showed 11:17.

Every few minutes the secretary would stick her head out the door and call out a number. The first he heard was 9.

"Damn!"

He glanced at the paper on the clipboard a couple minutes, grimacing at the prospect of completing the form. Sitting next

151

to him, he found a pudgy, bespectacled guy wearing a shiny, well-worn suit and a thin tie, who looked nervously back at him.

"Will you help me with this?" he asked. "I hurt my eye. Can't make out these words too good." He rubbed his eye, and it watered quickly as he handed the clipboard over.

"Well, I...don't know if I'm supposed to...."

"It'll be all right," Buckley said. "I'll tell em I ast you to do it. It'll be okay."

He got his bluff in on the guy, and the fellow said, "Last name?"

"Buckley."

"First name?"

"Jeter."

It went on like that with birth date, gender, race, address, education, and more. So much more that Buckley finally got sick of it and said, "That's enough. Just gimme that thing," he said, indicating the clipboard.

"We ain't through," the fellow whined. "And you got to sign at the bottom."

"I can do that," Buckley said, grasping the clipboard and scribbling perfunctorily. "You did good," he told the man. "I owe you, buddy. What's your name?"

"Slover. Gene Slover. Same last name as that tall guard downstairs. He's my cousin from Harriman."

"That's good to know," Buckley replied. "I owe him, too."

All the other men in the hall were listening in, which irritated Buckley. He stood up, waving the clipboard. "You all too scared to talk your own selves?" He glared at the bunch of them, then asked, "Anybody got a smoke?"

152

It was quiet until one guy down at the far end near the door said, "Yeah, I got smokes." He brought out a pack of Camels. Buckley traipsed down the hall feeling big as all get out, took a cigarette the guy offered as well as the light, and returned to his seat puffing with a grin, loosening everybody up. More cigarettes were passed around, lit up, and soon several conversations were underway. Buckley told himself, *Now we're cooking with gas.*

He signed the form as the woman opened the door and yelled "10!" The hall had instantly gone quiet when her face appeared, and she hesitated before closing the door, a bemused look on her face as she noticed the smoke throughout the hall. Number 10, a stocky fellow in a dress shirt and tie, went in after her.

Over the next hour and a half Buckley learned about Slover and his cousin who had joined the Army in 1941 right after Pearl Harbor. Gene stayed on the family farm outside Harriman, helping his folks work tobacco and planned to do so for the duration, but, when he learned about the good salaries paid for jobs at CEW, he talked his father into letting him come looking for employment.

"What kind of work you want?" Buckley asked.

"What kind you got?" Slover grinned. A happy fellow, young, too. Buckley estimated maybe twenty years old with reddish brown hair, freckles spread across his cheeks. His teeth weren't so good, crowded too close together, but the boy wasn't self-conscious.

"Hell if I know," Buckley said. "What skills you got?"

Slover shrugged, searching his past. "Well, I reckon I can chop wood, cut tobacco, run mules to plow."

"I don't expect they're gonna bring mules onto the CEW Reservation, buddy. Can you use a hammer and saw?"

153

Slover brightened up. "You bet. I helped Daddy and George put up the new part of our barn two years ago. I got good arm strength."

Buckley crossed his legs and leaned back as the woman called out the next number. "I bet you do," he told Gene. "Is George your brother?"

"Yes, sir."

"You don't have to say 'sir' to me, Gene. Call me Buckley."

"Yes, sir."

Buckley shook his head and took another look at the Negroes a few chairs down from him. They looked older than most of the whites in the hall, but not dressed so well, wearing weathered overalls and mud-spattered shoes.

Buckley called to them, "What's your names, boys?"

They looked to one another without answering.

"I'm Buckley," he said. "This here's Gene. What's your names?"

The largest of the three, a tall, gangly, dark ebony fellow, said, "I'm Pompey. This here," he said, elbowing the fellow seated beside him, "is Stanley, and the little feller's called Zander."

"Zander, you say?" Buckley asked, studying Pompey's companions. Stanley was caramel colored with broad features, especially about his nose, unruly, kinky hair, and arms that stretched well beyond the sleeves of his jacket. The one called Zander didn't look up. He was a light-skinned Negro with finer features, possibly part Creole.

"That's right," Pompey said. "His granma calls him Zander, and she's a good woman."

154

"Well, if his granny calls him that, I will, too," Buckley said, speaking up so others could hear him say it. "Glad to meet you, Pompey. You, too, Stanley and you, Zander. Maybe I'll see you all around the Area when we're working for the CEW."

"Yes, sir," Stanley said. Zander nodded, as did Pompey. They were studying him.

The woman went through the numbers, and she fussed at the smokers near the Personnel door for dropping ashes on the linoleum. "You can't drop ash on our clean floors, boys. This won't do." Once when a fellow who had just gone in got ushered right back out, she brought out some little tin plates for ashtrays. Somebody brought one down to Buckley who nodded at him as he set it down. The fellow said, "We wouldn't of thought to smoke if you hadn't brought it up."

Buckley said, "I thank you."

"Who're you anyway?" the fellow asked.

"I'm Buckley."

The fellow nodded. "That your first name or your last?"

"Buckley," he replied. "That's how I'm known."

Pompey got called before Buckley, and he said, "You want my number, Mr. Buckley? It'll get you in quicker."

"Naw," Buckley said. "But, tell you what, let's go in together on your ticket."

"Huh?"

"Just let me do the talking. It'll save time."

Pompey looked back at his buddies, shrugged, and said, "All right."

They went down the hall and into the Personnel Office like old friends. The fellow who had loaned Buckley the cigarette said, "Come back and give us a report when you're done."

"Sure," Buckley said. "You bet." He winked, and the hall chuckled quietly until Pompey opened the office door. The secretary, a cheerless, dark-haired woman with horn-rimmed glasses and a hawk nose, said, "What's this? We only do one at a time."

"Oh, we're together," Buckley explained. "Because, you see, I'm the only one around willing to work with niggers, and we thought that would interest the boss man. They ain't many willing to work with niggers, is they?"

"This won't do," she said, screwing up her face. "You can't change how we...."

"Just tell the man what I'm telling you," Buckley insisted with a little flint in his voice. "He's gonna want to see us together."

"I don't know," she said.

"I'll explain it to him," Buckley said, glancing at Pompey who stood half a foot taller. "This don't have to blow up on you. I can take it on." He toned down his face so as to smile his most polite smile. And that worked.

She knocked on the inner office door and went in. A moment later she emerged, saying, "Mr. Williams will see you...both."

Pompey held the door open so Buckley could go in first. The secretary scrambled around her desk with papers, handing one to each of them. Mr. Williams, a round-faced fellow with red splotches on each cheek, sat behind a larger, more elaborate desk than the secretary's. Buckley noticed the inlaid patterned wood on the desktop, the polish, the trim, and figured he could probably sell such a piece of furniture for $700 or more, and here the man was sitting behind it every damn day of the week, probably without no idea of what it was worth. No real appreciation for it.

Mr. Lawrence Williams held out his hand without even looking at their faces, and they gave him their forms. Right away Buckley didn't care for Williams, but did his best to hide it because he needed to persuade the man to his way of thinking. He had some momentum built up so far, and he was hoping to ride it right on through. Williams remained seated, his glasses perched halfway down his nose, peering over them. Buckley noticed the man's hair was much like his, streaked with gray. Williams' hair was longer, with more curl to it, more pomade. Buckley thought, *I got this guy with the hair. I got him.*

"Boy," Williams said, not looking up. "What are you trying to pull?"

Pompey didn't blink. Respectfully, he said, "Listen to this feller," indicating Buckley, and he stepped back so Buckley was in front.

Williams sighed, removing his glasses. "I'm listening."

From Williams' general demeanor Buckley was thinking, *He's been seeing men across this desk for what? Six hours? Maybe he needs a break. Maybe he's curious about this here situation, a little white guy barging into his office with a big nigger. Longer he listens, the better our chances.*

"Mr. Williams," he said, "we want to work together."

Williams sat blinking, and Buckley thought he might have to push a little harder, and he was trying to decide what to say next when Williams said, "Explain how that might work out. You being white, and your friend here, colored. Here in Tennessee, in the South, how's that going to work?"

"Can we sit?" Buckley asked.

Pompey's eyes shifted back and forth between the two

white men, settling on Buckley, who sat down before Williams indicated it was permitted. Pompey took the other chair.

"It'll go like this," Buckley said. "I'm gonna be the straw boss for any crew of niggers you bring me. I'll teach em what to do, and make em toe the line. Pompey and his two buddies out in the hall will need to be on my crew because we got history. They'll follow me, and we'll have strong influence on other such crews, and we'll get the job done. I already got another white guy that'll work with us. Right out in the hall. We'll get a lot done for you."

Williams blinked again, and Buckley saw how tired the man was. *Must of had a bad night last night. Or maybe he's been doing this too long. Seen too many young fellers wanting jobs, trying to pick only the good ones. Which ain't easy.*

Williams turned to Pompey. "You got history with this man? Is that true?"

Pompey didn't hesitate. "Long as I've known him, he's been the leader. I'll foller him on any job. Me and my friends, we'll foller him."

Not bad, Buckley thought. *That might do the trick.*

Williams looked at Buckley's form, but Buckley saw that his gaze wasn't focused on the page. He was just going through the motions. Buckley told himself, *This idea we brung you's growing on you, ain't it? You need somebody who's willing to work with niggers, and he's setting right here in front of you.*

Williams made a show of studying Pompey's form, but not so long as he had studied on Buckley's. Then he leaned back in his chair which had the springs and casters on it so he could rock back and roll around the room if he wanted to. Now he wasn't rolling around, but he did loll back in it. Finally, he said, "I need a crew to haul water in the mornings and collect human waste and sewage in the evenings. It's ten-hour days, six days

158

a week. Are you interested?"

Pompey said, "Yes, sir. We'll take it. Me and my buddies will." As he finished, he glanced at Buckley.

"How much does it pay?" Buckley asked.

"Sixth-five cents an hour for the crew," Williams said. "Eighty for the supervisor."

We could argue about this, Buckley thought, *but maybe not. These salary figures are a hell of a lot better than anywhere else in Tennessee..* "Okay," Buckley said. "If I can be the super, I'm in, too. When do we report?"

"Go over to the Central Bus Terminal, and see Flanagan," Williams said, sitting back up, scribbling something onto their forms, then dropping them into a tray on his desk. "Tell Flanagan to take you to Happy Valley. That's a new section opening up. When you get there, find the truck marked H-17, and follow the route that's marked on the map. You'll find it inside the truck's cab. It's already loaded with water that needs delivering to every unit. No need to do the waste pick up run because nobody's moved in yet. Report to Joe Pyatt. Any questions once you get there, ask Pyatt. When you're done, you can go to Scarboro to the hutments."

"The what?"

"Hutments," Williams said, wearily. "That's what we call the living spaces we've constructed for Negro males. Not a grand hotel, by any means, but it's a roof over your head." He showed a hint of a smile. "Jeter Buckley, you're assigned quarters with your crew. No females allowed in male hutments. None. They got their own section called The Pen. We have guards patrolling The Pen day and night."

"No problem," Buckley said, but he was thinking about The Pen. *Might have to give it a visit.*

Buckley and Pompey went back out past the secretary, but Williams had followed them a few steps, explaining the arrangement to her. They waited a moment to see if he had any more words for them. He didn't, but she did. "Here's your temporary badges," she told them. "Pyatt will get your permanent badges with your photographs done at the job site. Wear these wherever you go. All the time. Even in the hutments. They got guards who'll be checking you regularly. No badge, no job."

The message was, *Can you handle this part of the deal? And, yeah,* Buckley thought. *I can handle that. Ain't no big deal for me. I wonder if Gene Slover can handle it.*

Out in the hall Buckley pulled Slover aside and told him there was a job waiting for him if he wanted it. Slover wasn't so sure about the hutment part of it, but he said, "Let me meet you over there. I got to think about all this. I might go another way."

"Suit yourself," Buckley said.

"I ain't ungrateful, mister," Slover said. "I appreciate what you done for me. I just...well, it's caught me unawares." He was looking back and forth from Zander to Pompey to Stanley. "I need to do some thinking. Shit Duty ain't exactly what I had in mind."

All this was being overheard by the waiting men seated along the walls, and Buckley turned to say, "Here's the best advice I can give you. Tell the man what you do best, not what you want to do. If that don't git you work, look me up at a new place called Happy Valley. The work me and my guys are gonna do ain't the cleanest. We'll be shoveling shit mostly, but it's work that's got to be done. And I got a feeling some who'll be doing it won't do it long. They'll need replacements, and I'll vouch for you. If you strike out here, come see me. Name's Buckley. Ask for Buckley."

As the four of them began the trek to the buses, Zander and Stanley were happy as pigs in mud. Zander did a quick two-step, slipped in the mud, and got his backside muddy from belt to knees, but he didn't stop laughing and wiggling as they went along. Stanley said, "Man, oh, man, that's gonna be good money!" He moved ahead to grab Zander around the shoulders, and the two of them hooted and squealed while they walked along. "Whoo-wee, boy! We're in the money!"

Pompey said, "What you think about all this, Mr. Buckley?"

"Just Buckley. Don't call me mister."

Pompey grinned. "Fine with me, Boss."

"Yeah, that sounds okay, too. Boss or Buckley, either one."

"So what you think, Boss? Is this deal good as I think it is?

"Take a look around this valley," Buckley said. "Tell me what you see."

"I see lots of buildings and mud everywhere," Pompey said, surveying everything around them. "The Central Bus Terminal a hundred yards ahead. The hospital across the Turnpike. Construction near the hospital. Dormitories, shops and stores a little farther up the ridge. Townsite above, and the high school farther up. Dirt and mud everywhere. Piles of lumber, pipe, shingles."

"You're right as rain, boy. They're building this place fast as they can go. And they ain't near through," Buckley said. "The bus driver who delivered me to the Castle this morning said that there's a new road cut into them ridges nearly every single day. Dirt and mud roads most of em, but they're hauling gravel in as fast as the dump trucks can deliver it to make em passable. This whole damn place is busting at the seams."

Pompey nodded, letting Stanley and Zander get farther out of earshot, which gave Buckley pause. "What I need to know,

Boss," Pompey said, studying his face, "is why you're gonna be working with us. I seen you talk your way into that man's office. Seen how you talked to all those fellers in the hall. You got the silver tongue. Yes, sir, you do. That's what you got."

"Sometimes it seems that way," Buckley said. "I admit that much. But not always."

"So why you pick us?" Pompey said. "You could do lots better. I think you can."

"Pompey," Buckley said, "I don't have to be on top of the heap to git what I want outta life. They's plenty of ways to enjoy life in the middle. Or even near the bottom. Right now I believe it's good to do the shit duty Williams has given us. It'll give us time to study how things is laid out here in the midst of all this hubbub. That way we'll learn what this Clinton Engineer Works is all about."

A smile crept into Pompey's face. "And you'll figure out how to take advantage somehow."

"Well," Buckley replied. "That's what I'm aiming for. That all right with you?"

"It is," he said. "It sure is. Specially if you take me with you."

They walked along a little longer, and Pompey wasn't sure he heard right when Buckley said, "If something happens to me, I want you to be the Boss Man. I'm gonna tell Pyatt that you'll be my number two man. That's the way it needs to go because you'll need to know all the ins and outs of the work if I move to something else. You could take over after I'm gone. And in case you hadn't been paying attention," he said rubbing his chin, "things happen faster around here than they used to. A whole lot faster. And Pyatt won't be interested in wasting time."

Photo courtesy of Deb Kile Hotchkiss

The Hereafter

Tressie Cook had just heard the news at church, staying late to talk with Colton Redd's parents. But she was disappointed. The Redds hadn't planned a thing. They weren't really into it yet. Her son, Reuben, had promised to meet her at church, but once again he didn't show. *He'll blame it on work somehow,* she thought. *Overtime's good, but not if it keeps him from sitting next to me in our pew.*

So after she'd been home at least an hour Reuben finally pulled his truck into the front yard. She met him in the hall ready to give him Colton's news, her cheeks flushed with excitement. She hoped he'd notice her agitation as soon as he laid eyes on her. *It would be best if he'd ask me what's up,* she thought. *He needs to be asking me.* He didn't ask, but that didn't stop her. She told him straight out, "Dinah Braden has got herself engaged to Colton Redd." This rocked Reuben to the core, but he didn't change expression, didn't let his mother see how he really felt.

In his mind's eye he was seeing Dinah, a slender, willowy blonde with intense hazel eyes. Two years younger than Reuben, she wasn't what others would call beautiful, but she'd always been a beauty in his eyes. He didn't want his mother talking about Dinah and Colton, who was one of Reuben's best friends. The Redd farm was on the north side of Poplar Creek, the Cook farm, just south of it.

Colton, aged eighteen, was in his last year of high school while Reuben, also eighteen, had quit school a year earlier to go to work in the Clinton Engineer Works, the new Federal District

165

that had built up rapidly in western Anderson County twenty miles west of Knoxville. Reuben ventured into that new adult world five or six days a week, working long hours on a carpentry crew, so Colton was around Dinah five days a week while Reuben was lucky to see her even twice a week.

Tressie was a petite, bright-eyed woman, her gray hair woven into a long braid down her back. As short as she was, her weight gathered in her lower parts, which was deceptive because she was always so animated. Today she was especially lively about this fresh tidbit of church news. Big news, actually, in the Marlow community just a few miles from the CEW, but Reuben didn't share her excitement. He simply couldn't see Dinah betrothed to Colton who Reuben knew had only one objective---to join the Army.

Whenever Reuben came home to visit his mother, he inevitably did some private reminiscing about his father who had passed away five years earlier: a logging accident at Woodcutter's Crossing. Tressie constantly reminded him how he favored his father, a handsome man, big-boned and square-jawed, with honest, pale blue eyes. "You're spitting image of your Dad," she told him.

All he had to do was step into Tressie's bedroom for a moment to take a look at the two-step platform he and his father had built for her when Reuben was just eight years old. The platform enabled her to climb onto the tall four-poster bed Tim had made for her when they were first married. She cherished Tim's bed and Reuben's steps leading up to it.

Whenever he ran his hand over the nail heads, smooth and flush into the top step, he was gratified by his father's patience which had paid off so very well. Tressie hadn't witnessed the aggravation of a clumsy boy with a hammer. Merely flattered Reuben had made them, she had no knowledge of what father had taught son about doing things right. Starting over if you needed to. Taking pride in what you'd accomplished, even if it was just two steps up onto Momma's bed. Nowadays when Reuben ran into trouble or got anxious about something, he asked himself, "How would Dad deal with this? What would he say?" And that always helped. Always. The answer was to take a deep breath, calm down, and think it through. "That's the way to go, son, and it's a good way to work and a good way to live."

There were times now and then when Reuben took a deep breath when Tressie told him something. She always wanted to gossip and speculate about folks they knew, but he didn't share things as easily as his mother did. This thing with Colton and Dinah perturbed him. He realized he'd never even told Dinah "I love you," but he'd kissed her, held her hand, danced many a slow dance with her. She fit herself to him perfectly. There was no one else but Dinah; she didn't have feelings for Colton. He knew this because of the way her lips parted ever so slightly when she kissed him, her mouth lingering on his, as willing as he was to explore one another. Dinah Braden was destined to become Dinah Cook someday. But now Tressie had brought news that put all this in doubt.

Colton had never really been in the picture. On the contrary, Colton had been totally distracted ever since Pearl Harbor, dead set on getting into the Army. All through 1942 and into 1943 Colton had been obsessed with leaving East Tennessee to go off to war. Mr. Redd had done everything he could to talk Colton out of going to see an Army recruiter. Why didn't Colton just get work at the Clinton Engineer Works? If you were sixteen or older you could find a good job in the CEW where the pay was almost too good to be true. Better than anybody anywhere else in Tennessee was paying, that's for sure. And CEW overtime was like finding gold nuggets in your own back yard.

When Tressie had got home from the new church called the Fire of Baptism Tabernacle set up in an old house on Highway 61, she had been intent on telling Reuben about Pastor Doug

Hightower and a load of church gossip. She was effusive about Dinah's father, Lloyd Braden, who she said prayed louder than anyone else. "There's times he seems to be speaking in tongues. Everybody's impressed when he goes off like that, but, you know, he scares me a little bit. I don't understand him." Tressie was just waiting for Reuben to make a brief comment about her news so she could go on and on about every little thing. When she spoke, it was all Dinah and Colton, Colton and Dinah. And a smidgen of Mr. Braden to top everything off. Soon she was nearly out of breath. "Aren't you pleased for Colton? For him and Dinah? And for the Redds and Mr. Braden, too?"

For an instant, he thought, surely, she understood that, no, he wasn't pleased at all. But she revved up again. "Her Daddy was the one that pushed the idea. Ain't it nice what Lloyd Braden's done for his daughter? David and Anna Redd are good people, too, and they agreed to do for Colton just like used to be done for all young folks. Your Daddy, if he was still alive, he'd let me pick the best gal around here. I know you're close friends with Dinah, but we can do better than her."

Reuben wasn't quick enough to head her off. She had always reveled bringing news home to his father, who had worked as a logger, carpenter, and journeyman laborer. Tim Cook had earned a reputation as a reliable worker, a man who didn't waste time gabbing. Tim had always deferred to what he called Tressie's "Great Social Need." She couldn't resist passing things on to whoever was patient enough to hear her out. Lloyd Braden, was somebody who couldn't deny her any better than Tim had. Mrs. Braden had died giving birth to Dinah, and Mr. Braden hadn't found a woman to agree to be his mate, much less mother for Dinah, so there were times Tressie could suggest something, and Lloyd would follow her advice. Etiquette and stylish topics mostly. Lloyd didn't have anybody at home to keep him in line. Tressie sort of took care of him at church, and he was always right there on the fourth row at New

Hope Baptist with Dinah. That was before the CEW had done away with New Hope. Now the Bradens were set up on the fourth row at Tabernacle.

After his father's death Reuben had adopted his father's way of listening respectfully with only a rare comment when one was absolutely necessary, paying close attention to his mother's expressions, her choice of words, her tone of voice. So long as she felt the joy of telling, he let her do what she did best. Talk about neighbors and kin in Dossett, Marlow, and Frost Bottom, bucolic communities one valley removed from the bustling industry in the CEW.

During her nearly constant palaver Tressie tended to philosophize about the essential questions young girls faced in their lives. Who to marry? Whose proposals to turn down? Whose to accept? Which path to take in life? "Young females have fewer options than young males," she liked to say. "You males can leave home to make your way in the world. Or you can work the family farm. Start a family or remain a bachelor. One's just as good as the other, but a female has just the one honorable path, and it leads to marriage and family." Reuben was reminded of all the women and girls employed in the CEW. Typists, waitresses, secretaries, drivers, technicians. They didn't fit the order Tressie relied on. In fact, she didn't know they existed. Only five miles away just past Black Oak Ridge, the CEW was a separate universe. He worked in that universe, but came home to Marlow when he could.

When her husband died, Tressie gradually forged a private bond with her son that put him in charge, merging into his deceased father's role while his mother became less the matriarch. She let Reuben handle things as Tim had done. She told him, "I'd like you to come with me to this new church, this Tabernacle." She was sitting at the kitchen table when she said it, and he was standing, looking out the window. She had put it so succinctly he was caught off guard, thinking she would need

169

more preamble.

He didn't want to go. "Momma, I'm not ready to find another place to worship. And besides that, sometimes I can't go with you because of work. You understand me, don't you?" He was distracted and unsettled by the news about Dinah. Not thinking straight. Staring at his shoes.

When she took his hand, pulling him close, he was surprised how cold her hands were. "Just come see the place," she said. "The pastor is Billy Hightower's brother, Doug. You remember Doug. He's been to Memphis to get ordained." She kept on like that, wearing him down until finally he agreed to go to Tabernacle the next Sunday.

But the service was unremarkable. Pastor Doug was a long way from matching his brother in the pulpit. His sermon didn't hold together with a compelling scriptural message the way Pastor Billy's sermons always did. Nevertheless, after the service when they shook hands with the pastor, Tressie was effusive. "Pastor Doug, that was a powerful message you gave us. I was touched by every word."

A short, wiry fellow with dark hair receding slightly, the pastor took her hand in both of his, thanking her, "I appreciate that, Mrs. Cook. I really do." Yet he had already turned his attention to Reuben. "Hello, young man," he said, clasping Reuben's hand tightly. "Haven't seen you here before."

"This is my first time," Reuben said. He didn't feel anything else was necessary, and Tressie filled the brief void, chattering about the rousing final hymn, *The Church in the Wildwood*. Reuben was barely listening, absorbing the images of faces among the exiting congregation, nearly all familiar to him, former members at New Hope. After Reuben delivered Tressie home, he made an excuse to head back into the CEW. Marlow was still home, but, as strange as it now seemed, the place was no longer home as much as it used to be. Marlow

170

hadn't changed. Reuben had.

After work at the Y-12 plant he stayed in the CEW, sleeping on an extra cot in one of the trailers at a brand new trailer park called Happy Valley. A guy he worked with gave him a key, and Reuben paid ten dollars a month for the convenience of not having to drive back home. Happy Valley was one of the new places built up in the Federal District, which made Reuben guess there would be something else going up soon near the trailer park. He was close enough to Grove Center to get most of his meals there, which helped him make a go of his work. Reuben's job at Y-12 had him framing and roofing the out buildings around the larger buildings where the scientists and technicians worked. Nobody on the carpentry crew knew exactly what was happening at Y-12, but they built the place according to Government specifications. It was good work, and there was plenty of it.

The CEW was a constant hubbub, literally changing every day with buildings thrown up all the time, one- and two-story wooden structures along every block. Brush piles pushed up along brand new gravel roads. Trees and shrubs were cut down, pushed into long rows, and set ablaze to clear building sites. Men tended the fires, which were still smoldering from yesterday's deforestation, the gray smoke billowing in columns that gradually spread out to disguise the valleys and ridges where the CEW was still in the throes of being born.

When he went back home to the farm, Reuben escaped the hustle and bustle of the Federal District as he drove east, exiting through the Elza Gate and continuing on Tennessee Highway 95 until it intersected with Highway 61 where he turned up the long hill toward home in Marlow. He could feel his work tension dissipate as he crested the hill and coasted down into the valley. Part of this slow release was because he was usually worn out from working all day long in the sun and wind. He found himself gazing at the pear trees which were just coming

171

into their early April splendor. Cherry blossoms, already waning. Jonquils opening up white and yellow in the pastures. He cracked the driver side window to let in some fresh air, colder than he'd thought it would be.

When he got to the Tabernacle it was almost six o'clock. He looked for Momma's Ford coupe, but didn't see it. The church was an old house with tar paper showing through where the siding had peeled away. Parking in the gravel, he started up to the front door when Randy Holloman burst out the door. "Reuben, quick! Drive me to my house. Quick, quick!"

"Sure," he said. "What's going on?"

They piled into the truck, and Randy said, "Dinah's hurt." Randy was a big, pudgy fellow with slicked back blond hair and what everybody termed a baby face that was flushed red now, splotchy red. "She fell onto a pew. Hit her head. I need to call Dr. Tiller from my house. The Tabernacle don't have a phone yet."

Reuben opened his door. "I need to see her," he said.

"No, damn it!" Randy said. "The girls told me to call the doctor. You got to drive me. Come on, come on!"

Randy lived less than a mile away. Two minutes tops. He said, "Come on. We got to hurry." So they took off like Snider's pup. As they drove, Reuben said, "Tell what happened," trying to keep his voice calm.

"Mary Lou and Jackie had mopped the sanctuary, but Dinah and Shirley didn't know that, and they came running in from the kitchen. They slipped on the slick floor. Shirley slid into Mary Lou, but Dinah spun around bottoms up. The back of her head hit a pew. Hit it hard. We laid her out on the floor. She's got this big old goose egg on the back of her head. Her eyes were open, but she never said anything." He gulped air. "We need the doc quick."

172

When they got to his house, Randy ran inside to make the call. Reuben kept the engine running. Drumming his fingers on the steering wheel, he decided he should go listen to Randy. He opened his door just as Randy came back out, and the tires threw gravel as they turned around for church.

"Doc Tiller's at Albert's house," Randy said. "He'll come soon as he can."

When they got back to the Tabernacle, people were crowded around, mostly girls. Linda Jo, Mary Lou, Jackie, but a few boys, too. Jimmy, Bill, and Colton. Dinah was lying on the floor under a gray cotton blanket. Shirley was holding a wet cloth to her head. Not a word was spoken until Randy said, "Doc's with Albert. He'll be here quick as he can. They might get somebody else." The two of them pushed through the group to get up close to Dinah. Colton was seated on the pew nearby, looking pale, maybe sick to his stomach, his dark hair down in his eyes.

Randy said, "Why's she on her side like that?"

Shirley glared at him. "The back of her head's swole up where she hit the pew. We don't want to make it worse. Stop asking stupid questions." She was so unnaturally belligerent Reuben could tell she was scared. She might just bust out crying. But she had taken over; everybody was watching her tend to Dinah.

Reuben moved in and knelt close to Dinah, peering at her face. "I'm going to touch her arm," he said.

Shirley looked at him. "Why?"

He hesitated. "To let her know I'm here." But that didn't really make sense.

"We're all here," Shirley said, her irritation rising.

Reuben said, "You all helped her already. You've moved

173

her, covered her up. I ought to do something." He touched Dinah's elbow, rubbing back and forth a few inches up her arm. She felt clammy, her breathing shallow, almost undetectable. Her chest shuddered, and she was still. Her eyes open, but unseeing.

Shirley pushed Reuben. "What did you do to her? Move back! Move back!"

He let her push him away, feeling almost combative himself, but also pretty useless. Shirley was still in charge. He wanted to help Dinah. Yes, but by doing what? Colton was just sitting there like a knot on a log.

A woman came in the door. She was that retired nurse, Mrs. Carmichael from Oliver Springs, one of those women more than a little pudgy, bulging at her midriff and upper arms. Her dyed hair had gray roots, but nearly blue tips. When she spoke, her eyes fluttered nearly shut all during her speaking so that she only saw the person she was talking to when she first met you and maybe again minutes later as you answered her. She shooed everyone back. "Give me room here." Blinking rapidly, she sat by Dinah, checking her eyes, breathing, and pulse. Dinah was not moving a muscle. Reuben wished she'd move a little bit. That would help.

"You all need to get back a little more," Mrs. Carmichael said, huffing and red-faced. It took her nearly ten minutes to look Dinah over, shaking her head now and then. Her eyes, a flittering paroxysm. She put a finger to Dinah's neck, then moved her fingers a few inches, still assessing vital signs, her pulse mostly. She stood up abruptly, her voice louder than it needed to be. "She's passed away." Her eyes fluttering faster and faster. "Dinah Braden's dead."

The air was sucked out of the room. No one spoke. Mrs. Carmichael stood with eyes trembling shut, waiting for a reaction. The girls erupted in tears, collapsing on each other.

Shirley and Jackie turned out to be the shoulders to cry on, and there was plenty of it going on. Mostly quiet whimpering. "Oh, my God, my God!"

Randy moved beside Colton, placed a hand on his shoulder, and said, "I'm awful sorry, Colton. I...I just can't believe it."

Colton had turned pale. "She was just here a minute ago," he said. "Dinah was right here with us. She...she can't be dead, can she?"

Mrs. Carmichael said, "She ain't got no pulse, and she's turning cold. She's gone to the hereafter, and there ain't nothing to be done for her now. So that's it. I need everybody out of here."

A shot of terrible sympathy for everybody there moved quickly through Reuben, not the least of which was self-pity. He was devastated; he had no breath, no words. Without knowing what else to do, he went to his truck and backed around to head out on the highway, inadvertently heading east on Bush Road. When Sulphur Springs Road came up, he took it, climbing slowly up the winding road to the top of the ridge and then coasting down into Clinton. When he got to Main Street by the courthouse and Hoskins Drugs, he turned west, following the Clinch River back toward the CEW. He wasn't really thinking where he wanted to go, his mind wandering through other concerns, trying not to think about Dinah. He was numb in a way, but extra sensitive in other ways. He felt like a hopeless fool, totally unready for death.

He went through Elza Gate, irritated that he had to stop and show his badge. Suddenly grumpy that the guard made him turn off the engine and pop the hood to be searched. He wanted to get going, to floor the gas pedal, blasting down the Turnpike, but he stopped himself from that kind of thinking. A couple of times he choked up just visualizing Dinah's face as she was lying on the floor, and, hearing the croaking distortions of his

175

own voice, he stopped abruptly, breathing deeply and slowly, trying to gain control. After the first pitiful episode, he thought he'd be all right, but a moment later, it happened again. He completely lost it. He stopped trusting himself to achieve any degree of composure, ignoring the moans and snuffling he produced as he drove. That worked. He made it back to Happy Valley, rushed into the trailer, lying down on his cot. But it wasn't restful just lying there. He wiped tears away more than once, not knowing what to do, and when he closed his eyes, Dinah's face was all there was.

He attempted to control his breathing, taking longer, deeper breaths, and then waiting. This soothed him slightly, but he hadn't lost agitation altogether. He was afraid to think about Dinah, but also afraid not to. Suddenly, he wanted to go home. That would mean talking with Tressie, but maybe that could be a good thing. She'd probably talk too long, but that might be a good thing, too, filling up the incredible void surrounding him.

***

Dinah woke to bright light even though her eyes were closed. It was so quiet she thought she could hear air molecules knocking into one another. She could not remember anything. Where was she?

She felt as if she'd collided with something---what it was she didn't know. She thought somehow she was removed from one moment in time, transported to another, then back again, and she didn't know where or when she was. She wanted to open her eyes, but didn't seem to be able to do that. It was as if she had forgotten how to see. She moved her hand, thinking, *That's good.* Just as that thought had fully formed, she lost what little energy she had and slipped back into oblivion.

When she woke again, she was able to remember being at church and that others had been with her, but every other memory was patchy. She wasn't certain she could open her

176

eyes, and that was beginning to worry her. *What's going on with me? What's happened? Am I ill?* Something horrible must have happened. Whatever it was had left her impaired and very weak, unable to see anything. On the edge of her consciousness she questioned everything. Her health. Her sanity. Her existence.

She probed again, scraping her knuckles on the side barrier, knocking them against what was above her, and she thought the sound was like knocking on a wooden door. Like the door to her bedroom. Her father always knocked like that before coming to see her at bedtime.

She used both hands to push the surface just above her, and it felt like wood as she pushed upward. It didn't move much, but when she tried harder, it did. Just an inch or so, which gave her hope. The stuffy, closed-in sensation was altered, too. She had cracked something open, and she wanted out. She panted as though she'd just run a mile, and she couldn't seem to stop. Dizziness came on her, and she did her best to slow down. To breathe deeper, not so rapidly, and gradually that helped.

She pushed the top off her, but was still cramped by barriers on each side. After giving the top another push, she heard it slide away, crashing onto the floor. Abruptly, she pulled herself up. The room was dark, but she could discern a sliver of faint light under a door. She had no idea where this room was or why she'd been confined, but her eyes were working fine. She was so relieved she climbed out of the container and almost fell flat on her face. She had skinned a knee, and it hurt. Her head hurt, too, and when she put her hand to the back of her head, she felt a soft lump. No blood, but there was swelling under her hair.

She made her way toward the door, which was locked. She put her hand out to explore the wall and found a light switch. She flipped the switch and was blinded by overhead lights. The table was in the middle of the room, and the container she'd escaped was an odd shaped box. She came back to the lid, studying everything. When she realized what the box was, she slumped to the floor. *Was I dead? Am I still dead?* There was a trickle of blood at her shin. So, no. Not dead.

She wore one of her Sunday dresses, sky blue, and her best black shoes. Blood trickled down a little more on her shin, and she reached down to staunch the wound, her fingertip coming back bloody. She found the door latch and exited the room to discover she was in the Tabernacle, and it was full dark outside, the only light coming from the room she'd left. Shirley's family lived just down the road. Surely, the Merediths were home. She could walk down there, knock on the door, and they'd tell her what had happened. Shirley was her best friend.

Dinah walked through the big front room of the Tabernacle and out the door. The night was breezy, and right away she got chilled. A crescent moon gave some light so she could follow the gravel road. The Meredith house was about a half mile away. No lights on anywhere. As Dinah trudged along, she hoped that Shirley would be the one to answer the door. But it would probably be Mr. Meredith. He was a nice person. Mrs. Meredith could be prickly.

A few minutes later Dinah walked up the steps to the Meredith's and knocked on the door. No answer. She waited to see if any lights would come on, listening for footsteps approaching the front door. She knocked again and called out, "Shirley, it's me, Dinah. Can you let me in?"

When no one came to the door, she was puzzled. *Are they gone?* She turned to look for their vehicle and couldn't recall if she was looking for car or truck. Mrs. Meredith didn't drive. *What does Mr. Meredith drive?* Then she remembered how he had driven them to Norris Dam for a picnic in his Studebaker sedan. Dark blue. She stepped off the porch and walked into the yard a few steps so she could see the spot where he always parked. *No car.* She called out again anyway. "Mr. Meredith?

178

Shirley? It's Dinah. I've been hurt." She was getting colder. She began to weep again, so tired of this, whatever had happened to her. And there was no one to help or explain any of it. *Why is this happening? Why am I out here?*

Her shin had stopped bleeding, but a narrow track of blood had crusted down nearly to her ankle. She walked back down the driveway. The moon had moved westward, but she could see how the driveway led down to the road. When she got down there, she could either turn right and go to Frost Bottom or left to Laurel Grove. There was no traffic and few houses in either direction. She heard a barred owl calling for its mate somewhere up the ridge. When she got to the road, she turned toward Laurel Grove, hugging her arms to keep warm, walking along the shoulder, listening to burbling Poplar Creek.

***

When he got home, Reuben saw lights on in the kitchen. Tressie was up. He walked in the front door, headed for the kitchen, and there she was at the table, playing Solitaire. She got up, walked quickly to him and embraced him. "Oh, Reuben," she said. "Mrs. Meredith told me about Dinah's passing. It's so tragic. The girl was going to get married, but now…she…she…" She muttered more words into his shoulder so softly he couldn't understand her.

He remembered very well five years ago when his father got killed he'd wept with her before gaining his composure, taking deep breaths, whispering, "It's all right, Momma. We're going to be all right." He had walked her into her bedroom, helping her lie down. He'd sat on those steps he and Tim had constructed. It was the best possible place to be. He thought now about what his father had given them. A quiet confident assurance that sometimes things might look bad for a while, but in the long run the family would manage. He realized just coming home was all he really needed. He had touched base,

179

and that was enough.

He led Tressie into the bedroom, saying, "We're both tired. Let's talk tomorrow. I'll stay a while to help you get to sleep. Then head back to Happy Valley."

Tressie said, "Why don't you stay here tonight? It's been too long since you stayed over."

He said, "You get ready for bed, and I'll just wait on your steps. Then I need to go." He said those last words with the same firmness his father had always used when opposing a frivolous notion; he lowered his voice, looking at her face with calm determination, maintaining eye contact until she blinked or turned away. He had more strength of will than she did.

Half an hour later he was heading into Frost Bottom. It was close to 1:00 AM, and there was light fog rolling through his headlights, obscuring the rolling sloping pastures on each side. He took his foot off the gas, thinking, *Good idea to slow down.* Carefully, he scanned the road ahead for movement as he more or less coasted north. No houselights on anywhere. A possum waddled lazily in front of him, disappearing in darkness.

The idea that Dinah was gone haunted him. He had been trying to deal with that depression, that despondent and morose feeling because he'd lost the love of his life. He thought of the things he should have told her. Words that should have made sure she knew he loved her. Now he was approaching Walden Ridge Road, and he was thinking about turning the truck around and just taking a more direct route to Happy Valley. He was in the middle of a three-point turn when his headlights swung around so that he could see someone standing on the side of the road, not twenty feet away. He stopped right there, listening to the motor idle. He blinked and looked closer as his heart leaped in his chest. His mind staggered, wrestling with what he was seeing. If he wasn't hallucinating, it was Dinah Braden gazing back at him.

He shut off the engine, opened the door, and walked toward her.

"Dinah," he said. "It's me."

She flinched when he got close enough to touch her, but she stood still, dazed and shivering. "What's happened?" she said, her voice croaking.

"I don't know," he whispered as he folded his arms around her. She didn't flinch at that. He said, "But I've got you now." She shuddered slightly, but never answered. They stood like that for a moment before Reuben said, "I'll take you home."

She pulled away so she could see his face and said, "I'm going to be all right now." He didn't know if she was telling him or posing a question.

"I think so, yes," he said, his mind racing to make sense out of what was happening.

They drove up winding Walden Ridge Road to Dinah's house. She was quiet and still, but had scooted over on the bench seat to be close to him. He had a multitude of questions, but thought it best to wait. She seemed to be in a kind of trance, awake, but exhausted. He wanted to give her room and time. When they got to her house, he pulled up next to Mr. Braden's truck, his headlights illuminating stacked firewood in the gravel.

He came around to help her out, and they walked slowly up to the front door of the darkened house.

"Let me do this," she told Reuben. "Daddy," she called out, her hand trying, but not moving the knob at all, surprised the door was locked. "Daddy, let me in. I've been hurt. I've come home."

A light came on in a back room. Then it went off. There was a noise inside. Then another.

181

"Daddy," she said. "I'm cold. Please let me in. I'm hurt."

Reuben whispered, "Where are you hurt?"

She turned to face him, whispering, "The back of my head."

"Do you want...?"

She held up a hand. "Let me try again."

Why wasn't her father coming to the door? Reuben had heard the noises inside, but couldn't understand what was taking so long. *What's Mr. Braden doing?*

"Daddy, please!" Dinah wailed, louder than before. "I'm tired. I'm hurt. Let me in."

Suddenly, they heard shouting from inside. "Git away from here, Satan! Git away!" Then it was quiet again.

Dinah didn't move. She felt completely bewildered. She began taking shallow breaths. Reuben touched her arm as she leaned toward him. She had goosebumps. He whispered, "You're cold."

She shook her head. "That doesn't matter."

Her father yelled again, "Leave me alone, Devil! My daughter's gone. I won't let you inside this house. Not now. Not ever. Git away, git away!" His voice hoarse and distorted with rage.

Dinah turned away, weeping silently, and as they got into the truck Reuben said, "You need to understand, I thought you were dead. We all did, but if your father would just . . .I don't know . . .We need some time to think about all this." He yawned, and that surprised him, but he willed himself to stay alert and get on with what needed to be done. "I'm going to find a place for you to sleep tonight."

She said, "All right," slipping back against the door, eyes

182

closed.

Maybe thirty-five minutes earlier he had just come through the Elza Gate to get to Frost Bottom, and he'd hardly slowed down at the guard house. Now he was passing through the gate again, going the opposite direction. He knew the fellows on duty there. Not their names, but their faces. They'd checked him through scores of times. Usually, they recognized the truck before he got right up to the gate, and they'd wave him through. Sometimes, if they were feeling talkative, he'd stay a couple minutes to chew the fat. But tonight it was chilly. The guards waved, and he waved, and they let him through. Dinah had slid down in the seat. The guards never saw her.

As always, the CEW was busy. Not so many cars and trucks on the Turnpike, but the gray buses were making their stops at the dormitories all along the way. He turned onto White Wing Road and parked in the big gravel lot out front of the trailers at Happy Valley. Dinah had been so quiet as he had been driving that he thought maybe she was asleep.

He was mulling over Mr. Braden's tirade. It concerned Reuben that he'd turned his own daughter away. Reuben considered going back on his own during daylight hours. It would be easier to explain in daylight. But he was recalling the tone the man used renouncing his daughter. Did he really think she was Satan? It seemed impossible that he had forsaken his daughter when she so desperately needed him. If it had been up to Reuben, he would have made the man see that it was no devil, no ghost outside his door, begging to be let in. It was his only child, for God's sake.

This reminded him of some of the new things going on at Tabernacle. Growing up, he'd always felt comfortable at New Hope Baptist, especially with Pastor Billy there leading folks through the Apostle's Creed and the Lord's Prayer. All of it comfortable and predictable. The Communion and Baptism and what should come to pass hereafter. It was good to be right with Jesus for the rest of eternity. It gave you comfort. It gave you grace. It gave you peace.

It all fit together, and Mr. Braden had been one of the New Hope Deacons, one of the first to volunteer any time Pastor Billy pointed out a family in need of help, whether it was putting on a new roof or towing somebody's car stuck in the mud or moving a neighbor's livestock to the slaughterhouse. When Pastor Billy had left, Mr. Braden seemed lost. Without Pastor Billy, all bets were off.

When New Hope Baptist was demolished, the Feds had condemned and purchased hundreds of acres, essentially running a lot of folks out of what would become the CEW District, Pastor Billy had moved away. Reuben thought it odd that his brother, Doug, had tried to fill the spiritual void with the new congregation, the Fire of Baptism Tabernacle, but maybe Pastor Doug could be as good as his older brother. The man had brought in new rituals, some less formal, simpler phrasing, modern ideas that New Hope had never entertained. Tabernacle was so different from New Hope that Mr. Braden had sometimes got flustered. Reuben could tell just by looking, studying Mr. Braden's expression to see how the man was feeling. If Mr. Braden wasn't flustered, Reuben could talk to him. But if Mr. Braden showed any sign of stress, Reuben would be sure to steer clear.

Dinah was still slumped down in the seat. "You can sit up now," he said. "I'm going to take you to see someone I know to see if she can find a place for you to sleep." He watched as she sat up, adding, "You look worn out."

"I *am* worn out."

"I've got questions for you," he said, putting a hand out to touch hers. He was still amazed she was right there next to him.

184

"Not sure I have answers," she said. "Where are you taking me?"

"To T & C Café," he said. "Her name's Roxy Sandlin. One of the owners. She's a little older, a big redheaded girl. She was in a jam, and I did some cabinet work for her for cost of materials only, saved her a lot of money. She said if I needed a favor, I should come see her." He squeezed her hand. "I think we could use one now."

The T and C Café was a tidy place on Jackson Square. Red and white checked curtains at the windows. Same look on the tablecloths. Maybe a dozen round tables. It felt cozy. He went to the front door, peered through the glass, hoping to see a light on somewhere, but there was none. He knocked on the glass, listening for a response, watching for movement. Finally, a light came on in the back, and he saw someone headed his way.

Roxy looked disheveled and put out about being waked up, but when she got up close, she brushed hair out of her eyes, smiling at him. She wore a long maroon robe that reached the floor. "Reuben Cook, is that you?" She unlocked the door. "What's going on?"

Reuben looked back at the truck. Couldn't see Dinah. "I got to ask a favor," he said. "I need you to put somebody up for the night. My girl friend."

"Your girl?" Roxy said. She brushed her hair out of her eyes again, backing up a step, holding the door open. "I've got a cot in the back. She can sleep there."

He got Dinah out of the truck, his arm around her shoulders, and walked her to the front door. She perked up a moment as Roxy said, "Welcome, welcome," then turned to Reuben. "Who's this?"

"Dinah Braden," he said.

"This way, Dinah." Roxy led her back through the dining room to a hallway, and Reuben followed. At the far end of the hall was a small room with a cot along one wall, shelves of canned goods on the other walls. Dinah slipped off her shoes and slid into bed. Roxy said, "Honey, you just holler if you need something." She turned to Reuben. "You want to tell her good night? I'll wait in the hall."

Reuben knelt by the cot, and Dinah's eyes opened when she felt his hand on her shoulder. He said, "Roxy'll take care of you. I go to work in the morning, but I'll try to beg off. If we need to go to the hospital about your head, we will."

"I don't need that," she said. "I need sleep."

"I'll call you in the morning when I know if I can get off work." He leaned down to kiss her forehead, but she took hold of his shirt to pull him closer. She kissed him very lightly and lay back on the pillow, staring at him as long as she could. Which wasn't long.

In the hall Roxy said, "She's not in trouble, is she? You ain't broke any laws, have you?"

"We haven't broke any laws," he said. "But we got a sticky situation. I'm not real sure how to get through it."

Roxy went to a cooler and pulled out two beers, "Want one?"

"No. I'm kind of tired myself."

"Good. How about a Nehi?"

He nodded. They both took an orange Nehi, and he said, "Let me tell you what's happened. Then I need to get a couple hours sleep so I can go to work. I'm hoping I can get off and come back in the morning."

Roxy sipped her Nehi. "Tell me the story. Don't leave

186

anything out."

"Roxy, you're a life saver."

"Yeah, yeah, I know."

He started with the surprise engagement.

"She's engaged to another guy?"

"Not really," he said. "Her daddy set it up. The guy's my best friend, and he's trying to get into the army. That's all he wants. She's not marrying him."

"You're sure?"

"Dinah loves me, not Colton."

"Keep talking."

So he took Roxy through all the rest of it, finding Dinah on the road, and Mr. Braden calling her Satan. Roxy asked a few questions along the way, but when he had finished, she took another sip, and said, "You all got a lot going on."

Reuben finished off his Nehi and stood up from the table. "I'll be back quick as I can." He took out his billfold. "I can give you some money."

"Keep your cash, buddy. If we need to get square, we will. Now go on. We'll see you when we see you."

Reuben got back to the trailer, fell into bed, and slept soundly for a while, but something woke him up while it was still pitch dark outside. He thought for an instant he'd forgotten something important, and he couldn't think what it was. Normally, he would tell himself what his father advised in such situations, *Don't waste time worrying. Relax. It'll come to you.* But he had trouble not worrying, and he was still agitated in general. Eventually, he went back to sleeps, but the alarm roused him only moments later. He put on some fresh clothes, decided a shave would take too much time, and headed to work. The crew was beginning a storage building, so they'd need to work outdoors all day. The sky was overcast with darkening clouds moving in.

A steady shower began as soon as Reuben found the boss, who said, "From the looks of it, we're shut down today. Can't even get the concrete poured til it dries out. Might be down tomorrow, too, if it keeps raining."

Reuben went to the phone at the check-in desk and called the T and C. He asked Roxy, "Is she doing all right?"

"Still asleep," Roxy said.

"Here I come," he said. "Be there in ten minutes."

He parked on the opposite side of Jackson Square, noticing how busy the shopping center was. Shoppers and people getting breakfast. Cars filled the lot, and there were no free tables inside T and C. Roxy was taking orders at a table near the entrance and caught sight of him as he came through the door. She pointed him toward the back.

Dinah was exiting the room where she'd spent the night when she saw him. She wore a white blouse and denim slacks, her hair pulled back in a ponytail. She looked like a different person.

"How do you feel? You look good."

"I'm feeling better," she said. "I'm helping Roxy clean tables. She's loaned me these clothes. She's nice as can be."

"What about your head?"

She reached back. "Still swollen a little bit, but I feel okay."

She moved into his embrace. "Do you want me to talk to your Dad?" he said. "It ought to go better in the light of day. Or do you want to do it? I'm off from work, so I can do anything

188

you need."

"Daddy will listen to your Mom. I think he will. I'd like to have her help. But tell me this," she said, her voice quaking. "For a little while, did you think I was dead?"

He nodded. "I wasn't there very long," he said. "I couldn't stand it. I took off. Drove around an hour or so. Went back to my trailer. I don't know who made the final decision."

"What decision? That I was dead? That they would put me in a coffin?"

"Is that what happened?"

"That's where I woke up," she said. "I got out of the box, looked for help, but there was no one there. I started walking. You found me. That's all I know." She was coming undone, close to tears, and he didn't want that.

"I think you know I love you," he said, unsure if that was the right thing to say.

She stepped closer. "Why didn't you tell me that a long time ago?"

"I should have," he said.

Roxy stuck her head in at the end of the hall. "You two all right back here?"

"Doing fine," Dinah said as she took Reuben's face in her hands and kissed him.

"Yeah," Roxy said to Reuben. "She's not marrying your friend."

Dinah said, "What?"

Roxy said, "Reuben told me you're not in love with that guy who wants to join the army."

Dinah smiled. "I love Reuben."

Roxy clapped him on the back. "Atta boy, atta boy."

Dinah hugged him tight, and he said, "So you want me to talk to Momma? I can explain that . . . ."

"Just see what she knows. Just listen."

"That won't be a problem with Momma."

Through a raging downpour Reuben splashed back to the truck, headed for home. When he pulled up in the yard, it was only sprinkling, and Tressie met him at the front door. "I saw you coming," she said, giving him a hug. She had an uncanny ability to sense movement out on the highway, to know who went north on the road, who went south, who was driving, who sat in the passenger seat. Sometimes she even knew if they were running late. She was connected to the entire valley that way.

"Come back to the kitchen," she said, eager to play hostess. "You want breakfast?"

"Just coffee," he said. "We need to talk."

She brought a plate of biscuits out of the pie safe as they sat down. "I can warm these up if you want."

Reuben shook his head, but she put the plate in the oven and turned on the heat. "I'm glad you came home," she said. "I'm so upset I don't know what to do. They're saying Lloyd's taken Dinah away somewhere. Everybody's fit to be tied."

"What do you mean?" Reuben said.

"Don't you know about this?" she said.

"I was right there when Mrs. Carmichael told everybody she was dead. But I couldn't stand to stay around any longer. I had to get out of there. Carmichael's creepy."

Tressie said, "It must have been horrible." She patted his

190

hand. "I'm sorry, son."

Reuben reached for his coffee. "Tell me about Mr. Braden."

"Oh, it's heartbreaking, that's what it is. Lloyd went into a funk when they told him Dinah had died. And who wouldn't? It came out of the clear blue. Shocked all of us, but Lloyd most of all." She patted his hand again, which he wished she wouldn't do, but not enough to move his hand. "Anyway, Mr. Meredith and that nurse, Mrs. Carmichael, they took over. They shooed all the kids out and phoned Lloyd to get him to come to Tabernacle. Well, of course, he wasn't home, so Mr. Meredith went looking for him. She told Meredith he was just to say, 'She's had an accident. You need to come see about her.'

"But Joel Meredith hasn't got the sense God gave a goat," she said. "Somehow he let on to Lloyd it was bad, bad news, and Lloyd rightfully guessed it was worse than serious. Left to his own devices, Lloyd Braden got himself worked up something fierce. He ran into Tabernacle, and there lay Dinah with her friends all red-eyed and sobbing. There was Colton, struck dumb, poor boy. Mrs. Carmichael ordering people around, telling everybody what to do, to give her more room, don't touch the body. All that stuff. She was going to be the one to get Dinah ready for viewing, dressing her up just so, making her presentable and all. Lloyd was just baffled about the whole shebang, just devastated, letting Carmichael do what she was bound and determined to do anyway.

"Lloyd went straight over to Dinah. That's what Shirley said. I wasn't there, of course, but I talked to Shirley and the other girls, and they told me about it. Anyway, Lloyd fell down next to Dinah, crying his heart out, sobbing, moaning, and groaning such that he drove all the kids out of there. Shirley said he was it was the saddest thing she'd ever seen. Pitiful in every way. Mr. Meredith said so, too. Finally, it was Mrs. Carmichael seeing to Dinah and Lloyd just muttering in the

191

corner. She sent him home to get Dinah's best dress and shoes. He did that, but then she told him to go away. Now Lloyd's gone, and guess what. Go on. Guess."

"I don't know," Reuben said. He hoped she hadn't heard the irritation in his voice. He was losing patience with her. She was like the expert on tragedy, and he thought she relished the role.

"He took Dinah with him. Took her body and the coffin. Everything."

"What?"

Tressie leaned back in her chair. "I expect he went absolutely out of his head. Running off like he did, with his child's dead body. Maybe he's burying her himself somewhere. God only knows. Lord, have mercy on his soul."

Something nagged at the corners of Reuben's consciousness, but he couldn't quite see it. He needed to find Mr. Braden and explain things, if the man would let him. Even as he thought this, it sounded unlikely. Even impossible.

"I guess I'm not hungry, Momma," he said. "Don't even want this," he said, waving his cup. "I need to get back to Y-12."

"Y-12?" she said, like she'd never heard of the place. "Where exactly is that? What kind of place is it? You never talk about your work or the Y-12 Company. Stay and tell me about it." Her eyes were bright with anticipation.

Reuben stood up. "Another time, Momma. I don't have time for it right this minute."

She stood, too. "But you will, won't you? Sometime soon? Please say yes, Reuben. I don't see you near enough any more. You're always...."

He cut her off. "I come most Sundays, Momma. We both

192

know that's how it goes. And I give you money to meet expenses. You don't lack for much." He removed two twenties from his wallet, offering them to her.

She accepted the money and hugged him tightly. "Reuben, I know you're not always delighted with me. There's times you look as though you barely tolerate me. You think I'm silly and foolish, and maybe I am. But there are times when I'm exactly right, and you know it. And you're as good at providing as your Daddy was. Every bit as good. He'd be proud of you, if he was here."

And with that Reuben knew almost with complete certainty that she was changing her tune, just to keep him there even longer. He started edging toward the door, and she came right along with him, her hand on his arm. He stopped only to kiss her cheek and pushed quickly out the door.

She stood at the threshold, entreating him to come back Wednesday night. "I'll see if I can. Not sure I'll be able to. We'll see." He was trying to persuade them both that he'd see her often enough, but enough meant different things for different people.

For Tressie it meant his living at home, taking care of the yard and the garden, working at the Woodcutter's Crossing just like Tim had done, bringing home that lumberyard paycheck. Reuben would be the new Tim, a caretaker for the household and tolerant of, even eager to hear her sentiments on every topic, no matter how trivial.

For Reuben it meant getting out of Marlow, entering the burgeoning metropolis of the Clinton Engineer Works where thousands of men and women were busy with new, often secretive work. It meant working on the carpentry crew as many hours as they'd give him. Maybe when Y-12 was finished he'd move over to that new plant, K-25, which was closer to the trailer park in Happy Valley. And he'd marry Dinah. She'd find

193

a job somewhere in the CEW. Maybe they'd get assigned one of those little flattop houses. Save as much as they could. Start a family. Momma would fall in love with her grandbabies.

When he got back to T and C Café and he saw Roxy taking orders at a table. She nodded at him, indicating he should go back in the hall. She tore a page off her notepad, handed it to the cook, and followed Reuben. "I want to hire Dinah," she said. "She's a natural."

Everything was happening too fast. He said, "Does Dinah know about this?"

"She's the one that brought it up." Roxy grinned. "I like your girl, Reuben, and I'm glad I could help you two. But..." her brow wrinkled, " . . .I don't aim to get this place all tangled up with anything."

"What do you mean 'all tangled up?'" Reuben said. This thing Roxy had said, maybe it was what he'd overlooked. One of many things he'd failed to consider.

"It's not every day I get people begging for a bed in back of my café. Not every day the girl who's slept here's been disowned by her father. That's all I know. So I'm thinking legal charges might be filed by one somebody against another somebody else. That's why I'm wary," she said, "because I've been burned a couple of times before by folks in a quarrelsome romance. Not folks as nice as you and Dinah, but, well, I just don't know enough about you all yet."

Then Dinah found them. She looked fine, but he wondered how she felt. And would she tell him, if she had any discomfort? Was she worried about her father? Did she really want to work for Roxy? He wanted to hold her, kiss her, whisper in her ear. But Roxy was there, and they owed her answers. He asked, "How are you feeling?"

"Better. My head's got a knot on it." Grimacing, she

194

reached around to it.

Roxy said, "Maybe that's a good place to start. Tell me how you got hurt." She was looking at Dinah. "Not now, of course. We might get some time after the lunch crowd clears out The other waitresses can handle things. That's the best I can do. And," she grinned again, "I'm curious as I can be to find out what you two've had going on."

Dinah caught her lower lip in her teeth, then let it go. "It's been...I don't know what you'd call it," she said. "We need some kind of plan."

"You're right," he said, "but you're distracting me."

"How am I doing that?"

"Just being here," he said, grinning. "Not with Colton."

She blanched and said, "Daddy was the one that...."

"I know, I know," Reuben said. "Momma told me about what he arranged with Colton's folks. I should have asked you before Colton did. I was stupid. I thought you knew that...." His face was bright red. He could feel it. "I thought...."

"I knew you were the one," she said, "if that's what you're asking. It was me who should have said something."

"What?"

"To Daddy," she said. "He caught me off guard. I had no idea he wanted me to marry Colton." She put a finger to her lips, thinking, and he waited to hear what she'd thought of. "It might have come from Pastor Doug. Everything's different at Tabernacle. Pastor's brought in new things. Maybe too much new, so he might have wanted to do something like old times. When parents paired children off as they saw fit. Daddy was listening to Pastor Doug."

"Your father's not much of a talker, is he?" Reuben said.

195

"Neither are you," she said, kissing him. "That's not what I mean. We need to go see him. Set things straight. Probably wasn't a good idea to see him after dark. I can see that now."

Reuben tried to keep his face blank, but Dinah caught something in his expression. "What? What is it?"

"I'm going to tell you what Momma said. Your daddy's not home now. He...."

"What?"

"Momma said he took the coffin, and he's just gone. She thinks he plans a secret burial somewhere else. Nobody knows you're still alive but me and Roxy."

Dinah stared at the ceiling, taking everything in. "We need to find Daddy and explain about what happened after I woke up. I'm not dead. Anyone can see that."

"And you're not Satan," Reuben said.

"When he sees me, he'll understand," she said. Reuben could hear the urgency in her voice. It wouldn't have surprised him if she'd said, "Let's go find him right now." *She's got her Daddy's intensity,* he thought. *Can't see it in herself, but she's sure got it.* And for a fleeting moment he wondered how he took after Tim or Tressie, which others could see, but he could not.

"I tell you what," he said. "Let's tell Roxy the whole story. See what she thinks."

At 1:15 they were through with lunch, and Roxy had time to listen. Dinah told her part first, which didn't take much time. She finished up describing her father's stormy, anguished reaction at home. Reuben described finding her on the road, which was what still bewildered him. He tried to explain to both of them how stunned he was to think her dead one minute, and the next minute find her standing on the side of the road. He got whiplash just thinking about it.

196

Roxy sipped coffee, asked a few questions, nodding here and there. They were done by 1:50, and Roxy said, "I think I got the big picture."

Dinah said, "We know what we want to do, just not exactly how to go about it. Especially what to do first. Who to start with."

Roxy got up for another cup of coffee and said, "Dinah, if you don't get your Daddy to understand pretty quick that you're not dead, you'll never get him to believe you."

Reuben chuckled, which caused Dinah and Roxy to give him a funny look.

"How can you say he won't believe she's alive?" he said. "If she's standing there right in front of him, how can he doubt it?"

Roxy said, "It seems to me your Daddy's one of those really devout persons, struggling to keep up with new ideas, trying to relate to a new pastor. Sometimes church people can go off on a tangent, especially when they're fending off evil."

"I don't get you," Dinah said. "What evil?"

"Your Daddy had a shock. He'd lost his daughter. Sometimes a person will look real hard for something to make sense out of horrifying things. To blame on somebody else. The Devil is something people are scared of, and the nighttime is when they're most scared. Sometimes if you ask them the next morning what all the yelling was about last night, they can't tell you. They don't remember."

Roxy said, "What's important is to get them talking about trusting somebody. Not being so afraid. That's not easy, and what works to save one person won't necessarily work for somebody else. Everybody's special in the way that works for them."

197

Dinah said, "Where'd you learn this? It makes sense, but where'd you get it?"

With a rueful smile, Roxy stood up. "My Uncle Dexter Harmon was sheriff of Roane County for 14 years, and I've heard him tell stories about criminals as well as victims. All kinds of people in trouble. I used to visit him at the Kingston jail, and I watched him testify in court." Her smile grew wider. "I loved him at our kitchen table talking about helping people. 'Sooner or later,' he used to say, 'everybody gets scared. Everybody needs help.'"

"He sounds like a good man," Reuben said. "I'd like to meet him."

"He died last year," Roxy said. "Lung cancer." She laid her cup down on the counter. "I was up too late last night, so I'm going to lie down a while. Come get me in 15 minutes, will you?"

After Roxy went down the hall, Dinah told Reuben, "I want to see Daddy."

Reuben said, "Me, too. The sooner your father sees you're alive and kicking, the better." She slid her chair over to his and grasped his hand as he said, "Maybe we start with Colton. That'll be easier. See your father after Colton."

She said, "Yes, that will give us more time to decide how to talk to Daddy." They talked a few more minutes about Roxy and last night. Then Dinah headed for the dining room, leaving Reuben drifting in thought. He thought, *Take a deep breath, and think it through.*

After the supper crowd thinned out at T and C they decided to leave around 6:30 or 7:00. Reuben was confident they could get Colton to see how Mrs. Carmichael screwed up. It was a crazy mixed up story, but they could explain things to Colton. And with that under their belt, they'd have a better idea how to get through to Lloyd Braden. How to get him to welcome his daughter back into the world of the living.

***

Tressie was rinsing supper dishes at the sink when she noticed a truck going past on the highway. A red Chevrolet pickup. Male driver. Female passenger. Looked like Reuben's truck, but it wasn't turning in at her driveway, heading instead for the Redd's place next door. Because of the curve in the road, the truck slowed down, and she was able to see both faces clearly.

"Oh, my goodness," she murmured to herself as a chill wind blew through her. She thought, *That's Reuben! And the girl looks like Dinah. How can this be? Carmichael said Dinah was dead and gone.* But her eyes had not deceived her. She'd seen Dinah and Reuben. Bold as brass. In the flesh.

She didn't know what to do. Go to the Redd's house? She didn't see their car in the driveway. *What's going on? Why doesn't Reuben bring her here? I can help him with her. I can....*but as these thoughts materialized in her brain, she felt a twinge of uncertainty based on how many times Reuben had chosen not to tell her about something important. She could help him with nearly everything that might trouble him, but he had to ask, didn't he? He needed to ask.

Oh, but not about work issues. No, she wanted social issues, relationships, and the like. Talking to people with hurt feelings, embracing people who looked like they needed a hug. But, like his father before him, Reuben kept problems to himself. Tressie had pleaded more times than she could count, "Bring me your troubles. I can help. I know people. I can fix things." But she always found out later, so she was torn: *Do I go over to the Redd's to help? Do I go look for Dinah's father?*

She made up her mind quickly without knowing who she

would run into first. She'd just go out visiting and deal with whoever she happened on. So she packed up a basket, taking selected items out of her pie safe. It bothered her that she wasn't able to help Reuben directly. But she was determined to help him indirectly. From the Braden side.

She changed into something presentable. A sweater, clean blouse, fresh skirt, comfortable shoes. She wished she had better shoes to make the best possible impression. She took one last look in the mirror and headed out to the car. She hesitated a split second, searching her pocketbook for the house key, failing to locate it. While most Marlow folks never locked their doors, Tressie tried to lock hers. Of course, remembering where she'd left the keys would have helped.

She drove the hundred yards to the Redd's house, thinking how she'd go about talking to Reuben and Dinah. She rehearsed a few opening lines before she noticed Reuben's truck wasn't in the yard. She got out, went to the front door, and knocked, but there was no answer. She pushed at the door which opened, stuck her head inside, and called out for the Redds. "Hallooo! Anybody home? It's Tressie. Anybody here?"

No answer.

"Durn it!" she muttered, closing the door. She considered leaving Anna and David a note about Dinah, but she didn't know want to give away the best part. She wanted to see their faces as they processed astounding news. *Where are they?* she wondered. *Where's Colton?*

She thought about Pastor Doug. *Maybe he knows where they are. Reuben and Dinah could have gone on to Tabernacle. Could be with him right now.* She got back in the car and backtracked down the highway to Tabernacle. No cars outside. But sometimes Pastor Doug walked to his new church. If he was there, she'd give him the news, ask for guidance. Help him tell the story to everybody who'd listen.

200

She parked and walked up to the front door. "Pastor Doug, are you here? It's Tressie Cook. Hallooo!" Her voice echoed through emptiness. It wasn't a large sanctuary since the church was merely a vacant house Pastor had refitted for worship. She called out again as she went into the kitchen, also empty, but a shadow moved outside the back door, which was slightly ajar. Was someone out back? She went to see. Then she heard a noise around the corner of the house. A dog maybe? Pastor Doug had a beagle named Chester, a sweet little meddlesome dog. It would be just like Chester to be into something he shouldn't be.

"Chester, are you there, buddy? Come here, come here, Chester." She walked that way, watching for the dog, but, when she turned the corner, it wasn't Chester. It was Lloyd Braden, staring at her like he didn't know her from Adam. He looked like he'd been lost in the woods. Scruffy, circles under his eyes, wearing sweat-stained overalls.

"Lloyd," she said, as natural as can be, if she'd been looking for him all along. "You look terrible." She thought, *Maybe I shouldn't have said how he looks.* She studied him as she thought he might not answer. He might be sleepwalking or something. She felt uncomfortable standing there with him, so she went another way. She said, "Are you hungry?"

He flinched at the word, "hungry," which she took for a yes.

"Wait here," she said. He stared back at her, and she said, "I'll be right back." She left him there as she went to get her basket from the car. When she got back, he was seated against the back wall, his legs splayed out in front of him, looking more worn out than hungry.

"I've got biscuits," she said, placing the basket next to him. His hands were calloused and dirty, and he smelled of sour sweat and mud and a profound lack of washing. "Let me get something for you, Lloyd. Do you like apple butter or peach jelly?" She thought she might be talking too much, but she heard no complaint so she lifted the dishcloth covering the food. She held a red-and-white checked napkin out to him. But he didn't move, watching her handle the food. She fixed two biscuits, one with the peach jelly, one with apple butter.

"I don't have anything to drink," she said. "Is that all right?"

"Yes," he said in a quiet whisper, staring at the biscuits she handed him.

He began with the peach biscuit chewing with bovine single-mindedness. The apple butter biscuit took him only four bites, and he sat there, blinking, breathing slower. She had no idea when he had last eaten, and she wanted to ask him about that. Wanted to ask about where he'd been. About Dinah, too. *What in the world has he been doing?* She wished she could be in two places at once: here with Lloyd to find out his story; and with Reuben and Dinah to find out hers.

She wished someone else would break the ice. Once it was broken, she could take the conversation anywhere she wanted. Pastor Doug or Reuben or somebody else needed to talk first and then get out of her way. But there wasn't anybody there with her but Lloyd Braden. Unless somebody arrived pretty soon, it was going to be up to her.

As she made up two more biscuits, she said, "Lloyd, something wonderful has happened. I can't tell you about it til I know what's been going on with you. Where you've been. What you've done." She studied his face. There was no hint of how he felt about what she was saying. "You can answer my questions. Then I'll tell you what I know."

"All right," he said, a little louder this time.

It took Lloyd a little longer to finish the last two biscuits she'd fixed, and he sighed heavily.

202

"Better now?" she said.

He nodded.

She said, "So tell me where you've been, Lloyd. I'm listening close here, and when I start talking, you're going to listen to me just as close, you hear?"

"I don't exactly remember where I been," he said, stopping short of what she'd hoped for.

"Just tell what you know for sure," she said.

In fits and jerks he started talking about how Carmichael had said Dinah was dead. "I thought she was making some horrible joke. I tried to read her face," he said, "but her eyes get to me. I couldn't do it."

"I've heard about how she does her eyes," Tressie said, settling down by him. "Keep talking."

He said, "I'm ashamed of how I acted, sobbing and blubbering over Dinah lying there. Carmichael fussed for me to get clear so she could care for the body." Then he was sent home to gather clothes for Dinah to wear. "You know, in the coff...the coff...." Telling this choked him up.

She saw that lost feeling come over him as he stared up at the sky. He told about going back home later, only to realize every room smelled so much like his daughter he had to walk around outside for an hour or so or he'd break down crying. He didn't get to bed until after midnight and had only just gotten to sleep when he woke to a ruckus at the front door. Somebody pounding on it in the middle of the night. Trying to get in.

"I was overtired," he said. "You know how it is when you've been going full bore too long. Too tired for sleep. I was going to answer the door, but then I asked myself, 'Why's somebody knocking on my door this time of night? Can't be nobody I know.' They ain't nobody I know cruel enough to barge in on me like that." His face altered as he spoke until finally he erupted mournfully like an animal caught in a trap, wailing and keening for release. He was not doing this for Tressie. He was reliving a time and place when he'd been horribly wounded in his soul.

Tressie took a few steps back, trying not to stare at him, gazing instead across the pasture toward Black Oak Ridge. She needed to give Lloyd some room, and that was difficult to pull off. She tried to count silently to mark time, but even that was tough. After nearly two minutes, she said, "All right now, Lloyd. You got to get a hold of yourself. You got to use your words." When he was quieter, she said, "You want any more biscuits?"

She was surprised when he said, "I ain't had anything to eat since yesterday morning."

"A man's got to eat," she said, confident he was in agreement, overdue as he was. She brought out the remaining biscuits and used up everything left in her basket to fix them. She didn't have to announce he could go to it. He jumped right in. When he was through, she said, "Remember I said I got something wonderful to tell you?"

He nodded warily, but she didn't let that bother her. The ice had been broken, and she had some momentum, so she said, "I'm going to tell you something wonderful, and you're going to sit and listen to everything I got to tell you. Part of it needs explaining, but most of it is easy. And like I said, it's wonderful."

He nodded.

"You've been spooked pretty bad. You're still spooked, but sooner or later you got to face your fears. Nobody else can do that for you." She noticed his stolid expression. "Just be patient. I'm getting to the best part." Again he nodded, and now she saw him relaxing his gaze. His eyes didn't seem so alert as they had before he'd eaten. She figured all the blood was moving to his middle for digestion.

"You think you're just a simple fellow," she said, "but you're not, Lloyd. You're just not." She wondered why she'd said that last part. It was true, of course, but had taken them off the path she'd been following. Now she was flummoxed for an instant, standing in front of him, not knowing how to get to what came next. She needed Pastor or anybody else really. Somebody to jump in right here.

Gazing back over his shoulder through the screen door to the kitchen, she glimpsed movement inside. Somebody was making their way to come out the door. It was David and Anna Redd who came out with Pastor Doug and Colton bringing up the rear. They were surprised she was there, but even more surprised to find Lloyd there, too.

"Mr. Braden," Pastor said. "You're back. We were worried about you."

Tressie said, "He's worn down to a nub, trying to get his mind straight about Dinah." She patted him on the shoulder. "But I've brought him good news. It's good news for you, too, Colton. Good news for all of us." She felt warm, almost glowing, fanning herself with one hand, looking from face to face.

Anna said, "Well, for goodness sake, Tressie. Don't keep us guessing." She was a slender, lanky woman, an inch or two taller than her husband. Anna had zeroed in on Tressie.

Pastor Doug said, "The Redds have just come back from the Army Recruiting Office at the courthouse over in Clinton. Colton reports to Chattanooga in thirty days, so we've had a patriotic gesture made today. A grand gesture, if you ask me."

Colton shifted back and forth, uneasy on his feet. Tressie

noticed Lloyd doing the same thing. She was in danger of losing the spotlight, so she said, "Dinah's not dead."

"What?" Anna said.

Tressie smiled with compassion for her audience, letting the moment linger. Then she said, "I saw Dinah riding in Reuben's truck about half an hour ago." She wanted to watch Lloyd's face, but couldn't keep from watching all of them in snippets and peeks. Lloyd didn't flinch, like he was the great stone face. David turned red, looking to Anna and then to Colton. Colton blinked, staring at Tressie. There was general commotion in everybody's head. Pastor Doug was listening intently, as yet uncommitted. But there were no more questions, so she started filling in gaps.

She explained how Lloyd had gotten spooked when somebody banged on his door. How she had caught a glimpse of Reuben's truck on the highway, Dinah riding with him. Exuberantly, she said, "Things are going to be wonderful because Dinah isn't gone. "She's with Reuben," she said exuberantly. To her what she'd seen on the highway when that red truck went by, well, it was unimaginable good fortune. That imperious Carmichael woman had been mistaken. Everybody had been fooled into believing everything Carmichael had said, but Dinah had merely been knocked out. "That was all it was," Tressie said, feeling a fierce joy for the wonderful news she was sharing.

Pastor Doug said, "If all this is true, it's plainly a miracle." He clapped Lloyd on the back, which seemed to activate the big man. Lloyd shook the pastor's hand vigorously, moving to David and Anna, shaking their hands. Finally, he approached Colton who seemed lost for words.

"Are you still wanting to marry her?" Lloyd said.

Colton had turned pale. "I've just signed up," he said.

"Would you want Dinah to be one of those war brides? What if I got killed? Is that fair to Dinah?" He'd gotten over the idea of marrying Dinah. Which intrigued Tressie. She didn't care if he did or didn't marry her, but she wanted to ask questions. Many, many questions. And she craved getting every single answer.

Tressie was thinking how she'd calm Lloyd down after he realized Colton was calling off the wedding, but actually Lloyd had heard it and seemed okay with it, too. A surge of relief had engulfed Colton and Lloyd at the same time, but from different directions and separate purposes. That caught her off guard, and she could feel things drifting away again, trying to understand what had just happened.

They heard a vehicle pulling up in front of the Tabernacle, and Colton, who was standing so he could see through the screen door and out through the front window, said, "Looks like Reuben's truck." They heard car doors slamming shut. Then footsteps approaching inside the church. Tressie would have given anything to stand where Colton stood so she could watch her son's face as he came in. She'd be interested in studying Dinah's face, too, but she'd want to see her son's face above all others. She wanted to remember his exact expression when he came through the screen door to find her there with these people. She wanted to speed things along, but also to relish the moment as long as she could. Suddenly, she had a thought: she wanted to be the one to tell Carmichael she'd made that colossal mistake.

The screen door swung open, and she saw her son holding it for the girl everyone had thought was dead. The implications of this gathering behind the Fire of Baptism Tabernacle would surely provide Pastor Doug with the basic elements of many a sermon. But for Tressie this situation was the most sensational event she'd ever been a part of. She was still trying to pin it all down so she could study it proper. It had been one long, roundabout trek to get to where they'd all come together, but she wasn't letting any of it go to waste.

She'd been slowed, but not deterred.

Keep Her Safe

The Director of Intelligence for the Clinton Engineer Works had been on the job since September, 1943. Captain Clyde Hubbell, a heavy-set man with thinning, sandy-colored hair, was inclined to listen first, ask questions later. He had a square jaw and steel gray eyes. This was how Theo saw him as the man sat in the living room talking with General Groves. Theo handed Hubbell a glass of tea, handed one to the General, and took one out to the car for Marcus.

When he handed the glass to Marcus, Theo asked, "Hubbell works for Groves? I thought Intel was run by a young lieutenant. Guy named Blankenship, I believe. Do I have that right?"

"Blankenship's still there," Marcus said. "But Groves wanted someone with more experience. Hubbell's in charge, and Blankenship's there, too. Everybody works for Groves," Marcus said. "Thanks for this." He wiggled the glass and took a sip.

Theo said, "So he's not just a visitor here?"

"No, he's here at the Castle," Marcus said. "Here all the time, not just once in a while like Groves. He gets to keep everything legal day in and day out, and only has to answer Groves face-to-face when the General's in town." Marcus shook his head. "Not a job I'd want, I can tell you that."

"So he's an attorney?" Theo asked.

"No."

"How can he do legal then?"

"Oh, I didn't mean legal," Marcus said. "I meant secure. Safe."

"Well, tell me about...."

"We probably need to stop right there," Marcus said. "The General don't want me talking about him. You know, 'Loose lips sink ships.' Right?"

Theo raised his eyebrows.

Marcus said, "Groves blessed me out yesterday when he heard me talking to a guard. I thought he was going to fire me right then and there. He's real security conscious, that's all. And he expects everybody else to be that way, too...so I can't really tell you anything. You know how it is."

"Okay," Theo said. "Forget I asked."

"Oh, you can count on that," Marcus said, handing back the empty glass. "I got the best damn job I ever had, driving for Groves. I ain't going to do anything to risk losing it."

Theo went back into through the kitchen door. He opened the fridge to take inventory and found some coca cola along with some Nehi orange drinks, which Groves sometimes preferred. Placing the empty glass in the sink, he walked quietly to the door that separated the kitchen from the rest of the house, stopping to listen for conversation in the living room where Groves and Hubbell sat talking.

He heard their voices, but couldn't make out every word said. He had an impulse to stay where he was, ear to the door, but thought better of it. He didn't know what they were talking about, and maybe he was better off not knowing. If Groves ever asked him, "Have you heard anything top secret? Anything you weren't authorized to know?" Theo would be able to answer honestly, "No, sir. I don't know a thing." Of course, you couldn't help picking up tidbits here and there. Groves had a strong voice, which was difficult not to hear. Even when he was talking on the phone in the living room, Theo and Bashie could sometimes hear him emphasizing a point, and he did a lot of talking on the telephone. Sometimes he'd make a dozen or more calls after he'd had supper, most of them to stations west of Tennessee. Chicago. Washington State. Someplace in New Mexico. Once in a blue moon the phone would ring at the Hackworth House, and the voice on the other end would say, "Call for General Leslie Groves. Urgent." Everything involving Groves was urgent.

Hubbell and Groves were all right for a while, so Theo went out to talk to Marcus again. When he got close to the sedan, he saw Marcus in the backseat, lying down, so he backed away. There wasn't much to do, so he went and sat on the front steps to wait for the next visitor who was supposed to be coming soon. Marcus had said as much. "A guy working with Hubbell." Too late to find out more now.

But seeing as how Marcus was relaxed enough to take a nap, Theo wasn't exactly worried. More like curious, wondering how these men who reported to Groves…how they would look and talk and interact with General High Pockets. It always tickled Theo to see how high the General's waistline was. Not that he ever let on it was funny. Lord, no.

Half an hour later a Jeep came up the driveway, and Marcus stirred, sitting up, peering out the car window. A uniformed man got out and walked up the walk carrying a stack of folders in his arms as Theo stood, wiping off the seat of his pants. This soldier was older than Hubbell, slender, wiry in a way that said he'd done hard labor, heavy lifting, and could still do it. But his face was an open, honest face. That's what Theo thought. "Welcome to Hackworth House," he said.

"Thank you," the soldier replied. "Captain Frye. Here to meet with General Leslie Groves."

"We're expecting you. Come in."

Knocking on the front door that opened directly into the living room, Theo waited for a response. The General called out, "Enter."

Holding the door open for Frye, Theo let him go in ahead.

"Frye," the General said, "you brought today's assessment?"

"Yes, sir, General. Three copies."

"More than we'll need. Next time bring only two copies. But all right. Let's get to it."

Theo passed through to the kitchen, brought cookies and a cherry pie in, went back for the drinks, leaving tea and soft drinks where the men could choose their own. Finally, he brought in an ice bucket and glasses plus a stack of napkins. Satisfied he'd set it up right, he retreated to the kitchen again, but Groves called out to him. "Mr. Kincaid, can you come take this? It's trash. We don't need it." The General held out crumpled pages in his hand. "See that every scrap of this is incinerated."

"Yes, sir."

He had his hand in the cupboard pulling the matches out of the cup where Bashie kept them when he heard a loud thump in the bedroom. He stuffed the papers into the cupboard and went to see about her.

"Honey," he said, softly, "you all right? How're you doing?" He noticed a book had fallen off her nightstand.

She smiled sleepily. "Better, thanks. What time is it?"

212

"Six twenty," he said. "The General has two men with him. I took in the platter and drinks."

"And Marcus?"

"He was napping in the car, but he's up now."

"No headache for me," she said. "That's the best thing. And my stomach feels all right." She stood and headed into the bathroom. "Go on. I'll catch you in the kitchen."

The next three hours were special because Bashie was so happy, so upbeat that Theo didn't want Groves, Hubbell, and Frye to leave. The two of them had served the officers soft drinks and sandwiches, checking on them every quarter hour, but not needing to do much. It was a charmed event, a halcyon type of change that caught him off guard. She was energized. If he had known this was going to happen, he would have taken pains to see that he had something really special for her. She couldn't resist milk chocolate, and he cherished the expressions on her face whenever he surprised her with milk chocolate or caramels. Valentines was a big deal usually, although in February she'd been sick as a dog all that day, hiding in the bathroom with severe diarrhea. After her ordeal, she'd slept almost a day and a half. It had been a bad, bad day. Not like today.

Groves finally called out, "Mr. Kincaid, these gentlemen are leaving now. I'll be in the bedroom. Got calls to make. Thank you for the refreshments."

The front door was closing, and the visitors were headed down the front steps by the time Bashie and he entered the living room. They heard the General dialing from his bedroom. The bedroom door remained slightly open because the General's voice was easily understood. After a while, he closed the door, his voice becoming just a murmur.

Bashie sat where the General had been sitting, and Theo

213

gestured silently, pointing toward the General's bedroom, whispering, "What if he comes back in here?"

"He won't," she said. "He's on the phone. Relax." She offered him an olive. He shook his head, but was finally warming to her mood.

"You are...something else," he grinned.

"I'm finally feeling good," she said. "It's been a long time."

"Seems like it has," he agreed.

"Tonight is something special," she said, her voice taking on a tenor that puzzled him. He didn't know what she meant. Her face was aglow, unnaturally so.

He sat down quickly. "What is it?"

"You've been so kind, so generous all this time," she said. "Come here." When he was close enough, she pulled his face to hers and gave him a luscious, lingering kiss unlike anything he'd experienced in months. Nothing else was said as they straightened up the living room and kitchen. Theo had difficulty keeping his eyes off her, just the way it had been when he'd first met her. She was moving un-self-consciously, which he had never understood how she could do when she knew he was watching her...and he knew she knew.

She came by, touched a finger to his lips, and went into their bedroom. He had a glass to put away, so he opened the cupboard, and there were the crumpled papers Groves had told him to destroy. He noticed something. At the top of each page: "Six Immediate Military Requirements for Adequate Security." He left the papers where they were and closed the cupboard.

While she was in the bathroom, he got into his pajamas. He pulled back the coverlet, lying in the very center of the queen-sized bed, waiting for her to finish up in the bathroom, which was a rarity these days. Usually, she was in bed before he was.

214

Sound asleep.

She turned off the bathroom light as she entered the bedroom which was dark already, and with the paucity of moonlight coming through the window he could make out her shape, her nightgown, her bare shoulders as she slid under the sheet beside him. His heart caught in his throat as he recalled similar entrances she had made when they were first married, and he was pleased when she used his arm as a pillow and snuggled close to him, fitting herself perfectly to his frame.

But she stiffened. "Let's not get too excited here," she whispered, which doused any fire he had thought might get kindled. He waited to see what else she might say, not knowing what he should say, trying to slow his breathing.

Finally, he could stand it no longer. "You're not interested?"

"That's not it," she insisted. "We're not alone here, Theo. What if we made some noise?"

It was quiet again for an extended period. "Besides," she added. "I'm still a little fragile."

"Oh?" he said. "What is it exactly? I mean, do you still have the headaches? Or the pain in your chest?"

Theo was afraid he'd broached something forbidden, but he felt her relax in his arms, and her breathing slowed noticeably. He thought she might have fallen asleep as he awaited her answer.

"I'm much better," she said. "But not back to normal. Sometimes I have a slight...I don't know, discomfort. But mostly I feel just disconnected from what I was before. There are nights when I dream about a little girl. A dear, dear little thing who talks with me about anything and everything. I entertain her with stories. I try to keep her safe, but I'm afraid

215

something terrible will happen to her when I'm not around. I don't know how to protect her. This dream confuses me. It bothers me so much. I wish it would stop. I'm...I'm...." She never finished.

"It's all right," he whispered. "All right. Let's just hold each other a while." He thought she'd begun holding her breath. "Is that all right with you?"

He felt her nodding at his shoulder and kept listening to hear what she would tell him, but she never offered any words of clarification. He could see what she was getting at. He'd been so eager physically that he had discounted the fact that Groves was just down the hall. And he'd been oblivious to her recuperation or lack thereof. She'd been ill so long that he had become inured to everything. He'd been so constrained that he'd forgotten what passion felt like. Compassion he knew well. Passion was forgotten. Until now. Apparently, it wasn't going to happen tonight. But she had said it was really because of Groves, and High Pockets wouldn't be around much longer. He might be gone tomorrow. Theo took a deep breath and told his wife, "It's okay, Bashie. We can wait a while. You'll be getting better, right? We'll be able to...to do whatever we want to do. Whenever we want to do it. We'll be all right again. I know we will."

He waited for her reply, for some indication she agreed. Hoping she agreed. Knowing she would want to please him if she could. If she was able. The more he thought about what she had said about how she was feeling, the more he realized she wasn't really back to normal. Part of him had known that all along. Another part was desperate for her to come back as she had been before she got sick. He thought about that as he lay with her in his arms until they both fell asleep.

The next morning he was up at the regular time, five thirty, and, as was his custom, the General was, too. Coffee was all the

216

General ever needed, and Marcus knocked on the front door at six fifteen. The two of them were gone a few minutes before six thirty.

Theo made the General's bed and straightened up in the bedroom and bathroom. He tossed the used towels in the hamper in the kitchen. When Bashie came into the kitchen, Theo said, "Let me show you something."

"What?" she asked, sipping her own coffee.

He handed her the crumpled papers---two identical pages--- and she looked them over. She glanced up. "Is this official? Are these the General's?"

"He told me to burn them."

"Are you going to?"

"Probably. I mean, yes, I am."

She took a longer look at the list. "Here. You read this one, and I'll do the other one."

1---Keep strangers out of area
2---Keep project members free from harm
3---Reduce chances outsiders could learn of any explosions
4---Safeguard public outside the area from fallout
5---Plan for emergency evacuation
6---Forestall any national press reports that might
      alert Japan or Germany

Theo put his copy down with a dozen questions rushing through his head. Bashie seemed lackadaisical, not intrigued. She was scanning the page slowly. When she finally looked up, the telephone rang, and Theo held up a hand. "Let me get that."

Bashie said, "What's this fallout thing?"

He held his hand up again. "Just a minute, honey."

He answered the phone and listened a moment, then said,

"Thank you for letting us know. I'm awfully sorry. Good bye, sir."

"What in the world?" Bashie said.

"That fellow, Frye," he said. "The second guest last night."

"Yes," she said. "What about him?"

"He had a stroke when he was walking up the front steps to his dormitory last night," Theo said. "Had another this morning at the hospital. He's dead."

"My God!" Bashie said. "Who was it that called you? Marcus?"

"It was General Groves," he said.

"Groves called us?"

"He wants to have another visitor here tonight," he said. "Along with Hubbell. The replacement for Frye will be here. It will probably be a late night. Are you feeling up to a full supper for three?"

"And something for Marcus and for us," she said, happily.

"You seem awfully sunny," he said, grinning. "You must have slept well."

"I did," she said. "But it wasn't as long a sleep as it might have been."

"It wasn't?"

No. You kept me occupied longer than I expected."

"Oh, yes," he said, feeling his face warming. "That's right."

"Poor Mr. Frye," she sighed, and they stood by the phone a while. Finally, she said, "What's fallout?"

B & E

Buckley called the hutment Pompey's Place. It was like all the other hutments, merely sixteen feet square, built of quarter-inch plywood tacked to four-by-four posts, with no insulation whatsoever. No windows, just the one door. No electricity. Rough, unfinished plywood flooring. Outhouse a few steps away. Communal bathhouse a little farther down, servicing seven more hutments. A cot pushed into each corner plus one in the middle of the room. Each nigger got three nails in the wall to hang his clothes on. The Housing Authority promised to put in a pot-bellied stove come cold weather, but that meant the guy in the center cot would have to go. On a summer day Pompey's Place sweltered like a furnace, so Buckley and Pompey sat outside most of their free time after work, swatting flies and skeeters, smoking, drinking hooch, and playing cards. Zander and Stanley only came home after meeting gals from The Pen, finding some hidey hole to roll around in. Both boys were making time with females every chance they got, and they had a lot of competition because there just weren't very many women on the Reservation. But those who were there were young and more than willing to enjoy life after their shifts ended. Just like Stanley and Zander were.

That was something that affected Buckley, even though he had a few years on those young black boys. Shoot, he was probably twice their age. There was a shortage of white gals around the CEW, too, but Buckley'd been doing okay in the Fooling Around Department. In fact, better than okay. He often found his privates were still a little sore and chafed. He thought,

I might need to rest up a bit. Too much fooling around will do a man in as sure as too little. Lately, he'd seen a lot of Roxy Sandlin, a gal from Oklahoma who liked to dance and go to the Ritz Club in Clinton every time she got asked. She was a redhead, heavy hipped, but small up top. He brought her black market lipstick, which she overused, but they always had a good time, drinking, dancing, fooling around with one another. He liked to slip a hand down her hip when they embraced, tugging her skirt up, and usually she'd guide him, pulling his hand where she wanted it to be. He couldn't help but smile a bit remembering where she wanted it last time sitting in the booth in the darkest corner of the Ritz Club. That was pretty good. Ought to have been enough to make him anxious to get back there.

But when he did get back there talking to folks, the conversation just naturally came around to Clinton Engineer Works. A lot of people at the Ritz had found work at the CEW plants, and folks usually talk about what they know. So there was talk about the CEW, even though the Army discouraged employees saying anything about their work. The way Buckley saw it, the Army could discourage talk, but they couldn't actually forbid it. There was a lot of easy talk about ordinary things like riding area buses or avoiding all the mud. Easy talk about standing in line at the drug store or the barber shop or the grocery or even to get on a damn bus.

He'd started hearing whispers about something which was going to help win the War. Nobody knew what it was or what it could do, but there were whispers about this thing that provoked the hell out of him. It was not knowing what it was that ate him up. He didn't give a shit about winning the War. That was Army business over in Europe and way out in the Pacific. It was the damned secrecy that got his goat. He'd be damned if he wasn't going to find out what it was all about. Now and then he'd run into somebody who talked hard, hinted like they knew a little bit about it, but sooner or later they'd get spooked and shut up. It was like he was one of those Intelligence agents trying to catch them talking out of school. And when he figured out what they were thinking, that they were afraid of getting turned in, there wasn't much he could do. He couldn't just tell them, "I ain't one of them undercover guys. I'm just curious, that's all." When he said that, they tended to clam up anyway. He read people good as anybody else, and it pissed him off when they turned him down. So, one night, sitting in a dark booth at the Ritz Club, after getting pissed off over and over, he told Roxy, "I'm gonna find out what that damn thingamajig is."

She laughed and took a pull on her Pabst. "Sure you are." And the way she said it prickled just a little bit. It got on his last nerve. He decided right there he was going to get into Y-12, if it was the last thing he ever did. If the thing he was hunting wasn't there, he'd do X-10. Then into that K-25 place. And even S-50.

"I'm gonna see for my own satisfaction," he said.

She laughed again.

"You just watch me," he grumbled. Then he turned and headed toward the exit.

She called after him, "Buckley, wait. Watch you do what?" But she didn't come after him.

He found the taxi driver and said, "Take me back to the CEW."

"Now?"

"Yup."

"Where's the lady at?"

"She'll be coming later. Come on. Let's go."

221

The driver drove him the eight miles to the CEW Central Bus Terminal. Then he got on a work bus for Y-12 which ran down Gamble Valley Road to Scarboro Road, and he got out at the Bear Creek Road checking station with everybody else. The warm September evening was humid, and the lights at the guard house attracted moths and other flying insects whirling up into the lights overhead. Buckley hung back as the bus crowd moved in a loose group toward the chain link fence and the gate where they'd have to enter one-by-one, showing their identification badges. He noticed right away that the badge he wore was the wrong color. His blue to their yellow. Under his breath, he muttered, "Shit."

This is gonna require some maneuvering, he thought. And he started looking around for some kind of help or distraction. Couldn't find a thing, so he turned around and got in line to board the bus he'd just left. The line for boarding was longer than the one for getting off, so he had more time to examine his surroundings. Just as he was about to climb the steps onto the bus, he took a last look at the entry gate and found a familiar face. *What was that fellow's name?* he asked himself. He could see the guy's face from a few weeks ago. He'd seen the guy in a group, but where? Couldn't bring up the name in his mind.

When he got on the bus, there were no seats available, so he stood up near the driver and did some thinking about how he might get into Y-12. Maybe without riding the bus all the way to the gate. That might be worth a try.

Then he remembered. *The guy's name is Gene Slover. He's a guard now? Whaddya know? He's found hisself a pretty good job at Bear Creek.*

Buckley rode all the way back to Gamble Valley thinking how Gene Slover might be able to help him. Or maybe he'd just slink in through the woods another night. He fingered his badge, and a scheme started forming in his mind.

222

He was seeing how Gene Slover might help him get into Y-12. It was too late now that it was 10:43 p.m., but Momma had always said "Patience is a virtue," so he would try again to get into Y-12 tomorrow night. He was lucky he'd made the bus ride because now he saw a better way to pull it off.

The next evening around 7:15 as he was riding the work bus toward the Bear Creek Road, it started raining steadily. Some on the bus had brought hats or rain gear, and they covered up as they exited at the gate, but others who had not anticipated rain simply held their hands over their heads and pushed hurriedly toward the guard checking badges. Buckley did likewise, holding an arm over his badge because it was blue when it should have been yellow. He had his head down and couldn't see if Slover was even there, and he was walking right up to the gate. When he was third in line to go through, he heard a voice tell somebody, "Okay, you're good. Next." He decided not to worry about Slover. He pushed closer as the woman in front of him stepped up to the guard, and he heard, "Okay," and then he was right there at the gate.

The guard said, "Okay," and Buckley moved quickly to go through, planning to catch up with those who had already passed inspection. He was three or four steps inside when the guard called out, "Wait a minute." His heart froze, and he stopped.

A hand on his shoulder as the rain fell faster. He made sure to keep his arm covering his badge.

"Don't I know you?"

It was Gene Slover right at his side. "You're Buckley, right?"

The man was smiling even though he was getting as soaked as Buckley was.

"Yeah, it's me," Buckley said, hunched over, trying not to

let his badge show.

Slover seemed delighted to see him, and Buckley didn't want that. The last thing he needed right now was to have Old Home Week right there at the gate. He wanted to be dismissed so he could disappear among the Y-12 employees, but Slover seemed excited to connect with him again.

"What you doing here?" Slover asked.

"Pyatt from Happy Valley sent me down here to talk with your Head Sanitation guy."

"Huh? Sanitation?"

"Yeah," Buckley said while the rain beat down a little harder. "The Big Boss, the General Whatshisname, wants us to talk with your people about how to do cleaner collections."

A crack of lightning exploded thirty yards from them, startling both men, and the rain came down in sheets.

"Go on," Slover shouted over the maelstrom, heading back to the little guard house. "Stop by on your way out. I want to catch up with you."

Several Y-12 employees slipped through the gate, and now there wasn't even a semblance of badge checking going on. Buckley hurried along with everyone else, headed toward the big building shrouded by downpour.

Twenty-five yards ahead there was another gate to go through, but nobody to check your badge. The rain had slowed some, and Buckley was looking for a place to stop and pour water out of one of his boots. He was making an audible squishing sound with each step he took. He was also looking for a way to get inside the building without running into anybody who would take a better look at his Badge. That would not be good.

The Y-12 building was huge, and they had put up a lot of lights on poles so that it was lit up like noontime. There was so much humidity everything was shrouded in cloudy aura, and the lights produced little rainbows all around. Buckley had never seen anything quite like it. Branching off from the crowd of employees who were entering the main doors, he looked for a logical alternative route away from them, but not too obvious to anybody who might be watching. He noticed a light that had burned out on one of the poles, leaving not darkness, but an area that was dimmer than the surrounding sections. Buckley sidled in that direction, still searching for anyone who might be monitoring the shift change that was going on. All he saw was men and women intent on coming and going. He did find a door about thirty yards from the main doors, and he made for it, which was within the partially illuminated penumbra between light poles. At the door he tried the knob. No good. Locked. He checked to see if anyone was watching him. None he could see.

He pounded on the door just to see what would happen. *The worst thing that can happen,* he thought, *is nothing. The door doesn't open.* But that wasn't exactly right. The door opened, and a uniformed guard stood there facing him. The man didn't look as surprised as Buckley felt, and he sounded pretty sure of himself when he said, "Stand still."

Buckley considered making a run for it, but heard someone approaching on his left. Two more guards, one of them straining to hold a German shepherd on a leash as the animal whined and lurched at the restraint. Stepping back into the room, the lead guy said, "Come in here." By now the guards were right up on top of him, so Buckley did as told.

"How'd you get here?" the lead guy asked. "What do you think you're doing?"

"I'm looking for the head sanitation guy," Buckley said. There was no way to outrun the dog. He knew that, and he

225

couldn't take all three of these guys who he saw were younger, bigger, and probably a whole lot faster than he was. The lead guy was about five foot ten and slender. The other two were over six foot, thick-necked and muscle-bound.

"What's the guy's name you're looking for?" the dog handler said. The noise inside the building was louder than outside, a pervasive mechanical humming sound, which puzzled Buckley. He looked around the place while he was trying to come up with a name, taking note of all the big machines in the room. It was a huge three-story tall room, and there were workers, both male and a few females, some in white coats, some not, all of them tending to business.

He took too long looking around, and the guy who wasn't holding the dog grabbed him around his upper arm and jerked him around a bit, saying, "Talk! Just what you doing here?" A couple of employees walked by, staring at the four of them.

The lead guy said, "This ain't a good place for this. Cuff him and take him to the holding cell. We'll get what we want in there where we won't have an audience."

The fellow putting the cuffs on wasn't real polite doing it, and he glared at Buckley after he was finished, adding, "You're in a shitload of trouble, old man."

"Where's the sanitation boss?" Buckley said. "I forget his name. Where's he at?" He figured these guys didn't usually have visitors coming through the door he'd chosen, and they were doing their best to intimidate him. He stuck with his original line, thinking the only chance he had was to out talk them. Of course, that wasn't looking too good since he was handcuffed.

The four of them walked down the hall and got more stares from the employees they passed. As they turned a corner, the lead guy stopped them. "You know, it might be good to take this guy to see Blankenship. He's Hubbell's baby, and I don't have a good read on him yet. We need to show him how good we do our job. Cavanaugh says he's a good guy, but he seems like a hard-ass to me."

Buckley studied his captors and sat back to make the best of the situation. He had the spirit of carnival in his blood. He saw the entertainment was about ready to begin.

"I don't know, Charlie," the guard holding the dog said. "I mean, this old man made it inside the plant. Maybe it wouldn't be real smart to show Blankenship that somebody actually got inside the perimeter."

"Perimeter, hell," Gary said. "This old man has got inside the plant itself."

The lead guard reconsidered. "Maybe we ought to take him back outside then."

Buckley said, "Lots of people's already seen me inside, boys. You need to come up with something better than that to impress the boss."

They thought about that. Gary frowned staring first at the leader, then at Eddie. "So don't let Blankenship see this guy? Is that right?"

The leader said, "Let me think." He glanced around again. "We got to get this guy out of sight. Come on this way."

The Security Office was a cinderblock structure on the second floor. Inside were several desks in a front room, two private offices, and a large closet that served as a holding cell. It wasn't a big room, maybe eight by ten, with a cot on one wall. Gary led Buckley to the cell door, held him at the threshold and frisked him, collecting items from his pockets, wallet, matches, cigarettes, and a small pocketknife. Then he unlocked the cuffs, pushed Buckley inside, and secured the door behind him.

Charlie stepped up to the bars, looking Buckley over, then turned and said, "When Blankenship gets here, let me do the talking. We'll say we got him for B & E."

Gary said, "Huh?"

"For breaking and entering."

"Fine," Eddie said. "I'm going to take the dog back out so he can do his business, and I need to feed him. Be back in fifteen minutes. Come on, Geronimo. Come on, boy."

Gary asked, "You need me here?"

"Nope," Charlie said. "Probably better if you're not here."

Gary said, "Okay. I'm going to do a walk-through around the west building. I'll be down at Break Room C if you need me."

Buckley settled onto the cot and did some thinking of his own. He was feeling all right. Things hadn't worked out the way he planned, but this wasn't a bad hoosgow. The cot was clean. The room had a good smell. Better than Pompey's place for certain. He went through what would probably happen when the boss man arrived, this Blankenship fellow, and he considered how it ought to go, running through several different possibilities, and he ended up with what he felt was a pretty good plan. He got bored after all that calculating and figuring, so he napped a while.

Sometime later he woke up, and there was a fellow standing beside Charlie, looking through the bars. This fellow wasn't much taller than Buckley, probably five foot seven or eight, wearing dark-rimmed glasses. A young guy with neat, close-cropped light brown hair. He said, "Mr. Buckley, I'm Lieutenant Robert Blankenship. We need to talk, you and I. If I bring you out of your cell, will you promise to cooperate, not

228

try to escape?"

Sitting up, Buckley said, "Tell you what. Get me out of here, and give me something to drink, and I'll promise you not to run away."

Blankenship nodded, saying, "Deal. Bring him out, Charlie."

It tickled Buckley to watch how Charlie kowtowed to Blankenship seeing as how Charlie and his buddies were probably ten years older than the lieutenant. Blankenship took a seat at a table and motioned for Buckley to sit opposite him. Blankenship appeared to be making himself comfortable, as if he and Buckley were down at Nash's Grocery, chewing the fat. Buckley liked him right away.

"Tell me about yourself, Mr. Buckley."

"I was born and raised here in East Tennessee," Buckley said. "Moved around a bit though. Lived a while in Karns, Wartburg, LaFollette, Clinton, Robertsville. I know this whole area. Or I did before you Federals started tearing it all to pieces." Charlie brought two glasses of water, and Blankenship sipped his. Buckley let his glass alone, asking, "Ain't you got anything better than water?"

"No, sir. This is it," Blankenship said.

"Okay."

"Mr. Buckley, how did you get inside our plant here? That's what I'm curious about."

"Your guards brung me in, didn't they?"

"But how did you make it to the door where they discovered you?" Blankenship said. "We don't encounter many visitors right at that spot. In fact, the fellows tell me they've never had any unauthorized person to venture so close to our operation here. So, what we need to know is how did you manage it, given all the guards and dogs we have patrolling the area? How did you do it?"

"What is it you all do here?" Buckley asked.

Blankenship smiled. "That's classified. I cannot divulge that."

"Well, hell's bells!" Buckley said. "I don't know classified or divulge from next Sunday's picnic. I just want to know what's going on here." He spread his hands, palms up. "Really. I see all the construction going on. I can tell this building we're in ain't halfway completed. You got no cause to worry about me. I'm just curious, is all. Why all these guards? Why all the hubbub? Why all this construction and building like they's no tomorrow? Got to be something important. Tell me what it is, and I'll go away happy. Won't tell a soul. I just need to know."

"Mr. Buckley, I...."

"Call me Buckley. I don't qualify as a mister."

Another Blankenship smile. "All right, Buckley. I don't actually know what they're doing here. It's none of my business. The man in charge, General Leslie Groves, says we're performing work essential to the War Effort. He says nobody here deserves any more information than that. Just do your own job. Don't worry about what anybody else is doing. If you have a need to know something, you get that particular piece of information. If you don't have a need to know, you don't get that information. So, you see, we're in the same boat with you, Buckley. We're curious, too, but we don't need to know. And we've got our own work to do. I can tell you this: anybody who asks too many questions, anybody who gets too close to a place where they don't work, a place where he or she is not authorized to be...."

"Like me," Buckley said.

"Exactly like you," Blankenship agreed. "Anybody who's too nosy in the wrong places gets locked up, interrogated, and some of them get shipped out permanently. Never to return...."

Buckley shook his head, and Blankenship said, "What is it?"

"Damn," Buckley said. "I hate to hear you saying all this because I just got to know what all this secret stuff is all about. I got to know!"

"What things?" Blankenship asked.

"Like what is this secret thing I'm hearing about?"

Blankenship's eyebrows went up, and, although Buckley could tell he was trying not to show surprise about the secret, that little cat was already out of the bag.

"That's important, ain't it?" Buckley said. "You're trying to pretend like it ain't special, but it is. Sure enough, it is. Right?" He leaned back in his chair, smiling, and said, "You don't need to answer that last question I asked."

"Why?" Blankenship asked.

"Because I know it's important. And I bet you ten dollars we're going to talk some more."

"You'd be right about that," the lieutenant said. "You are one interesting person, Buckley. Ordinarily, we would just terminate you and ship you somewhere far, far away. However, there is something intriguing about you. About the way you don't try to hide. The intuitive way you interact when being interrogated. All this makes me think you and I might be able to help each other. I mean, you don't have any desire to get shipped out, have you?"

"Nope."

"And you have a powerful need to uncover secrets, don't

you?"

Buckley shrugged. "You probably got something there. I like to know what's going on. Always have."

Now Blankenship leaned back and took a deep breath. "Let me share something with you I haven't told my associates here. I'm not supposed to divulge this information, but I have a hunch about you. And that hunch tells me you wouldn't cooperate with me if I didn't share this information with you."

"Let me hear it," Buckley said.

"I have special permission from General Groves to think outside the box."

Buckley blinked at that. "So? What does that mean?"

"It means that while I don't know exactly what's going on here, I do know that if the United States and its allies are going to beat Hitler and Tojo. If we're going to win this war, we need to be willing to try everything we can to win. We need to get every able-bodied soldier into the fight. We need to provide him with the best equipment. We need to give him the best weapons. The most jeeps and tanks and airplanes and ships. Groves has got the clout to get anything done that he wants done. He's not waiting to try one thing and find out it won't work. He's trying everything at once. He's going like a house afire."

"I'm listening."

"Groves has me working as a special ombudsman. He's letting me try anything I think might work to help the Clinton Engineer Works operate better."

"What the hell's a home buds man?"

"Ombudsman," Blankenship said, pronouncing the word slowly. "It's a person who's in charge of investigating complaints. Solving problems."

'Well, I ain't complaining. What's that got to do with me?"

"Groves is the one complaining," Blankenship said. "He's assigned me to check into every hair-brained idea, every possible danger that might slow him down with the big secret or anything else he thinks might help win the war. So I've got permission to follow any lead I think is promising. I believe the latest lead I've run across is you."

Buckley frowned.

"Oh, don't worry," Blankenship said. "I'm not sure why or how you're going to assist me. But I do know you're one slippery character, the cleverest we've encountered so far here at CEW. And I want you to help me identify security loopholes. Security risks. I want you to find ways to hurt us before someone else does. If you'll do that, we can fix those problems before some bad guy uses them against us. Does that make sense? Have I told you enough? So there it is, Buckley. I'm asking if you'll be a part of the War Effort with me?"

They went on talking like that, and Buckley wasn't sharing much about how he'd actually got right up to that side door. He'd tell a little how he did it, but not everything he'd observed about Y-12's security measures. He gave Blankenship just enough to impress him, but not everything. The guards came back. Then they went out again, and most of the time it was just Blankenship and Buckley sitting there talking at the table. Buckley started feeling better about this young lieutenant. Like maybe he could make friends with this fellow. But he had other ideas, too.

Eventually, Buckley stood up from the table. "I need to take a piss. Is that okay?"

"You've given your word you won't try to escape, right?"

Raising his right hand as if testifying in court, Buckley said, I give you my word that I won't run away."

"All right," Blankenship said. "Rest room is just around the corner, down on the left."

"I think I can find it," Buckley said. "Appreciate it, buddy."

As soon as he said that, he wished he hadn't because it sounded something like good-bye, which, if properly translated by the lieutenant, would get him back in handcuffs locked in the cell again. He went out the office door, strolling toward the rest room, but actually he was making as break for it. A slow-motion break. He wouldn't run. He'd slow walk his way out of there, if he could. He by-passed the rest room and eventually came to a T-intersection.

Left or right?

Left looked good so he sashayed in that direction, doing his best to blend in with the crowd of men already going that way. He negotiated a few more turns and decided he was pretty much lost inside this huge building that never would end. He started paying more attention to faces and badges, searching for a friendly, unsuspecting face he could persuade to talk a little bit. Not wanting to start any commotion, but he sure would like to know what in tarnation this Y-12 outfit was all about.

Eventually, he saw a familiar place, and area he'd already been through, and that slowed him down a bit. Not sure that was good. He turned to look back the way he'd come, and whoops! There's Charlie coming up on him pretty quick. And focused on him. No doubt about that. Buckley did a U-turn to get away, if he could, and whoops again. There's Blankenship not ten feet away, stern, shaking his head at Buckley. "You gave me your word," Blankenship said when he was closer. "You said you wouldn't run."

"Never did run. Just walked away."

Blankenship grinned and frowned at the same time. "Is that how it's going to be between us?"

"Doesn't have to be," Buckley admitted. "You could let me go. Or you could help me want to stay."

"No," the lieutenant said. "We won't be letting you go just yet. I'll be more careful with words in the future, and I'll expect you to keep your word. No more games."

"Okay, okay. You got me. I won't try nothing more. Which way we going?"

Blankenship pointed, and they headed back to the office. "The more I talk with you, the more I sense you can help us. You could make a valuable contribution to the War Effort. But let me do some legwork on something for you that I think will make all the difference for you. Will you give me an hour or so to get what we need to seal the deal?"

"What you talking about?"

Blankenship offered a mischievous smile. "Admit it. You're curious what I have up my sleeve."

"You're right. Go on then. You're wasting time."

They got back to the Security Office, and Blankenship said, "Stay here. I'm not going to say any more. I'll be back soon as I can."

Buckley held out his hand, and they shook hands. Which, he had to admit, felt right. So he asked a question. "What's your first name, buddy?"

"My given name's Robert," he said.

"Good to meet you, Bobby. Real good."

Blankenship told Charlie, "I'm going to go see Captain Hubbell. See that Mr. Buckley gets anything he needs."

Obviously fired up about what he was witnessing, Charlie said, "You're not going to get friendly with this guy, are you?"

Blankenship stared at Buckley a moment, answering, "I believe I'm already friendly with him." And he walked away.

To keep Charlie happy Buckley walked into the cell he'd occupied previously and lay down on the cot. Charlie did a doubletake when he saw where he was, stood up with the keys, and made a great show of locking him in the cell. "I believe this is where you're going to end up," he sneered.

"Might be right about that," Buckley answered. "How about bringing me a co-cola?"

"In your dreams," Charlie said.

Buckley put his arm over his eyes to shield from the overhead light bulb, and he dropped off to sleep waiting for Bobby's return. Later he heard Blankenship saying, "Ferguson, what's he doing in the cell?"

"I was just making sure he wouldn't escape."

Blankenship said, "Let him out of there."

"I tell you what," Buckley said. "I'm happy where I am, but I would like a cocola. I already asked Ferguson."

Blankenship looked at Charlie. Didn't say a word. Just stared at him.

"What?" Charlie asked. "You mean…?"

Blankenship nodded as Buckley grinned, and Charlie skulked out of the room.

"What have you got for me?" Buckley asked. Blankenship handed him a sheet of paper through the bars. "Oh, you need to read that," Buckley said, passing it back. "Read it out for me so I can ast questions if I need to."

"All right," he said. "Here's what it says:

WAR DEPARTMENT

CORPS OF ENGINEERS

OFFICE OF SECURITY AND INTELLIGENCE

CLINTON ENGINEER WORKS

CLINTON, TENNESSEE

September 21, 1943

To all departments including Medical, Transportation, Food Services, Administration,

Scientific, Waste Management, Housing, and Intelligence: you will see that Bearer of this

Notice is allowed safe passage with or without showing Identification.

You will further see that Bearer is supplied with necessary items he may request to

Expedite his passage to his destination up to a value of one thousand dollars ($1,000).

Requests for documented reimbursement for said items or equipment to be forwarded to

The Office of Administration CEW.

By Order of the Officer Commanding

Captain Clyde Hubbell

Intelligence Department

"So what do you think?" Blankenship asked.

"Read it again."

Blankenship read through it again and waited a while,

watching Buckley's face. Eventually, he asked, "Deal?"

"Oh, hell, yes!" Buckley said with a huge grin. "Deal."

So Blankenship set it all up, knowing it was a long shot. That it might not work very well or very long. But General Groves had told him to think outside the box and try anything that might work. *So,* he thought, *there's that.*

Photo courtesy of Deb Kile Hotchkiss

Guardian Angel

Kathleen sat cross-legged on the floor, examining her shoes, which were pretty old and kind of loose, and they had holes in the sole bottoms. A week ago she had poked a finger through the leather. "Daddy," she said, "can't you get me some better shoes? Looky here. Look at this." He put down his newspaper and looked at her finger wiggling through where it shouldn't have been able to wiggle.

"I see it, Little Sister. And it makes me ashamed and at the same time proud. Do you want to know why?"

Daddy never passed up an opportunity to educate her about the way the world worked. And he knew a lot about that stuff. He knew what to put in the grocery so people would come buy it. He knew just when to toss stale bread or mealy vegetables. He knew when the boys had not finished their chores, but he also knew when Sister Etta had liked the book she was reading. Etta was the smartest Woodson. One night when they thought she was asleep Kathleen had overheard Momma telling Daddy Etta was smartest.

Etta was in the bathroom, brushing teeth, and she would be coming to bed soon. Momma and Daddy were waiting on her, and they thought Kathleen was asleep, but she was only pretending to be asleep. Momma told Daddy Etta was smartest, and Kathleen was prettiest, the best dancer, and should have been born to royalty. Daddy liked that. He was the sweetest in the whole family. This made Kathleen happy for Etta and for herself. It was too bad Etta wasn't pretty. After hearing what

239

Momma said, Kathleen started paying more attention to Etta, who unfortunately looked like Daddy while Kathleen looked like Momma, much luckier than Etta.

Daddy asked her, "Want to know why I'm proud and ashamed, too?"

"Yes, sir."

"Because you're a trooper, Rebecca Kathleen. You thrive on doing what's right so far as you understand what it is. But you also take great pleasure in exercising imagination, which opens up a whole universe of fantastic characters and situations for subsequent exploration. So I'm awfully proud of you, and at the same time ashamed you've got a hole in your shoe. I need to do better taking care of you."

"Holes, Daddy. Not just one hole. More than one," she corrected him. "In both shoes. See?"

He reached out to push a strand of her hair behind her ear. "You never miss a thing. Not one little thing. Like your mother. And I love you both."

Kathleen said, "I mean, this doesn't bother me. This hole in my shoe. I'm one of the Twelve Dancing Princesses. I danced so long last night my shoe has worn quite through, like in the story. I dance and dance all night with a prince in an underground castle where the leaves on the trees are gold and silver and diamond. Now my shoe needs mending. Even if I get new shoes, they will still get worn quite through. That's all."

Like Momma did, Daddy reached out, pulling her to his chest. She smelled cigars in his pocket, smoke on his shirt, and his own personal aroma after his working all day in the store. His was a different embrace than Momma's, but every bit as good. Kathleen had not decided how to say why exactly, but she was glad he had hold of her. And she was reminded of the story about the twelve who danced every night, but didn't tell their daddies where or with who or why they danced. If Kathleen was one of the twelve, she would tell him every morning about dancing. She would take Daddy with her no matter what the other princesses said. If they objected, she would defend him. She was not like those storybook princesses.

Daddy told her, "Shoes are controlled nowadays, Princess. So are cheese, butter, canned beans, canned tomatoes, many precious things. We can't buy you new shoes until we get a ration stamp for shoes, but I'll work on your shoes tonight. Maybe slip some cardboard over the largest hole. That ought to last a while. Is that permitted, Majesty?" She assured him it was indeed.

She loved Daddy. Although he didn't hear prayers as often as Momma, he was always anxious to hear them, so with him listening she strung everything out as long as she could to keep him right there next to her as long as possible. Momma never lied down, but Daddy did every time.

Next time she thought about the twelve she was with Miss Bashie down by the river sitting on a log listening to frogs calling in the weeds, looking at what Kathleen had found in the sumac. She held a little sky blue robin's egg in the palm of her hand.

Miss Bashie said, "I'll trade you something for your egg. Show me what you like in your Momma's store."

"All right," Kathleen said. "Let's go."

"No," Miss Bashie said. "Let me meet you there. I have to do something else first. You go ahead. I'll be there soon."

Kathleen went straight away, and when she got inside the screen door at the back of the store, there was Miss Bashie, smiling, waiting on her. *How did she get there so fast?* Miss Bashie was usually a little sad. You could tell by her eyes, her face, and how she did things deliberate and slow. *But how did she get here before me?*

"Show me your egg again," Miss Bashie said, so Kathleen did, and they decided that one robin's egg was worth one small piece of licorice. "Are you happy with that?" Miss Bashie asked.

"I don't know. I never had licorice before."

"Maybe we should wait until you know if you really want licorice," Miss Bashie said.

"No," Kathleen said. "I want licorice. My first licorice."

So that's what they did, with Kathleen making the black stick of candy last as long as possible. Miss Bashie cherished the egg in her palm, gazing at it a long time, so long that Kathleen wondered why that was happening. And that must have shown on her face because Miss Bashie said, "Things happen faster than they used to. Or maybe it's me getting older. We've had old times here longer than most other places, and I'm not used to the way things have changed so rapid and complete these days. Do you understand what I'm saying, Kathleen?"

"No, ma'am."

"Well, let me try again. What I'm trying to say is I like the old ways so I'll always choose a robin's egg over any kind of kitchen treat. Any sweet candy. The candy won't last. The robin's egg will."

Miss Bashie wanted things to stay like old times, and Kathleen could see when she was happy with things. Happy to keep it like it had been when she was a little girl herself. But when she thought more about it, Kathleen was not sure what Miss Bashie wanted was best. Maybe things ought to change when changing was better than old times. Daddy said the new tractors are better than mules. Momma said indoor toilets are better than outhouses. Ronnie said autos are better than horse-drawn wagons. Surely, Miss Bashie could see that. Kathleen did not know how she could tell the Sad Lady about getting ready for changes. Everybody needs to do that. You just got to be ready. But the Sad Lady wasn't ready. Kathleen could tell that. Miss Bashie wasn't going to be able to get ready.

Miss Bashie surprised her when she said, "You did good watching over your little brother, Toby. And just as good with sister Etta."

"Etta? I never watched over Etta."

"Well," Miss Bashie said, "you were a good listener when she read about the Twelve Dancing Princesses because Momma couldn't do it. Knowing you, I bet you had her read it over and over. How many times did she read that story for you?"

"I don't know. I like to hear the story. Love to hear her read it out loud for me."

"Why's that? Don't you know the story by heart?"

"I know it, yes. But it was Etta's voice that made it just right. It was the feeling when I heard her say the words I knew were coming. I used to think she just read and talked all day long, windy as a day in March. But she's better than that. Much better."

And at that exact moment in time Kathleen was startled to recognize how much she loved her sister. She choked, unable to say anything more, a tear sliding halfway down her cheek. There was this quick, unexpected feeling in her chest. *Why am I crying? I'm not hurt. Nothing's broken.* She wiped away the tear, and her cheek was dry long before she felt settled. She knew she'd be sort of touchy all day long. That's what Daddy called it. "You're a little touchy tonight, Kathleen. I wish you could be more tolerant of the world around you."

But standing there with Miss Bashie Kathleen was desperate to know how The Sad Lady could know what she knew about Etta reading the Twelve Dancing Princesses. "How'd you know?" she asked her, "How'd you know Etta was reading to me? You weren't there. I didn't see you." And as Kathleen said these words she got scared because she clearly recalled Etta had read the story in their bedroom three nights in a row. Momma and Daddy didn't know Etta was doing that. None of their brothers knew. Nobody else was around. How could Miss Bashie know?

She went straight up close to the Sad Lady, whispering, "How'd you know Etta read me that story? I never said anything about her doing that."

"Oh, didn't you? I thought you did." Miss Bashie's brief smile, an awkward, uncomfortable smile, gave Kathleen the feeling the Sad Lady was saying something untrue. She wanted Miss Bashie to say something better than "I thought you did." That was the thing they both knew was untrue.

"How did you know?" she asked again.

"I was closer to you, Kathleen," she said, "than you could possibly know. I was there, believe me. I saw. I heard. I just didn't want to interrupt. I know what Etta means to you, and, more importantly, I know what you mean to Etta."

Something was wrong now, dreadfully wrong. Kathleen felt odd, suddenly a little sick. Weightless, no longer inside her own skin. In her mind she wasn't in the house or the grocery any more.

She was climbing the closest redbud tree behind the house. The tree she had always imagined as her palace, with invisible rooms instead of branches. High in those branches she would carry Suzy Polineau into the Mystery Room where she would lay her baby into a crib perched higher still, way up in the branches. And Suzy Polineau would sleep well there. Kathleen would watch the child exchange her worried look for the gentlest smile in the whole wide world. Momma had said many times, "If a baby smiles in its sleep, it's listening to an angel."

Maybe Miss Bashie's one of those, come down to watch over me.

The End

Made in the USA
Columbia, SC
13 October 2021